I0593331

SILVERBELL
SHORE

Love me Like You Do

DL GALLIE

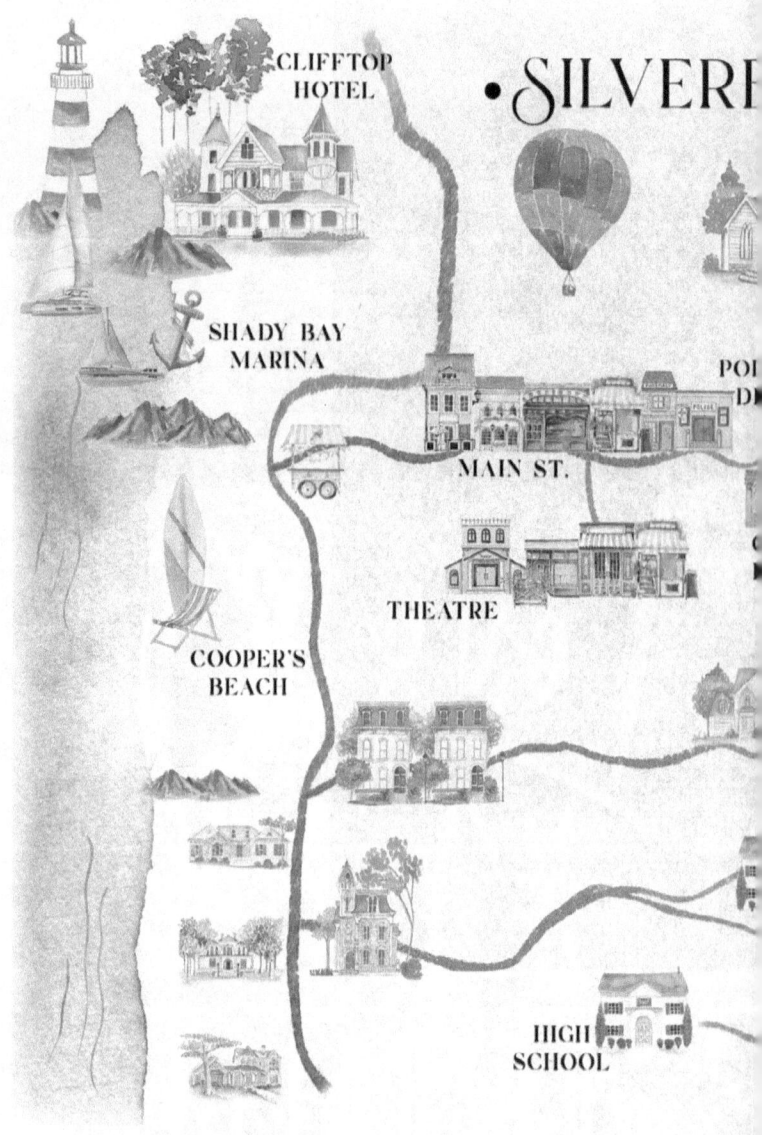

CLIFFTOP HOTEL

•SILVERF

SHADY BAY MARINA

POI D

MAIN ST.

THEATRE

COOPER'S BEACH

HIGH SCHOOL

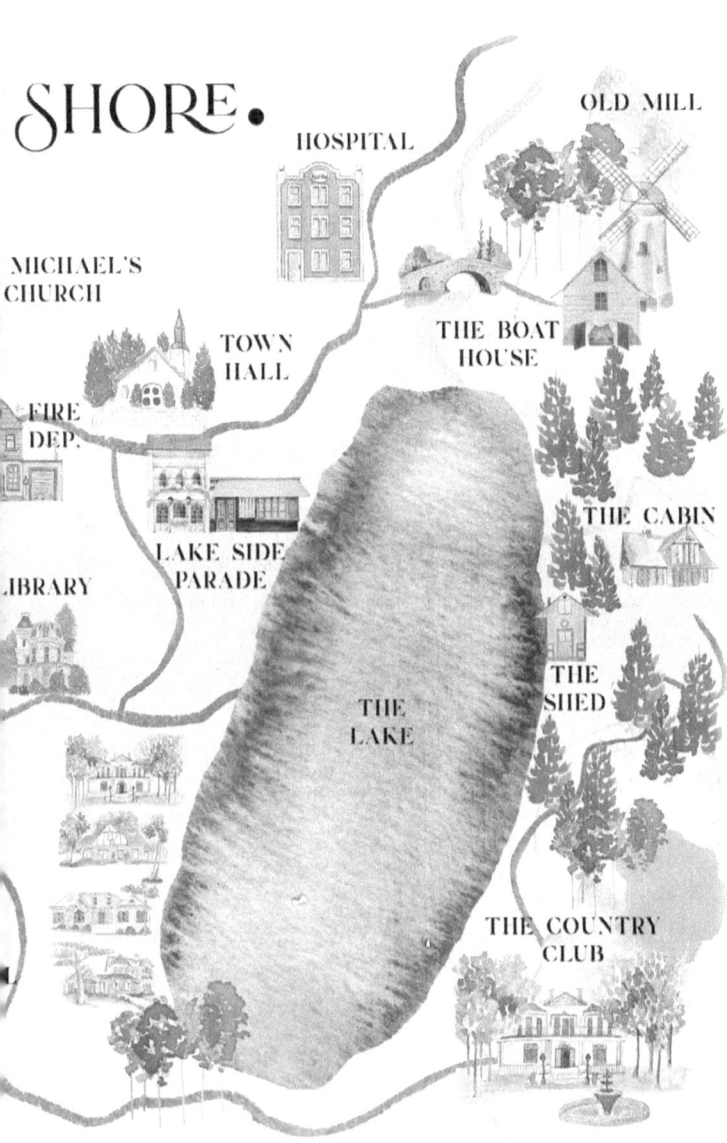

SHORE.

HOSPITAL

OLD MILL

MICHAEL'S CHURCH

TOWN HALL

THE BOAT HOUSE

FIRE DEP.

THE CABIN

LIBRARY

LAKE SIDE PARADE

THE SHED

THE LAKE

THE COUNTRY CLUB

Edited by *Karen Hrdlicka, Barren Acres Editing*

Proofread by *Lisa Edwards,*

Interior design and formatting by *Lou at LJDesigns*

Cover designed by *Alexandra Silva*

Series Information

Silverbell Shore is a (fictional) town on the East-Atlantic coast where the sea meets the rolling hills. Founded shortly after the Civil War as a fisherman's town, it's home to billionaires with private beaches, hotels and country clubs. As well as your everyday person—doctors, cops, EMTs, firefighters, farmers, teachers, students, etc.

Whether you're sunshine or grumpy, light or dark, the seemingly quiet and quaint town of Silverbell Shore welcomes you and all your deepest, darkest, forbidden secrets.

DL GALLIE

DEDICATION

To coffee and wine,
Thank you for being on this journey with me.

DL GALLIE

PROLOGUE

I never expected to fall in love with him, sure I always found him to be hot, like most warm-blooded women—young and old—and I'm sure a few of the men in Silverbell Shore did too. However, it will never be anything more than a crush, a silly schoolgirl crush, but fate has other ideas.

Several chance encounters with him set us down a dangerous path and one day we give in to those desires and everything changes.

The odds are against us and if our relationship is discovered, it has the potential to implode both our lives as we know them, but the heart wants what the heart wants, and my heart wants Kane Heatherington.

Just like his heart wants me.

No one loves me like he does, and I will do everything in my power to keep him and our love, even if it tears both our families apart.

CHAPTER 1

Cali

“ **I** need a piss,” Raven declares out of nowhere, leaving Fern and I shaking our heads as we watch him walk to the restrooms, waving to someone out of view as he saunters away.

"That boy is so crass sometimes," Fern Halstead, my BFF complains. She is my ride or die, the PB to my jelly. But there's also Raven, Raven Mitchell is the third amigo to our trio and the one with no filter … or tact, closely followed by Fern. Out of nowhere, just like Raven's pee declaration, she whisper-screeches, "OMG, Cali." She leans across the table, reaches out, and digs her nails into my forearm, squeezing me in excitement? Fear? I'm not sure which right now, but I think she's close to drawing blood.

"What?" I hiss, but she ignores me. Her wide eyes are locked on something behind me. The longer she stares, the more her nervous rash creeps up her neck and across her chest. The fact her nervous rash has appeared leaves me even more confused. Her eyes begin to move, indicating it's a someONE and not a someTHING and they are on the move.

Silently, she watches them walk behind me. Her nails digging deeper and deeper into my skin. Slapping at her hands, I snap, "Kindly remove your talons from my arm." But she still ignores me, she's still focusing on the someone behind me.

Pinching her arm, I garner her attention and she looks down at where I nipped her and finally realizes what she's doing. "Shit." She releases her grip and proceeds to rub my arm soothingly while still mutely staring behind me.

Clearly, it's a guy that has her all flustered because nothing flusters my bestie more than a guy, specifically a hot one. There's no risk of me wanting him because we have completely different taste when it comes to the opposite sex, so I don't bother to turn around.

Managing to pull my arm free, I rub at the nail indents before picking up my drink and taking a sip. "What caused you to go all grabby-grabby, stabby-stabby with your fingers just now?"

A look of contentment appears on her face and then she breathlessly pants a name, a name that I know all too well.

"Mr. Heatherington."

At the mention of his name, my heart begins to race. Putting my drink down, I anxiously run my palms up and down my thighs under the table. Kane Heatherington is the epitome of silver fox, but without the silver. He's hot. H.O.Double T hot. I know hot only has one T, but that's how smokin' he is AND he's the one and only man who we both agree is hot. Hell, even Raven thinks he's hot … and he's a dude.

"He's coming this way," she says under her breath.

Then I feel a presence behind me. Swiveling around in my seat, I come face-to-crotch with the man in question. Lifting my head, I run my eyes up his body and take in the Adonis before me. He can wear the hell out of a suit.

"Calliope. Fern," he says in greeting, and the timbre of his voice vibrates through my body. I normally hate my full name but hearing those four syllables—Ca-li-o-pe—pass through his lips, I don't mind at all. Hell, he could call me Sugartits Fartface and I'd be okay with it.

"Hi, Mr. Heatherington," we both singsong like schoolgirls, which technically we still are. Fern, Raven, and I graduate next week from Silverbell Shore High. I'm off to the Big Apple, where I'm attending Fordham University to study marketing. I got early acceptance to complete my degree and I can't wait to leave our sleepy lil' town and live it up in the big city. Mom and Dad were so proud of me, as was I. Fern thinks it's great because I've been accepted to FU. I sure am going to miss her and her crazy antics. She's leaving me and heading off to California to pursue her dream of becoming a makeup artist for the movie stars, and Raven is off to Chicago, currently he's undeclared but he has always wanted to live in Chicago because of deep dish pizzas and the Cubs. So come fall, the three of us will be scattered across the country.

"Congrats on your upcoming graduation, girls."

"Thank you, Mr. Heatherington," we both reply in unison. We both laugh at how in sync and school like our thank-you was.

"Calliope, I heard you got into Fordham. That's no easy feat."

"Thank you, Mr. Heatherington. It was tough but worth the effort."

"Please, call me Kane, we're all adults now. When you're done at FU." Fern giggles when he says FU. His lip lifts to laugh too but he schools it quickly, he is an adult after all. "Get in touch and I'll be sure to create a position at The Clifton for you."

"Thanks, Mr. H." He smirks at my use of Mr. H and I internally high five myself making him react like that. "I'll keep that in mind, but I want to get a job because I earned it, not cause the boss is best friends with my dad."

He nods and smiles. "I admire that. Speaking of your dad, he must be so proud."

"He is and I'm pretty proud too."

"As you should be. I wish Michael had your determination and tenacity. Instead, he's failing and likely never to graduate."

"He'll get there, Mr. H," I tell him, and without thought I reach out and squeeze his hand. A spark ignites when my skin touches his, it vibrates up my arm and directly into my heart and down to my lady parts. My heartbeat is currently going wild and pulsating in sync with my clit. *That's never happened before.* I'm ever so glad not to be attached to an electrocardiogram right now, my feelings would be given away by the loud beating sounds and there'd be little hearts on the screen in place of my actual heartbeat. "It's been a rough few years for him."

And rough is an understatement. Michael came home from school early one day to find his mom packing her things. Apparently, family life wasn't her style and she needed to get away from them all. As if his mom walking out wasn't enough, the following week, Nanna Heatherington—everyone in town called her this—died of a stroke. Michael and Konrad were the ones to find her. Nanna Heatherington's death was a shock for the whole town, she was the sweetest old lady and was loved by everyone, even cranky Mr. Barber and he doesn't like anyone. No one expected her to die suddenly like that, we all thought she'd live forever, especially Michael. They had a special bond, and with his mom and Nanna gone, he's become lost.

"It has, I don't disagree, but Konrad is managing fine." He smiles brightly and then adds, "He starts med school in the fall."

"I heard. Dr. Heatherington has a good ring to it. You mus—"

"You harassing my daughter?" Dad teases Kane as he joins us, interrupting my congratulations for Konrad. "Princess," he greets me with a kiss to my head. "Fern."

"Hi, Mr. Fischer," Fern sweetly greets him before she reaches over and picks up my iced tea, taking a sip since she's finished hers. I eye her but she just smiles and finishes what was left.

"Hi, Daddy," I singsong.

I'm a total daddy's girl and proud of it, but I'm so freakin' excited to spread my wings away at college. I mean, I can't remain a virgin forever, right? Sure, Raven has offered to pop my cherry for me, but he's like my brother and that's just too weird. I can wait a few more months for college to start and then I can find someone there to help me out.

"Keeping out of trouble?" he asks me, snapping my attention away from my virginity and to the present here at the country club.

"Always," I sweetly reply.

"Man, if pissing was an Olympic sport, I just won a gold medal," Raven announces, dropping back into his seat after using the facilities.

"Raven," Fern whisper-hisses, smacking him upside the head. "You are so crass ... and embarrassing at times."

"Yet, you love me." He blows her a kiss and then realizes we have company. When he sees who our company is, his eyes widen, his cheeks darken in embarrassment, and he sits up straight. Even though he's lived next door to us since he was three, he's intimidated by my dad. Probably because Dad caught us practice kissing one weekend when we were eleven. Raven and I wanted to see what the big deal was, but it was horrible. It was all tongue and slobber and teeth. As first kisses go, it was a disaster with a capital D and eleven exclamation marks. "Mr. Fischer." He nods at Dad then quickly looks to Mr. H. "Mr. Heatherington, how are you both?"

"Fine," Dad snaps through clenched teeth.

"I'm well, Mr. Mitchell, thank you for asking," Mr. H drawls, the tone of his voice once again vibrates through my body. "How are your mom and dad?"

"Dad's well," Raven replies, stealing a fry from Raven's plate and popping it into his mouth, chewing loudly. Then he adds, "Mom just finished chemo, but the doctors are hopeful they got it all this time."

"Good, good," Mr. H says. Resting his hand on Raven's shoulder, he squeezes in that loving parental way and I can see it reassures Rave that his mom is going to be okay this time around. "I have everything crossed for her. Please pass on my best wishes." Raven nods and then Kane looks to Dad. "Ready to go?"

Dad nods. "See you at home, Princess."

"Girls. Raven," Mr. H says.

Raven and Fern both speak at the same time. She says, "Bye, Kane." He says, "Mr. Heatherington." While I opt for, "Laters, Mr. H." He looks at me, a grin appears on his face and he does that little lip lift thing. That teeny tiny action does things to me that I shouldn't be feeling in public … or with my dad standing a few feet away from me. I know I shouldn't be lusting over my dad's best friend, but it'll never be so I don't need to worry, right?

Without another word, the two of them nod and leave us. I unabashedly watch Mr. H's ass as he and Dad walk away. Before he steps outside, he looks over his shoulder at me, totally catching me staring after him. We maintain eye contact for a few seconds and then he shocks the shit out of me and winks. We continue to stare at one another and something passes between us, I think.

My panties are currently damp and I swallow the lump sitting in the back of my throat and process the fact Mr. H just flirted with me, well, I think he was flirting with me. My mind replays his smile and wink over and over. Even though we were on opposite sides of the room, I felt that wink deep in my soul, and the little crush I have on my dad's best friend just ramped up into a full-blown teenage infatuation.

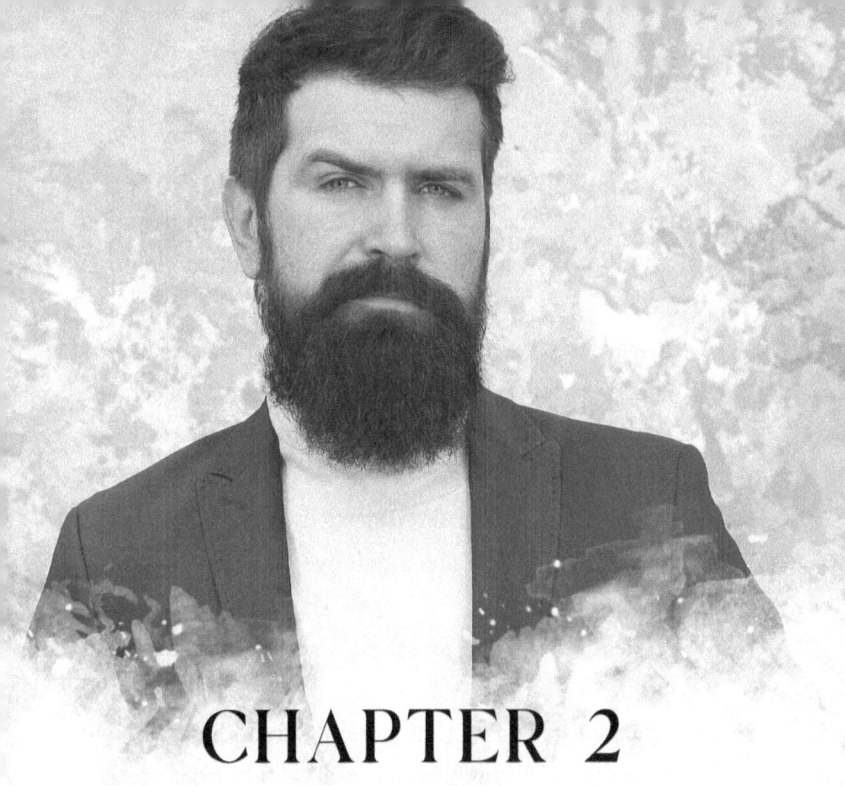

CHAPTER 2

Kane

… two years later

"I don't care, Danica, just sign the fucking papers. It's been nearly three years," I growl into the phone. "Just sign the damn fucking papers and end this farce."

"What are you going to do if I don't?" she sneers and pauses for dramatic effect. "That's right, fucking nothing … like always."

How I fell in love with this self-centered wench, I will never know.

"One question," I dejectedly ask, running my hands down my beard and tugging in frustration. "Why?"

"Why what?" she snaps, her voice laced with irritation that I would dare to ask her, the almighty Danica Heard, a question.

"Why are you doing this? Why prolong the inevitable? Still being married doesn't change anything between us. You left and we are never getting back together." Hell will freeze over before I ever take her back. She showed her true colors when she left like she did but when I look back, I should have known. Hell, she didn't even take my last name when we got married.

"'Til death do us part and then when you die, the hotel will be mine."

Of course this is about the hotel, I should have known. Shaking my head, I laugh. "You think I didn't change my will as soon as you left? You are delusional, Danica. Fucking delusional."

"What do you mean you changed it?" Her voice is raising and laced with shock that I would cut her out.

"Exactly that, I changed it. Why the fuck would I allow you to get your grubby mitts on what I created? What I worked hard to build. What—"

"You only created it because I was stuck and trapped at home raising your spawn."

"That's your children you're referring to."

"Those animals aren't mine."

"Wow." My grip on the phone tightens. "I knew you were a cold-hearted bitch but that right there, that's the icing on the bitch cake."

"Did you just call me a bitch?"

"If the bitch fits," I snap, and I'm ever so thankful she isn't in front of me right now. I don't condone violence, especially against women, but what she just said about our, no, my children is unacceptable. "Lose my number, Danica, all communication now will be through my lawyer. Just sign the fucking papers." Pressing the end call button, I throw my phone down on the desk. Then in frustration, I swing my arm out and swipe at it, sending everything flying off my desk and into the wall.

"Someone's having a bad day," a deep voice says from the doorway to my office. Looking up, I see Garrick standing there, concern on his face over what he just witnessed. "Wanna talk about it?"

"I just spoke to Bitchifer."

"What the hell did you do that for?"

"She sent back the divorce papers unsigned … again."

"What's her game?"

"Have a seat and I'll fill you in." Walking over to the bar in my office, I pour us each a stiff drink.

"If liquor is needed at eleven in the morning, she must have done something really bitchy."

"You have no fucking idea." Handing him his drink, I take a sip of mine and cherish the burn.

"So, what did she do now?"

"Apart from not signing the papers, she referred to the kids as 'my spawn' and wants me to die so she can get her grubby mitts on this." I wave my hand around the room.

"No fucking way."

"Yes fucking way."

"That's not possible, is it?"

"Fuck no. As soon as I realized she wasn't coming back, I changed the will so that all my assets go to 'the spawn'. She gets nothing."

"Good." He nods in agreement. "What are you going to do about the divorce then?"

"Chat with Stan and see what he thinks."

"As much as we all love Stan, maybe you need to bring in the big guns." I stare at him blankly. "Holly Miller."

"Chase's partner?"

"Yep." He nods. "She works at some big law firm in New York. Cali was telling me all about it, she's doing really well. Talk to her, there's got to be something she can do, or at the very least, she'll know someone who can represent you."

Nodding, I take a sip of my drink and the combination of the booze and the thought of hiring a new lawyer eases my frustration from a few moments ago.

"I was watching *Law and Order* with Jayne the other week and I remember this one episode—"

"Garrick, this is real life not some crime show."

"Hey, I'm just trying to tell you that it's possible. Call Holly, if anyone can help it'd be her. Just don't let Bitchifer worm her way back in."

"Hell will freeze over before that happens."

"Let's hope that day never comes."

Silently we sit here and sip on our drinks, then it hits me that Garrick is here in the middle of the workday. "As much as I appreciated the pep talk just now and your suggestion, what are you doing here?"

"Here to ask a favor."

"Shoot?" Taking his glass from him, I top it up.

"Cali wants to do some practical placement, get some hands-on experience. I was hoping you'd let her help out here."

"Are you just wanting her back here 'cause you miss her? Or because you think my marketing team can assist her?"

"Both," he nonchalantly replies but I know him, he just wants his princess back here so I call him out on it, "I call bullshit." And yep, he grins in that 'busted' kind of way. "But sure, I'll reach out to Hannah and see if it's something we can accommodate. How is Calliope doing?"

"Top of her class," he proudly declares, "but did we expect anything less from my princess?"

"You ever gonna stop calling her Princess? She's what, twenty-one now?"

"She'll always be my princess. You can't tell me that Finley won't be your munchkin forever."

"Touché."

Hannah walks past my office door and I sing out to her. She enters and I run the possibility of Calliope doing some work here. She agrees to have her intern here. I let her know I'll set it all up and get Calliope to be in touch. "I'm excited to see what Calliope can do for The Clifton. It might be time to bring in some young blood."

"You know, you're the only one to call her Calliope and get away with it."

"Really? It's her name, what else would I call her?"

"Cali, like most people."

"I'm not most people," I throw back at my best friend.

"Damn right you're not, and thankfully there's only one Kane-fucking-Heatherington, the world couldn't handle two of you."

"Fuck off, asshole," I throw back at him, finally relaxed after my phone call with Bitchifer. "Now that your princess has an internship of sorts, get the fuck out of my office so I can get some work done."

"Thanks for the scotch and helping Cali out, I really appreciate it."

"Anytime, you know I'd do anything for you."

He nods and exits my office. Throwing back the rest of my scotch, I grab Garrick's glass and pop it on the tray to be washed. Bending down, I clean up the mess I made after my outburst earlier. Once my desk is back in order, I google the firm where Holly works. Grabbing my phone, I call her before I chicken out, and ten minutes later, I'm booking a flight to the Big Apple to see my new lawyer.

CHAPTER 3

Cali

"**D**addy, I appreciate what you did arranging that with Mr. H and all that, but I'm not coming home for an internship that you arranged. I have repeatedly said, 'I want to do this on my own.'"

"But—"

"No, Dad, no buts. You need to back off and let me do this on my own. I'm an adult now."

"You'll always be my princess."

"And you'll always be my dad but please, let me live my life how I want." *Even if it is slowly falling apart and*

I'm lying to everyone, but I'm Calliope Victoria Fischer, I will get through this. Come hell or high water, I will make it work.

"Fine," he relents. "I'll tell Kane you don't want to come work for him."

"Thank you. Please tell him I appreciate the offer but it's not necessary ... my dad was just interfering, again."

We both laugh because Dad is the definition of overprotective, it's one of the reasons I applied to FU. Being so far away, he couldn't just 'pop in' to check on me. "I worry about you in the big city all on your own."

"I'm not on my own, I have Nicole and recently, I met this cool chick, Chelsea, who's dating a hockey player."

"You're not becoming one of those puck bunnies, are you?"

"Eeeeew, Dad, no. I don't even like hockey. Sports and I don't mix, you know that."

"Good, keep it like that."

"Dad, one day, I'm going to meet my Prince Charming and you're going to have to accept that I'm a grown woman and will be having S-E-X to give you all the grandbabies you keep harping on about."

"Not for another fifteen years, at least, and please don't ever mention you and sex again."

"Deal ... on both accounts. Now, I have an assignment to complete. I'll talk to you soon. Love you."

"Love you too, Princess."

Hanging up from Dad, I flop back on my bed and stare up at the ceiling feeling a smidge guilty that I once again lied to my dad. Life here in New York is hard, really, really fucking hard. This course is so much more challenging now but in saying that, I'm loving every minute of it, but it's the cost of living in NYC that is pushing me to breaking point. This city is crazy expensive, it's eating away at my savings and soon, I'm going to be homeless unless things change. *You can always tell your family that you are struggling and they will help,* I internally chastise myself, but the truth is, I'm stubborn, like my father, and want to do this on my own.

Things happen for a reason and I just need to patiently wait for all the stars to align for me, like they did for my roommate, Nicole. I just have to be patient.

She recently started working at a strip club to make some extra cash … and I'm talking really good cash. I'm not that desperate, yet, but if things keep going like this, I can see a spinning pole, sleazy businessmen, and nipple tassels in my future if I'm not careful.

The alarm on my phone pings and alerts me to the fact that I'm going to be late to meet Seth. He's a guy I met on campus last week. We've been texting back and forth and this afternoon is our first official date. I'm excited, however, my gut is telling me something is off with him but my vagina, she has other ideas. Ever since I popped my cherry when I first got here, she's taken on a new life and I'm horny all the time. I'm not a slut or anything, but I do like to ride the stallions on campus.

Blotting my lips, I take one last look at my reflection and smile. I look hot in an understated way. My long golden hair is down and I'm wearing a gray, almost black, wrap dress that accentuates my cleavage and stops just above my knees. Sitting on the end of my bed, I pull on my knockoff Louboutin black pumps ... one day I will own an original pair of Christian Louboutin 'So Kate' black pumps, with the classic pointed toe and signature red sole. For as long as I can remember, I've wanted a pair of Louboutin heels—I blame Carrie Bradshaw for this obsession. I also blame her for me wanting to live in New York City. That show made it look fabulous and don't get me wrong, it is, it's just freakin' expensive.

Grabbing my clutch, I sing out my goodbye to Nicole, who's currently in the shower belting out "Wannabe" by the Spice Girls. Walking down the street, I'm still humming along and miming the words to "Wannabe" when I bump into something, well someone, with a hard chest and a scent I would recognize anywhere. His hand reaches out to steady me and when I look up, my eyes widen, it's *him*.

"Mr. H, what are you doing here?"

"Just visiting my lawyer. You?"

We silently stare at one another and something passes between us, but it's quickly broken when I pull myself out of his grip. I immediately feel the loss and then I utter, "I'm ahh, on my way to a date." Pushing my hair behind my ear, I look up at him and smile.

"At three in the afternoon?"

I shrug, I too was shocked at him wanting to meet so early in the day but it just means more time for us to spend together, right? "Don't tell Dad," I quickly add. "You know what he's like. School is already stressful; I don't need him adding to my stresses by killing Seth because he took me out for coffee." *And hopefully more because since running into Mr. H my already antsy va-jay-jay is now thrumming like the drums part of* "In the Air Tonight" *by Phil Collins.*

"Your secret is safe with me." He mimes zipping his lips and I laugh.

It's been a few months since I've been home and I swear, now I'm older and not in Silverbell Shore daily, the man before me has gotten hotter. The older Mr. H gets, the sexier he becomes. He's like a fine wine, aging perfectly, and I just so happen to love wine, but we can never be because he's my dad's best friend and I'm, well, me. So I will just continue to appreciate him from afar and in secret.

"Thanks, Mr. H."

"Thought I told you to call me Kane?"

"You did, repeatedly, but you've been Mr. Heatherington to me all my life, it's weird calling you Kane, so I shortened it."

"Fair enough." He nods and smiles. "How's the big city treating you?"

That's the one question everyone always asks and I hate lying to them, but I don't want to let anyone down. "It's great, thanks. How's life back home?"

"Same old, same old."

"That sounds about right. Dad mentioned a renovation at the hotel, can't wait to see it. It was already beautiful."

"It's nothing major, just a splash of paint and I finally replaced that chandelier in the lobby."

My eyes widen because that light fixture was ugly as hell. "The ugly light is finally gone?" Then my eyes widen farther when I realize I voiced it out loud, but from the look on Mr. H's face at my kind of rude comment, he's not offended.

"Yes, I finally succumbed to pressure to update it and now that the new one is in place, I can admit the old one was hideous." He laughs at what he says and the joyous look on his face enhances his looks. My vagina is once again thrumming at his sexiness. *Down girl.*

"Hideous was an understatement. Mr. H, you really should fire the designer who chose that."

"I'm trying to divorce her right now so …"

Wow, I never realized his wife helped in the beginning, I didn't think she had anything to do with The Clifton.

"That was so rude of me, Mr. H, I'm so sorry." Dammit, I'm bringing out all the rude comments this afternoon. Mr. H is muddling my brain and causing me to not think before I speak.

"Don't be, Calliope, everyone is entitled to their opinion."

"Thanks." I smile at him and something lights up in his eyes when he sees me smile.

It lights something up in me too, but I need to smother it down and it seems to be working, until he says, "You've grown into a stunning woman, Calliope. You're glowing in the sunshine."

"Thanks," I mutter and I can feel my cheeks heating at this compliment. Then I internally berate myself, *If I say thanks once more, I'm going to punch myself.* This man has a way of twisting me up and seeing him in the flesh here in New York has reignited the crush I have on him, but I will admit, bumping into him has eased my nerves a little for my date with Seth.

"Well, I better let you get to your date."

"Okay, thanks." *Dammit, Cali.* "Mr. H, it was good to see you."

We step toward one another and he wraps his arms around me for a goodbye hug and surprising me, he leans down and presses a kiss to my forehead. My breath hitches when his lips touch my skin. Closing my eyes, I savor the moment, but all too quickly, his arms are no longer around me and he's pulling away.

In the middle of a busy New York City street, we stare at one another. A silence falls between us, it's not awkward per se, but it's not completely comfortable either. "Bye, Mr. H," I whisper, adding a finger wave before I step around him and head toward the coffee shop to meet Seth.

Those nerves from before are back, but this time it's because of the man I'm walking away from and not because of the man I'm walking toward.

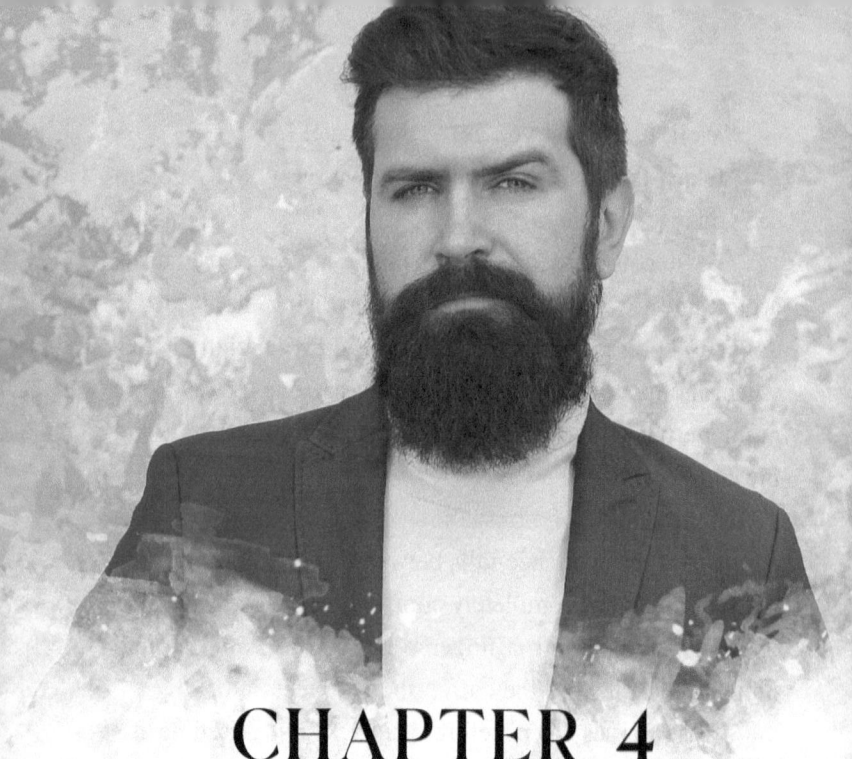

CHAPTER 4

Kane

"Thanks, Holly, I appreciate all your assistance in hooking me up with Alexandra." And I mean every word, in one meeting, I feel confident that Bitchifer and I will soon be divorced. Alexandra Woolley is a take no-holds-barred divorce attorney and with her now on my team, it will be smooth sailing to Divorceville.

"Anytime, Mr. Heatherington." Holly raises her hand to stop me. "And yes, I know you told me to call you Kane, but I was told to address my elders with respect and if I don't, my momma would have my ass."

"Less of the elders and I'll allow it."

"Deal." She smiles and offers me her hand. "Now, get out of here and let Alex get you divorced."

"Five nicest words you've ever spoken to me, Holly."

"No, the nicest five will be when Alex says 'congrats, you are officially divorced.'"

"I stand corrected." I nod. "Thank you again, Holly, I really do appreciate it."

"You won't be saying that when you get her bill." She winks at me. "Now, go explore the city and leave me in peace."

Nodding, I wave goodbye and exit her office, passing through reception and stepping into the waiting elevator. Pressing the button for the lobby, I lean against the wall and think over my meeting just now. I'm glad to have Alex and Holly on my team now, but I'm still betting that Bitchifer will contest it. Alex has a few ideas up her sleeve, if that occurs, but I'm pretty sure our divorce will be dragged through the courts and be decided by a judge.

This has gone on for too long now, I just want it over. I will never take her back after what she's done to our kids. Sure, walk away from me but not them. And her comment about wanting my hotel, that was the final straw. Alex has advised me to only communicate via text or e-mail now, so everything can be documented.

Stepping out onto the street, I'm met with the sounds of horns blaring, people everywhere, and that big city smell. I can't wait to get back to Silverbell Shore; give me my quiet, ocean-smelling small town any day.

Someone bumps into me and when I reach out, I'm hit

with the most stunning smell. It's familiar and when they lift their head, I stare into the beautiful hazel eyes of the one and only Calliope Fischer.

In the middle of the busy street, we silently stare at one another and something passes between us, but it's quickly broken when she pulls herself out of my grip. We discuss the hotel and the fact that she's on her way to a date. An irrational anger begins to simmer at the idea of her out with a boy, but what shocks me the most is how beautiful she is. She really has grown into an extremely attractive young woman ... and then I realize I'm checking out my best friend's daughter.

Shaking off that thought, I school the smile on my face and then we joke about her dad killing him ... and me, if he ever found out what I was just thinking now about his princess.

"Well, I'll let you get to your date."

"Thanks." Her smile widens farther when I mention her date and that feeling of rage reappears, but it dissipates when we hug each other goodbye and it morphs into something else. Something that leaves me feeling warm and fuzzy. Something that I should not be feeling toward this woman.

We hold on to each other for longer than is appropriate, and without thinking, I press my lips to her forehead and kiss her. It was only meant to be in a platonic 'your dad is my best friend' kind of way but as soon as my lips touched her skin, my body came alive. My heart kick-started to life, I haven't felt a jolt like this in a very long time, but quickly I pull away because it's Calliope.

She says another goodbye and then she's turning away

from me and heading off to her date.

Standing on the sidewalk, I watch her walk away. "What the fuck was that?" I mumble to myself as she disappears into the crowd. She looks over her shoulder and even though we're on a packed street, her gaze connects with mine. It feels like it's just the two of us, she finger waves again and I keep my eyes on her retreating form until I can't see her anymore. When she's out of sight, I shake my head, clearing the inappropriate train of thoughts currently playing in my mind.

I cannot go there.

I will not go there.

Stepping to the curb, I hail a taxi. Climbing in, I give the driver the name of my hotel and he pulls out into traffic. He weaves in and out and before I know it, we are back at the hotel.

A few hours later, I'm sitting in the hotel lobby bar with a glass of scotch when my phone rings. I answer without looking. "This is Kane," but I'm met with silence, "Hello?" I ask and again silence, "Is anyone there?" and then I hear a whimper and I don't know why, but I say the first name that comes to mind, "Calliope?"

"Yeah," she quietly replies, "it's me."

"Are you okay?"

"Yes. No. I don't know."

Hearing her so timid and meek causes something inside of me to snap, my heart is racing because the person on the other end of this call is not the brave and confident Calliope Fischer I know. This person is frail, distraught, and upset and not Calliope like at all. I want to protect her. Wrap her in my arms and never let go. "Where are you?" I ask.

"In a taxi," she replies with a sniffle. Hearing her so down and aloof affects me in a way like never before. Relief floods me that she's alone but I still don't like it.

"Tell him to come here." I demand, "Hotel Q on Fifth."

She covers the phone and I hear her muffledly tell the driver her new destination. "I'm on my way."

"I'll meet you out front."

"Thank you, Mr. H."

Before I can ask again if she's okay, she disconnects and once again, I'm met with silence.

Waving down the waiter, I order two scotches and a plate of buffalo mozzarella sticks, Calliope's favorite. I tell him, I'm going to meet my friend and will be back. He nods and I head outside to wait for her to arrive.

Just as I step outside, a taxi pulls up and from my position near the entrance, I watch her climb out. My eyes run over her. Her gray, almost black dress hugs her curves. It dips in the front, showcasing her tits, her gorgeous plump tits that I can't stop staring at. Shaking my head, I stop checking out my best friend's daughter and I look her over to make sure she's not hurt. She seems unharmed and it eases my worries somewhat.

She lifts her head and when she sees me, she pauses mid-step. She blinks a few times and then smiles shyly and finger waves at me. Smiling back, it sparks her into action and she races over to me. She throws her arms around my waist. Holding me tight, she begins to sob. Her body is shaking as I wrap her in my embrace. Holding her close to me, she begins to cry harder.

We stand here hugging one another until her sobs stop.

She pulls back and I cup her cheek in my palm. "Calliope, sweetheart, you need to tell me what's going on because you're really worrying me right now."

She nods and covers my hand cupping her face. She still has one arm around me, hugging me, and doesn't let go of her grip on me. To be honest, I like the feeling of being hugged like this.

She licks her bottom lip and my eyes track the movement of her tongue over her lip. "Can we go inside?"

"Of course." Lifting my hand from her side, I wipe the tears on her cheeks. Taking her hand in mine, I entwine our fingers together and escort her inside. Making our way back to the bar where I was sitting, I smile when I see our drinks waiting for us, and a steaming plate of buffalo mozzarella sticks next to them.

"You remembered my favorite?" Her eyes brighten at this revelation as she flicks her gaze between the food and me.

"Nah, these are for me," I tease her, shaking my head and picking up one of the fried cheese sticks.

"Ohh." She dejectedly sighs as I take a bite before shoving the entire cheesy morsel into my mouth, scorching my tongue in the process. I hiss and she grins in a 'that's what you get' kind of way. Pulling her chair out for her, she takes a seat and before I've sat down, she grabs the glass of scotch and chugs the lot back in one swallow, slamming the empty tumbler down on the wooden bar top. I notice she winces at the burn but it doesn't stop her from reaching over to grab mine.

Gripping her wrist with my hand, I stop her. Getting drunk isn't the solution right now, but I notice she's stopped breathing and she's staring at my hand on her wrist. I quickly release her from my grasp and she lifts her gaze to mine. She stares at me, rapidly blinking, her eyes glossy with unshed tears.

Breaking the silent stare off, I look and nod to the glass. "You can have that one, but only when you tell me what happened because right now, my mind is racing and I don't like any of the scenarios playing out in my head."

She nods, and again licks her lip but this time, she bites it. "I … I met Seth for coffee after I bumped into you. We had a great time and then he asked me to grab a drink. I was having a good time so I went to a bar with him. We had a few drinks, played some pool …"

"You weren't assa—"

She shakes her head. "No, but it felt like he could have. Thankfully, Dad made me take that self-defense class sophomore year because when he wouldn't stop getting all handsy, I kneed him in the balls and hightailed it out of there."

"But he didn't touch you?"

"No, he called me a dick tease and said he'd spread it around that I'm a lousy lay, but I just ignored him and got out of there before anything happened. I was so scared, Mr. H." She begins to cry again and seeing her so upset, affects me in a way that surprises me. Reaching over, I take her hand and squeeze it, letting her know I'm here for her. She jumps slightly when I first touch her, but she raises her eyes to mine and we silently stare at one another. In the dim lighting of the bar, she looks more beautiful than ever before. Even with mascara-stained cheeks.

She pulls her hand free, jumps off her stool, wraps her arms around my waist, and hugs me. The tears come harder and her body physically shakes. Hugging her tighter, I rub my hand soothingly up and down her back.

"Shhhh," I whisper into her vanilla-smelling hair. "I've got you. I won't ever let anything bad happen to you," I murmur into her hair and that feeling from earlier washes over me. It's something I haven't felt in a very long time but today, it's slammed into me twice. Calliope is the last person in the Universe I should be thinking about in this way but she's the first woman I've felt anything with since Bitchifer left me … I'm so screwed.

CHAPTER 5
Cali

Standing here in the middle of the bar, crying and breaking down in Mr. H's arms is not how I expected tonight to go. Then again, I didn't expect Seth to be such a sleazebag douche-hole dick-stain, but here we are.

My sobs finally subside to a slow trickle of tears and I pull back. Staring up at Mr. H, I tearfully smile at him. "Thank you," I whisper. He reaches out and cups my cheek, then with the pad of this thumb, he brushes away the tears and for some reason I start to laugh. Pulling away from him, I swipe at my cheeks, leaving my fingertips black from my smudged tear-stained mascara. "I must look like a mess."

"You look beautiful, Sunshine," he replies.

His words warm me deep into my soul. Without thinking, I reach down and take his hand in mine and, surprising me, he squeezes it. It's in that reassuring 'you've got this' way but still, it tugs at my heart. We silently stare at one another but the moment is broken when the bartender clears his throat. "Can I get you anything else, Mr. Heatherington?"

We each pull our hand away and turn our head to stare at him blankly. He repeats his question and Mr. H turns back to me. "Did you want anything?"

"A time machine to not go on that date." The barman and Mr. H both just stare at me. Shaking my head, I sigh. "But a glass of red would be nice."

"Coming right up."

The barman walks away to get my drink and I climb back onto the stool. Reaching over, I grab the remaining drink and chug it back. Mr. H is still silently staring at me. "What? You said I could have it if I told you what happened on my date, and I did."

He shakes his head and smirks as he takes a seat next to me. "Are you sure you're okay?"

Looking over at him, I nod. "I'm fine now. I have no idea why I called you."

"I'm glad you did. I hate the thought of you being upset and alone."

"It's New York, you're never alone," I reply, bumping his shoulder.

The bartender places my glass in front of me and without prompting, refills Mr. H's tumbler that I just finished. Picking the glass up, I bring it to my lips, close my eyes, and inhale. A smile appears when the scent of cherries and plums hit my nasal passages. Tilting the glass up, I take a sip and moan as the fruity tannins dance on my taste buds. Reopening my eyes, I see Mr. H watching me. His gaze drops to my lips and he watches as my tongue darts out and swipes across before I bite the corner nervously. "Sorry," I shyly say, "that's a good red. Being a student, it's been box wine for me for the last three years."

"I remember the days of cheap beer and mac and cheese."

"Whoa there, big spender, ramen noodles is my staple these days. Mac and cheese is expensive and only called for when celebrating." *As of late that is never. How I'm going to get through the next year without dying of malnourishment from only eating ramen, drinking coffee, and the occasional boxed red, I have no freakin' clue. Yes, you do, take up Nicole's offer and dance your way into less financial stress, amazing, yummy food, and non-boxed wine.*

He scrunches his face up at my statement. "Are you having money troubles, Calliope?"

Shaking my head defiantly, I laugh. "No, no, I'm fine." But I can tell from the look on his face he doesn't believe me. "Seriously, Mr. H, I'm fine. I'm just your typical broke student." He nods but we both know I'm full of shit right now, so I try again. "Really, Mr. H, I'm fine and I'm fully aware that when someone says they're fine they are usually anything but fine, but I assure you, I'm fine. It's all good."

"Okay, fine," he replies, and we both laugh when he realizes that he too just said fine. "You know what I mean, brat." He playfully bumps into my shoulder and I'm assaulted with his scent: sandalwood and leather. Then he shocks me when he says out of nowhere, "Dance with me?"

Staring at him, I blink rapidly. My heart rate accelerates. My mouth becomes dry. To show he means it, he stands up and offers me his hand. A force takes over and on autopilot I place my hand in his, and like earlier today when we touched, an electrical current zaps between us. Sliding off the chair, he holds my hand tighter, and we walk over to the little dance floor off to the side of the bar.

There are a few other couples dancing so it's not completely weird that he just asked me to dance. The current song stops and then "Just the Two of Us" by Grover Washington begins. Mr. H spins me out and pulls me back into him and as if we've done this a million times before, my arms go around his neck and he rests his on my hips. Locking into place as if it's where they belong.

Resting my head on his shoulder, I close my eyes and we sway to the music. My shit evening fades away and I focus on this moment. I focus on dancing with Mr. H and how amazing it feels being in his arms.

"You Are My Sunshine" begins to play and Kane begins to quietly sing it into my ear. His voice vibrating through my body. Lifting my head, I stare up at him. "Thank you," I murmur.

"Why are you thanking me?"

"For this. For making me happy—"

"When skies are gray," he adds, causing us both to laugh. He starts to sing again but this time he refers to me, Calliope, as his sunshine and I have to admit, my little crush on Mr. H is beginning to blossom further right now.

"I'll dance with a pretty girl any day of the week, but I'll only sing to a special one." He winks and then continues to sing, "You are my sunshine …"

A smile graces my face and I continue to dance and listen to him sing. The song finishes and we stop dancing. We stand on the dance floor and stare at one another as Train sings about bruises and fixing things. Like a scene from a romantic comedy, he begins to lean forward and for a brief moment, I think he's going to kiss me. My heart stops beating, it literally stops because holy shit, Mr. H is going to kiss me. He's getting closer and closer. He lifts his hands from my hips and he grips the side of my head. Closing my eyes, I wait to feel his lips on mine but I'm disappointed when, once again, he kisses my forehead … but I will say, if there was a medal for forehead kisses, Kane Heatherington would be a two-time, gold medal winning forehead kisser.

Pulling back, he stares down at me, his chest rising and falling in sync with mine but the intense and becoming sexual moment is broken when the barman yells, "Last call!"

"Guess, I better get home then," I whisper.

"Or you can stay for one more drink."

I'm nodding before he finishes the sentence. "I'd like that."

Mr. H and I walk back over to the bar and he orders two more drinks. He and I sit here while the staff cleans up and the two of us talk and talk until the wee hours of the morning. After the fifth yawn from him, I stand up. "I guess I better get going and let you get to bed."

"I can get a cab with you," he offers.

Shaking my head, I rest my hand on his. "Thank you but I'll be fine." I raise my hand to interrupt him. "And before you say anything, I've lived here for a few years now, I'm pretty sure I can get home on my own."

"Okay, but you need to text me as soon as you get in the door."

"Yes, Dad," I deadpan.

He smiles. "I couldn't bear the thought of anything happening to you. One heart-stopping moment for the night is enough."

"I'm sorry to have worried you."

"Never be sorry for reaching out. I will always be here for you, Calliope. Always." He pauses. "You are my sunshine after all."

"Thank you, and for what it's worth, I'm always here for you too. I'm your sunshine. Not sure what a college girl can offer a man like you but …" I end that statement with a shrug. Picking up my clutch, I open it to pay for my drinks, but Mr. H covers my hand.

"Tonight's on me."

Nodding, I offer him a grateful smile. "Thank you."

We fall silent. The air around us thickening with each passing moment. My tongue darts out and I lick across my bottom lip, and like earlier, his eyes follow the path of my tongue and then back up to my eyes. He reaches out and cups my face, running his thumb over the apple of my cheek. "If only," he whispers.

If only what? Does he feel this connection too? Or did I mishear him? But all too soon, he removes his hand and steps back. "Shall we?"

Nodding, I turn around and walk toward the exit, processing those two words—if only—that I *think* I just heard him whisper. We step outside and the bellhop hails a taxi for me—perks of living in NYC. There's one always there when you need it … unless it's pouring rain and you're running late—but to be honest, tonight, I wouldn't have minded waiting.

Mr. H waves the bellhop back and opens the door for me. "Good night, Mr. H," I murmur as I climb in.

"Good night, my little Sunshine."

He closes the car door and steps back onto the sidewalk. He slips his hands into his pockets and watches the taxi pull away. Leaning back into the seat, I stare at the roof of the car. As I've said before, Mr. H is an expensive fine wine and after tonight, I freakin' love fine wine. But my broke ass cannot afford fine wine and my heart can't have him either, so it doesn't matter what wine I can afford.

Fuck my life!

CHAPTER 6

Cali

… two years later

Today is graduation day. After four looooong years, I'm finally finished my studies and in a few short hours, I will have an expensive piece of paper in my hands confirming all my blood, sweat, and tears have paid off … well, it paid off to finish my degree. It didn't pay off and get me the six-figure marketing job I was hoping for, but thanks to my amazing roommate, it did get me a four figure a night stripping job.

Ohh, yeah. Did I forget to mention I finally succumbed

to being broke and became a stripper at the Nirvana Lounge? It was not long after my fight with Dad over him interfering and arranging the internship. One night when my card declined while I was trying to buy some wine, I knew I had to make a change. I couldn't admit to my family that I was a failure, so took up Nicole's offer and Miss Sunshine made her debut at the Nirvana Lounge. Finally, I had enough money to continue living and studying in NYC. As soon as my money woes disappeared, my grades picked up and I sailed through the rest of my studies. My boss, Miss Rhi, let me work shifts around my course so I managed to juggle both.

Sure, being a stripper isn't how I planned my life going, but I'm actually happy. And truth be told, I kinda love doing it. Who knew clumsy me would actually be pretty good at swinging around a pole? Miss Rhi said I was a natural and the money is phenomenal. It's all the mac and cheese and non-boxed wine for me now.

Speaking of mac and cheese, Mr. H—the cheeky man he is—after our evening together, he sent me a gift with a note that had me cackling like a hyena.

My Little Sunshine,
Every girl deserves a treat meal now and again.
Enjoy this mac and cheese ... I hear it pairs well with box red.
KH

Ever since the night of my horrible date with Seth, Mr. H has been here for me. Well, as much as I let him in. He, along with everyone else, thinks that life here in the Big Apple is grand. Little does he, and everyone else know, how close I came to losing it all, but with the encouragement of my roommate, I took a risk and made it work for me. I never imagined I'd strip my way through university but desperate times call for desperate measures, and now I only have a small student loan.

After the night when he was my knight in shining armor, my fantasies involving Mr. H became wilder and wilder. Luckily for me, dreams are free and I have an amazing vibrator because he and I can never be. This isn't a romance novel and the poor stripper girl doesn't end up with her dad's best friend. This is real life, so I have to settle for him being the number one star in my fantasies and a really good-looking, sexy as hell friend who I think about doing dirty, dirty naked things with.

I'm so thankful I ran into him that afternoon because that night he was there for me when I needed someone, and thanks to douche-hole Seth, a beautiful friendship blossomed. The friendship I have with Mr. H is one I treasure greatly. It's borderline inappropriate at times, but life's too short for it to be serious all the time.

Pushing aside my thoughts of Mr. H and my secret job, I finish getting ready for today. Looking at my reflection in the bathroom mirror, I take in my graduation outfit and smile. I'm wearing a kickass navy-blue pinstripe pantsuit that I bought myself. It cost me an arm and a leg, but how often do you graduate?

Picking up my mascara, I make that face you do when you apply it. Just as I begin to swipe the last coat, there's a knock at my door and it startles me. Jumping in fright, I nearly stab myself in the eye with my mascara wand but somehow manage to not smear black goo all over my face.

Exiting my bathroom, I head toward the door and they impatiently knock again. "Coming," I yell out and pick up the pace. Opening the door, I see a young delivery guy with a white box in his arms, "You Calliope Fischer?"

"That's me."

"Here," he snarls and shoves the box at me. Before I can say anything, he turns and walks away from me. Leaving me stunned holding a box in the doorway.

"Thank you," I sarcastically shout out. Kicking the door shut with my slipper-clad foot, I walk into the living room and drop to the sofa. Resting the box on my knees, I lift the lid and see another one inside, but my eyes widen when I notice the label before me. Throwing the lid aside, I run my fingers over the printing and grin.

Removing the inner box, I place it on the coffee table and drop to the floor, staring at the package before me. Stunned, I rapidly blink, thinking I must be hallucinating because surely, I'm not staring at what I think I'm staring at. Never in my wildest dreams did I ever think I would see, let alone touch one of these boxes in the flesh. Not anytime soon that is. Lifting the lid, I pull aside the tissue paper and cover my mouth, gasping with wide eyes. Before me are my dream shoes, a pair of Christian Louboutin 'So Kate' black pumps. I finally have a pair of my own Louboutins.

"Holy fucking shit," I mumble to myself as I pull

out the notecard in the bottom of the box. When I see the monogram on the notecard, my smile widens. "Mr. H, what did you do?" I mumble to myself as I flip the card over.

My Little Sunshine,
Every girl deserves a gorgeous pair
of shoes when graduating.
Hope they're the right ones.
Congratulations on all you've
achieved.
KH

Dropping the card, I gaze at my new shoes with a grin rivaling a carnival clown. With shaking hands, I carefully remove the shoes from the box and slide them onto my feet. I feel like Cinderella at the ball when they effortlessly slide onto my foot, they fit like a glove and feel amazing on my feet.

Wriggling my toes, I gaze down at my feet, still in shock at the gift from Kane. This is the best present I have ever received, but what does it mean? Is it just a 'congrats, you graduated' gift? Or am I reading too much into it?

Standing up, I walk into my bedroom and close my door so I can see myself in the floor-length mirror hanging on the back, and fuck me sideways, these shoes are everything. Dropping to the end of my bed, I snap a pic of my new shoes and attach it to a text message.

CALI: *Thank you so much, you really shouldn't have*

Walking back into my bathroom, I pick up the discarded

mascara wand and finish what I started before my gift arrived. I've just finished my hair when a text comes through. Grabbing my phone, I smile when I see it's from Mr. H.

Mr. H: You are very welcome ... with a heel that high, they look like they'll hurt

CALI: They felt like sliding through butter when I put them on

Mr. H: How do you know what sliding your feet through butter feels like? Do you have a foot fetish that I'm unaware of??

CALI: Ohh no, my secret sliding my feet through butter fetish has been revealed, what will I ever do now???

CALI: But seriously, Mr. H, thank you, best graduation gift

Mr. H: Be sure to tell your dad that LOL

Mr. H: Actually don't, not sure how he'll feel knowing I bought you such an extravagant gift

CALI: Your secret is safe with me. Thank you again, I love them.

Mr. H: Anything for you, Calliope. Anything!

Sitting here, I stare down at my feet and suddenly I'm accosted with a picture of me on my back, my Louboutin-clad feet digging into the muscular ass of Mr. H as he fucks me senseless. Lifting my hand, I squeeze my breast and rock forward, applying pressure to my throbbing clit, but my dirty daydream is interrupted by another knock at my door, and I know from the knock, it's Dad and Mom.

My sexy daydream quickly dissipates when I stand up. Letting out a sexually frustrated sigh, I shake off the thoughts and turn toward my bedroom door but my impatient dad knocks again. Even though I'm in my twenties, he still does our 'secret knock' each and every time he visits and truth be told, my inner ten-year-old loves it.

"Coming," I sing out.

Skipping out of my room, I race to the front door, swing it open, and smile at my parents. "Mom. Dad," I offer in greeting. Opening my arms, Mom envelops me. "Happy graduation day, Cali."

"Thanks, Mom." She grips my cheeks and stares at me, her eyes full of tears but a smile graces her face. "I'm so proud of you."

"Thanks, Mom," I voice again, and wipe at my eyes and sniffle. Before the moment can get more intense, Dad shoves—literally—Mom out of the way and wraps me in a bear hug.

"Happy graduation day, Princess."

"Thanks, Dad," I mumble into his chest.

Pulling apart, we walk into my apartment and Mom sees the shoebox on the sofa. "Did you get new shoes?" Nodding, my smile widens and I thrust my foot forward, spinning it from side to side. "Louboutin?" I nod, still grinning over my new shoes. "Calliope," Mom admonishes. I notice she uses my full name and I feel like I'm nine years old again, getting into trouble for using all of her Tom Ford limited-edition lipstick to paint Cari's face and turn her into a clown. "That's a lot of money to spend on shoes."

"It was a gift," I tell her.

"A gift from who?"

"A friend," I nonchalantly tell her, and I try to leave it at that but she presses me for more information.

"A boyfriend maybe?"

I wish, I think, but I keep that thought to myself. "No, just a friend."

I can tell from the look on her face she wants to know more but, thankfully, Dad interrupts. "We need to get going, otherwise we're going to be late and I refuse to miss seeing my princess walk across that stage. It's only going to happen once in my life."

"What about Cari? When she finishes design school, she'll have a graduation ceremony."

"Do they do that for design school?"

"Garrick," Mom admonishes him, slapping his arm. "Of course Cari will have a ceremony, I swear you don't think before you speak sometimes. Now, let's go."

Stepping between my parents, I offer them an elbow each and they loop their arms through mine. The three of us make our way down to Dad's rental and we head to campus for the graduation ceremony.

Later that evening, I'm lying in bed with my legs up on the wall above my bed, crossed at the ankle with my shoes still on my feet. Even after being squished for coming up on eight hours now, my feet don't feel sore at all. I don't think I will ever remove them. I'm still in shock Mr. H bought these for me, he really is amazing.

As I stare at my shoe-clad feet, I wonder if maybe he feels what I feel too. Or am I reading too much into this gift?

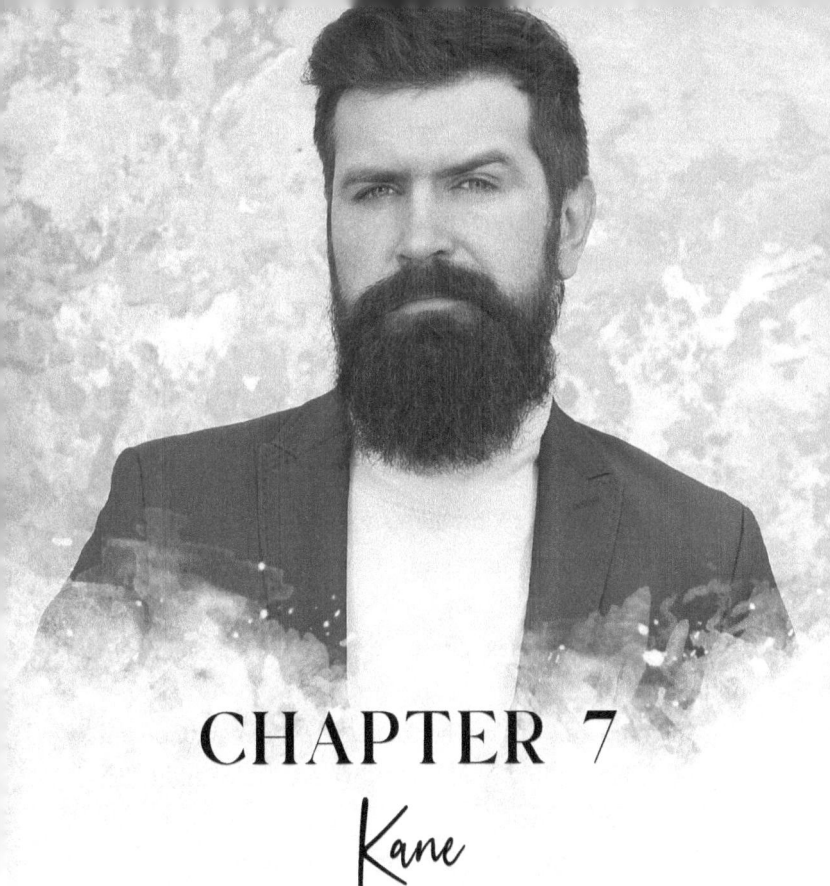

CHAPTER 7

Kane

... three months later

"**J**ust sign the fucking papers, Danica," I growl across the boardroom table in Alex's office at my ex-wife, well I hope, my soon-to-be ex-wife. This is my, I've lost count of the number of trips to the Big Apple trying to finalize my divorce from Bitchifer. She's blocked, stalled, and refused to sign every time.

"No," she sneers. "I want half the hotel."

"I fuc—"

Alex interrupts, "What my client means, is that the offer before you is final and more than fair. Ms. Heard has not had anything to do with the hotel," she pauses and then adds, "ever. And during the course of their marriage, Ms. Heard didn't contribute anything financially to the well-being of the three children they share, and since she up and left four years ago, she hasn't had any contact with her children or again, contributed to their lives. I'm more than happy to take this before a judge—"

"Can I have a few moments with my client?" Danica's lawyer asks, interrupting Alex, who was on a roll listing all of Danica's misdemeanors.

"Of course," Alex agrees, "Kane, let's give them a moment."

Standing up, I follow her out of the room and down the corridor. "Holy shit," I pant when we are out of sight. "You were amazing in there."

"Just doing my job," she nonchalantly replies.

"What do you think will happen next?"

"They'll sign," she confidently declares, leaving me shocked because I don't feel the same way at all.

"How can you be so sure?"

"Her lawyer wants this over and done with. My investigators have discovered that MacLaine and Sons are close to dropping Danica as a client."

"How—" She raises her hand to stop me.

"I know because I'm good at what I do, Kane. If she doesn't sign today, we go to court and trust me, she doesn't want that because she will get less than what's currently on the table. Her lawyers know that, but she's a deceitful, backstabbing, conniving wench and as it is, she doesn't deserve what you're offering her. You have offered her more than she deserves."

"But—" She raises her hand again and stops me from continuing.

"She's the mother of your children blah, blah, blah. Kane, and, yes, I'm aware I used your first name but that's how serious I am. She's no mother and from all accounts, she was a pretty shitty wife too. In the eyes of the law, she's entitled to very little—"

"But—"

Alex shakes her head and gives me the eye, reaffirming to me why she's the best at what she does. "Nope, no buts. I think you're making a mistake offering her what you are, but you are being the nice, kindhearted soul that Holly described to me. You're giving her more than she deserves but as your lawyer, I will follow your wishes."

Leaning against the wall, I rub my beard like I do when I'm agitated, and shake my head as I think about how this is all playing out. This is typical Danica, how I ever fell in love with her amazes me but our love did produce three amazing children, so it wasn't all that bad, except for the divorce part. When Danica and I said our vows, I meant the 'til death do us part' line and I hate that I'm in my forties and almost divorced.

"Let's go," Alex voices, snapping me back to the present. I was so far in my head; I didn't see the other lawyer come out and get us. Nodding, I follow her back into the boardroom. We both take our seats. Alex sits up straight and commands the attention in the room—see, amazing at what she does. "So, have we made a decision?"

My eyes dart between the lawyer and Danica. I can't read the expression on her face but then her lawyer utters four words, "We accept your terms." They turn my frown upside down and inside my head, I'm doing a little dance.

Alex and the lawyer discuss what happens next. I zone out and sit here stunned that she finally accepted, I still don't quite believe it. I was sure she'd draw this out to the courts. Dropping my gaze to my hands on the table, my eyes land on my wedding band. With my thumb, I mindlessly spin the ring around and around my finger.

Lifting my left hand, I remove the band and hold it up. Gripping it between my thumb and forefinger, I stare at it. Then I notice Danica staring across the table at me, standing next to her lawyer about to leave. With a flick of my wrist, I toss it over to her. "You can have this too; I have no need for it anymore."

She reaches out and slips the ring into her handbag. She shoves her lawyer out of the way and storms out of the boardroom. Her lawyer nods his goodbye and follows after her.

Shaking my head, I start to grin. "You did it, Alex. You really fucking did it."

"Did you doubt my ability, Kane?"

A laugh escapes me. "You? No. Her." I head nod to the corridor. "Her, hell fucking yes. When we left just before, I was positive she was going to draw this out and take us before a judge."

"To be honest, I thought that was how it was going to end up too. When he said, 'we accept' I nearly fell off my chair."

"You and me both. So, what happens now?"

"I draw up the papers, then you both sign them and then we file them."

"That easy?"

"As long as she signs them, yes."

"One can hope it will be that easy." I cross my fingers. "When will you have the papers? I fly back to Silverbell tomorrow afternoon."

"I can make sure they're done by lunchtime tomorrow, swing by here on your way to the airport."

"You're the best, Alex."

"Just doing my job. Congrats, you're almost divorced."

Holly walks into the room just as Alex says this and smiles at the news she just heard.

"Four of the best words," I tell her, slapping the table.

"If I remember correctly," Holly says, "you said the five best words will be 'congrats, you ARE officially divorced'?"

"Four is almost five and I'll take that win for now. Once it's all final, we can upgrade to are." Holly laughs, offers me an 'almost' congratulations and leaves me with Alex. "Call me if there are any issues with the papers." Alex nods and continues to gather up her things. "Thanks again, Alex. You have no idea how relieved I am that this is almost over."

"Probably as relieved as Mr. MacLaine."

"Poor bastard, I don't think he's ever had a client quite like Danica Heard before."

"I think you might be right," she agrees with me. "Now, go out and celebrate. I'll see you tomorrow."

Standing up, I push the chair back and stare down at

Alex. "I know, I keep saying it, but thank you."

"Just doing my job, Kane. It's why you pay me the big bucks."

"And a mighty fine job you did." She stands up and offers me her hand. I place mine in hers but I also pull her in for a hug. Stepping back, I smile. "I'll see you tomorrow." Turning on my heel, I exit the boardroom and walk down the corridor and step into the waiting elevator.

Walking through the lobby, I step out onto the busy street, turn left, and start walking. I lose myself amongst the hustle and bustle of the city. Stopping in the middle of the sidewalk, I drop my head back, close my eyes, and take a deep breath. "I'm free," I whisper to myself, "I'm fucking free." That tether to Danica has been removed from around my neck and for the first time in a very long time, I can breathe freely.

Tonight calls for a celebration and I want to do something I normally wouldn't. When I open my eyes again, they land on a neon sign. Thinking what the hell, I cross the road and walk through the doors of The Nirvana Lounge.

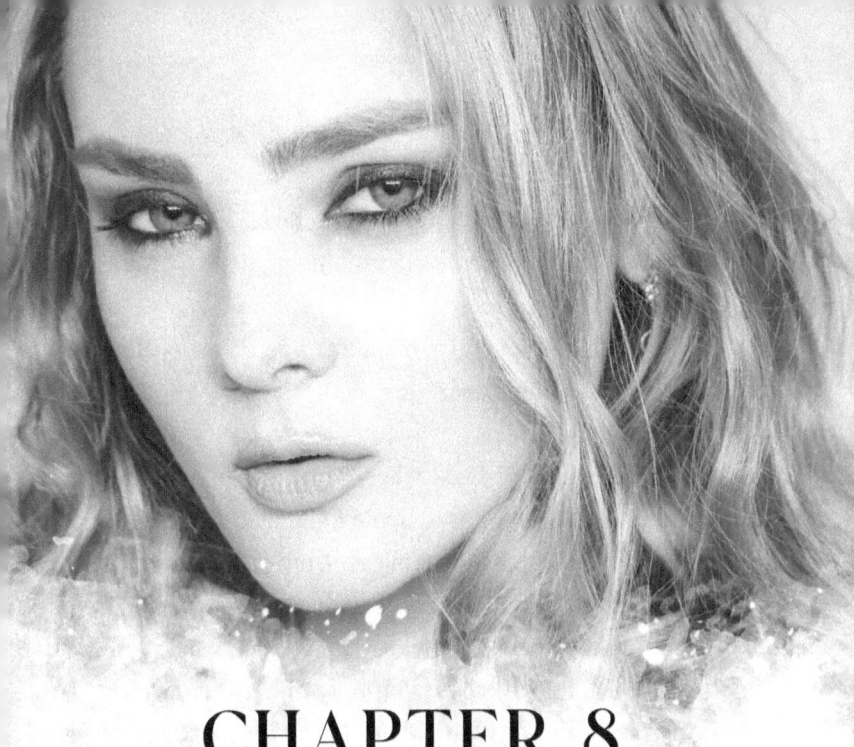

CHAPTER 8

Cali

The club is busy this afternoon, but then again, it's always busy here because it's one of the top ten clubs in New York. Tuesdays are generally quiet, being midweekish, so this is highly unusual but the cash boost is always the bonus of a busy day.

I'm in the dressing room in back, getting ready for the second set of my shift when Nicole drops into the seat beside me. She's all sweaty but she still looks put together and stunning—bitch. I look a sweaty mess when I get off stage. "Ugh, there's some right royal assholes out there today," she complains before taking a drink of water to rehydrate.

"Is it a full moon bringing out the crazies?" I ask her. "I ran into a sleazebag when I was coming in, never in my life have I been happy to see Zed."

"Wow, that's saying something when you willingly want to be rescued by Zed."

"I know, right?"

Zed and I briefly dated when I first started coming to hang here while waiting for Nicole to finish a shift. He was a little too intense for my liking so I broke things off, but he was another Seth and didn't understand no meant no. This was right around the time I was ready to pack it all in and head back to Silverbell with my tail between my legs, but after spending my last twenty bucks on cheap, crappy vodka that night with Nicole, she managed to get me to agree to give dancing here a go. Rhiannon, or Miss Rhi as she prefers to be called, gave me a shot. And I have to say, she is the most amazing boss in the world but her number one rule is, no fraternizing with staff or patrons. So luckily for me, it gave me the out I needed when it came to Zed. The only downside, he's very overprotective when it comes to me and handsy men. He always conveniently seems to be on break when Miss Sunshine—my stage name—is on and ready to swoop in and rescue me if I need rescuing.

Looking at my reflection, I sadly smile at myself. Deep down, I hate that I'm doing this, but facing up to my family and friends back home regarding my failures would be even harder to face, so I suck it up and dance. I've applied for fifty million different marketing positions but they all want someone with experience. How the hell am I meant to get experience if no one is willing to give me a try?

My last interview was at Luxe here in New York with some bitch named Scarlett. I wasn't too upset to not get that position, but working for Luxe would be a dream come true. I remember Mr. H talking about the CEO, Connor Crawford, one day, saying he runs The Clifton using the same business model as him. It's probably why The Clifton is always booked out through the summer each and every year.

Like always, when I start thinking about Mr. H, my lady parts start buzzing. Closing my eyes, I gently rock to the dull thud from the stage area in my seat and gently apply pressure to ease the want building between my thighs. FYI, it's not helping.

Hopefully, I'll get some relief when I'm up on stage in a few. Whenever out there, it's always him I imagine I'm dancing for. Makes it feel less dirty if I imagine him and it's a good way to dance out the tingles and get in my cardio exercise.

"You're thinking about him again, aren't you?" Nicole pokes my arm, snapping my eyes open and causing that buzzy feeling to immediately dissipate. "You always get this goofy grin on your face when you do."

"I do not," I protest, rolling my eyes at her. "And for your information, I was thinking about my next routine—"

"While thinking about him," she teases. Picking up a hair roller, I throw it at her and stick my tongue out. "You know what they say about people who protest too much?"

"Yeah, that their roommate will smother them with a

pillow later this evening."

Before Nicole and I can continue to tease one another, Miss Rhi sticks her head in. "Miss Sunshine, after you're done up there," she flicks her thumb to the stage, "there's a guy in VIP 3 waiting for you. He literally described you to a T when he listed the attributes he was after."

"Ohhhhhhh," the girls all around me coo.

"Someone's gonna get a big fat tip." Nicole winks. "And some money too."

Shaking my head, I roll my eyes. I know some of the other girls offer extra services in the VIP rooms, but I draw the line at that. Miss Sunshine will happily get naked, hello tips, but their penises stay away from her—my—vagina.

"You got it, boss lady," I tell Miss Rhi as I stand up. Walking over to the floor-length mirror, I take in my outfit to make sure it's looking fine. Tonight, I'm wearing stripper heels—duh—a sexy baby-pink G-string with a demi cup bra and over the top a darker pink, satin dressing gown that just covers my ass. Tying the sash, I open it at the front to show off the girls. Then I adjust my boobs before slicking some Vaseline over my nipples to make them shine, a neat little trick of the trade Nicole shared with me back when I was just here watching. With one last fluff of my hair, I spin on my heel and head to the stage, ready for my set.

"Have fun," Nicole singsongs and gives me a finger wave. Waving back, I step into the hallway and walk toward the stage. Standing off to the side, I shake my shoulders, loosening up my body. The lights go out, it's go time. I walk onto the stage and turn my back to the audience. Taking a deep breath, I close my eyes and an image of Mr. H appears, and that feeling of 'I can do this' washes over me. Nodding to the music man, he nods back, and the music starts; it's showtime. I always start my nights—and my VIP sessions—with "Closer" by Nine Inch Nails, you cannot get any sexier than talking, well singing, about fucking like animals.

My body moves to the beat, and I float around the stage, not paying attention to the audience, focusing on the image in my mind of Mr. H. Piece by piece my outfit falls away and just as the song finishes, I jump onto the pole in the middle of the stage and begin part two of my routine.

When I first started here, I was petrified of the pole, but now it's my favorite part of my routine. And I freaking love how I can seamlessly go from sexy dancing and stripping to seductive spinning on the pole. My next goal is to learn to strip on the pole, Nicole thinks I'm crazy, but I'm always up for a challenge.

Before I know it, I'm collecting the bills thrown on the stage and my second set of the evening is over. After a forty minute break, I'll return for my third set and repeat, four more times and then my shift is done. Occasionally, like tonight, I give private dances, therefore reducing my sets from six to five, but the private dance fee certainly makes up for the missed set.

Most shifts I walk away with about two grand in my pocket. Not gonna lie, that's why I do this. As an entry-level marketing assistant, I'd be lucky to be making nine hundred bucks a week, but I don't want to do this forever. No one wants to see a stripper with saggy boobs swinging around a pole. So my plan is to do this 'til my student loan is paid off and then I focus harder to get my dream job.

Stepping off the stage, Nicole reminds me of my private guest before she takes to the stage for her second set of the evening. Nodding at her, I race back into the dressing room to freshen up. My makeup is still on point so I slip back into my pink lingerie and gown. Quickly I grab a cool drink of water before I head to VIP 3 for my private dance.

Standing outside the door, I close my eyes and take a breath. As soon as my image of Mr. H appears, I nod my head. With my hand on the door handle, I push it down and open, just as the beats from my Nine Inch Nails song wrap themselves around me. Putting one foot in front of the other, I sashay into the room and drift into the zone. Lowering my head to make it more seductive, I step farther into the room. The sound of the door clicking closed behind me causes me to jump in fright. Taking another deep breath to calm my sudden bout of nerves, I lift my head, but those nerves come back with a vengeance and my eyes widen to the size of saucers. Standing in front of me is none other than the man of my dreams himself, Mr. Freaking-H.

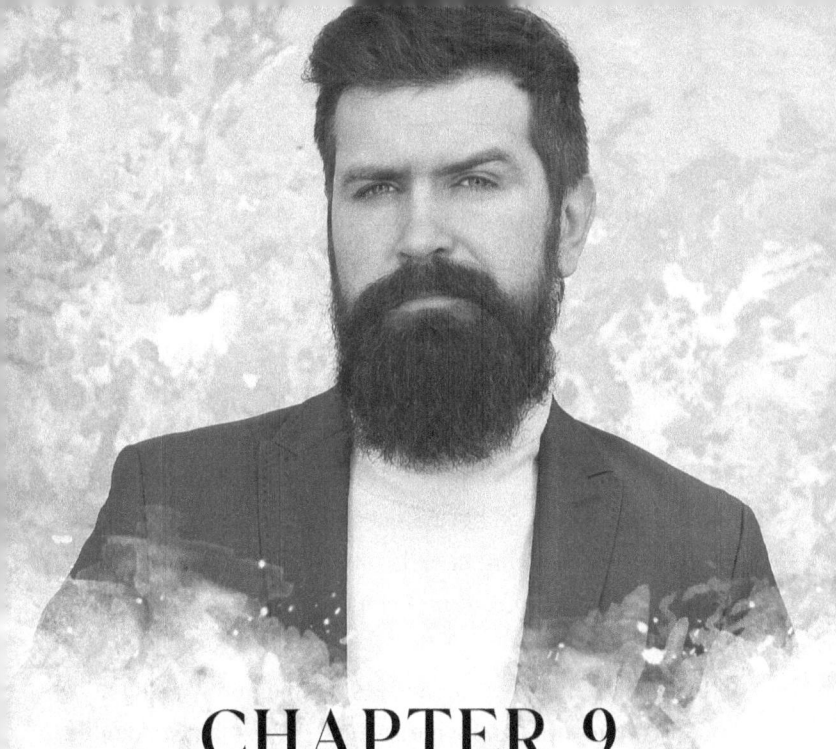

CHAPTER 9

Kane

While waiting in the VIP room for my private dance with Miss Sunshine, the nerves start to kick in. I haven't been in a strip club since Garrick's bachelor party, but this is the first time I've requested a private dance. As soon as I described the type of lady I wanted—golden blond hair, green eyes, fantastic tits, and legs that go on and on—the owner's eyes lit up like a Christmas tree. Then with a beaming smile she said, "I have the perfect girl for you, sir, but do you mind waiting? Miss Sunshine is about to go on but I promise you, she'll be worth the wait."

"Sure, I can watch her out here first."

She shook her head at me and tuts, moving her finger back and forth in my face like a pendulum. "Uh-uh, wait for her in the room, it will be more enjoyable for you, THEN you can watch her on stage later when she does her next set."

And that brings us to now. Me waiting in the VIP room for my dance with a stripper named Miss Sunshine. While I wait, my mind drifts to my Little Sunshine, wondering if I should reach out and have dinner with her. Garrick would appreciate me checking in on his little girl, it's what a good best friend would do. Before I can think on that further, the door handle rattles.

That little jingle has my nerves ramping up. Wiping my hands down my thighs, I wipe away the sweat that suddenly appeared. Closing my eyes, I take a breath, it eases my nerves slightly and when I open them again, I keep them focused on the entrance. After what feels like an eternity, music begins to pump through the speakers and the door begins to open. The room darkens, the atmosphere changing when the lights change color. The first thing I notice when she steps into the room is her long, lean, sexy as hell legs. My eyes drop to her heel-clad feet and then slowly I run them up her body and I like, no love, what I see before me.

My gaze lands on her head but she's looking down, swaying gently from side to side, anticipation building with each movement of her hips. Finally, she lifts her head and my heart stops, it literally stops beating in my chest. My eyes are as wide as hers and if this was a cartoon, they'd be bulging out of our heads.

Neither one of us utters a word. We silently stare at one another, each of us processing the situation we currently find ourselves in. I was just ogling the half-naked daughter of my best friend, the half-naked exact replica of whom I requested when I booked this. At that revelation, my brain kicks into gear. "Sunshine, what are you doing here?"

"Mr. H. ... I umm, shit, fuck, shit."

She turns to flee but she's trembling, her shaking hand can't grip the door handle. Finally, she gets it to move and pulls open the door, light from the hallway shines through the gap. Reaching over her shoulder with the palm of my hand, I slam it shut again. My front is pressed to her back. She's breathing heavily and I'm accosted with her scent. A scent I haven't been able to get out of my head for almost two years now. "Sunshine, sweetheart—" She shakes her head at the sound of my voice but I can't let it go. Spinning her to face me, I stare into her eyes. "What are you doing here? You work here? Why? What about marketing? Talk to me, Sunshine."

"I ... I ..." she mutters, unable to form a full sentence. She's still shaking her head, clearly, she's in shock because I know I fucking am.

"You work here?" I question again. "I thought—" But she interrupts me, pressing her palm to my chest.

"Please, Mr. H, can we just forget that you saw me?" she begs. The broken tone of her voice hits me deep inside. Then she pleads again, "Please?"

"I will never be able to get this vision out of my head, Sunshine." And that's the God's honest truth. Calliope Fischer, My Sunshine, is fucking gorgeous on any given day, but in sexy as sin lingerie, she'd bring the toughest of men to their knees; me included. My mind is running rampart with what I'd love to do with her scantily clad body, and let me tell you, the reality is much better than my imagination. I quietly add, "It's hard enough as it is." And I don't know if I'm referring to my dick, or the inappropriate thoughts I've had surrounding this woman.

Her breath hitches at my admission and she lowers her head. Reaching out, I place my finger under her chin and lift. Our faces, inches apart. I can feel her breath on my skin and if she was any other woman on this Earth, I'd cover her mouth with mine and kiss her, but I can't because she's my best friend's daughter. I know that's hypocritical considering I dream about her, but dreams and reality are two very different things.

"Mr. H," she whispers, "I … I—"

"You what, Sunshine?"

"I … I need to go." Staring at her, I see a broken and defeated girl before me and it hurts to see her like this. "Please let me go," she begs again, her eyes welling with tears.

"Okay," I relent, nodding at her but it's the last thing I want. I have so many questions right now. "I'll let you go, but this isn't over, Calliope." Removing my hand from her chin, I slide it down her arm and take her hand in mine, giving it a light squeeze before I remind her, "You and I need to talk."

She nods, causing a lone tear to fall down her cheek. On instinct, I let go of her hand and lift mine, wiping away the wetness on her cheek. Leaning over, I press my lips to her forehead, she closes her eyes and chokes back a sob. "Please don't shut me out," I whisper.

"I won't," she meekly whispers and before I have a chance to say anything else, she slips under my arm and I let her open the door. She steps out and closes it behind her. Leaving me standing alone in the VIP room.

When I came here earlier tonight, I'd hoped to see someone like Calliope, but never in a million years did I expect to actually see Calliope-fucking-Fischer, my little ray of sunshine here. After seeing her dressed like that, I'm even more screwed than I was before I entered this place where she's concerned.

Opening the door, I step out into the hallway and make my way to the exit but after what just happened, I need a drink.

"Scotch, neat," I tell the scantily clad bar lady as I climb onto a seat at the bar.

She nods and places two shot glasses before me. I lift my gaze to hers. "You look like you need a double." Nodding at her, I pick up the first glass and shoot it back, wincing at the burn but also savoring it.

My new best friend refills the glass I just finished and leaves me be. Picking up the second one, I shoot it back. Staring at the third, I know if I shoot this, it will knock me on my ass, so I pick up the glass and spin the chair around.

Leaning against the bar, my eyes dart around the club looking for Calliope but unfortunately, or maybe fortunately, I don't see her. Sipping on my drink, I keep thinking about Calliope and finding her here. The more I think about it, the more I need to speak to her. Pulling my phone out, I send her a text.

KANE: *We need to talk*

Four words that no one ever wants to hear, but we do need to talk. My eyes are glued to the door where I see other staff come out from but never do I see the blonde I want to see.

The lady who took my booking for the dance earlier glides over to me. She's smiling and I can tell that she's the big boss. She commands attention in the way she carries herself.

"I trust you enjoyed yourself with Miss Sunshine?"

"Umm, yeah, sure," I nonchalantly reply, and I can tell from my reaction that she's not impressed. The last thing I want to do is get Calliope in trouble. "I couldn't do it," I tell her with a shrug.

"Ahhhh, I see." She nods. "You are aware there's a no refund policy?"

Shaking my head vehemently, I raise my hand. "No, that's fine, I understand. I just hope I didn't upset the young lady."

"Miss Sunshine is one of my best, I'm sure she's fine, but I will be sure to let her know that you're sorry. May I offer you any of the other girls? I was sure with your specifics, matching you with Miss Sunshine would have sufficed your inner wants and desires."

Miss Sunshine, it's close to Sunshine, the affectionate name I call Calliope from time to time, and I find myself smiling. Does she think of me when she's here? Does she imagine me while she's up on the stage parading around?

"No no, it's fine. It's not her, it's me." Well, it was

both of us, but I can't tell this lady that I was about to get a private lap dance from my best friend's daughter, and that if she hadn't run away like she did, I would have allowed her to grind her sexy little body all over mine.

"Very well." She waves over the bartender. "This man's drinks are on the house."

"Yes, Miss Rhi." She looks to me. "Another?"

Shaking my head, I cover the glasses on the bar top. "Thanks, I'm fine. I think I'm going to head on out."

"I hope to see you back here again one day," the lady I now know as Miss Rhi says.

"We'll see." Nodding at her, I take one last look around, hoping to see Calliope but I don't. Knowing how mortified she is, she's probably hiding in the back, waiting for me to leave. Maybe I should sit here all night so she doesn't take that stage again but I know, well I hope, that she doesn't.

Waving goodbye to the bartender, I head toward the exit. While I'm waiting for a taxi, my phone pings with a text.

CALLIOPE: *I know we need to talk but I can't tonight … I'm mortified right now. I need to process everything*

KANE: *Take all the time you need, Sunshine. I fly out tomorrow night but I can extend if you need me to.*

She doesn't reply and I begin to wonder if I've overstepped the mark, offering to extend my stay, but I need to know why she's here. What happened to the great marketing job she told us all about? I have so many questions right now, but I'm also fretting about what I tell Garrick. Surely, he isn't aware that his princess is working in a strip club.

KANE: *I'm concerned, Calliope, please don't shut me out.*

CALLIOPE: *I'm so embarrassed, Mr. H*

Of course she's embarrassed. Her father's best friend was her next customer. Just saying that leaves a bitter taste in my mouth.

KANE: *Don't be embarrassed.*

KANE: *Please just talk to me.*

KANE: *I'm staying at Hotel Q on Fifth. Stop by when you're ready ... I'm not leaving New York until we talk.*

CHAPTER 10

Cali

"Shit, shit, shit, shit," I mumble to myself as I race down the hallway and away from my living nightmare. Of all the people in New York City, no, the entire world, it had to be Kane-freaking-Heatherington who was in that room just now. Entering the dressing room, I head for the tiny bathroom in the back. Once safely inside, I flick the lock and rest my hands on the vanity. Closing my eyes, I sigh when I'm accosted with a vision of *him* standing in the VIP room. I've dreamed of this scenario many, many times and I can say, real life didn't live up to the fantasy. Mind you, in the fantasy, I bump and grind all over Mr. H before we fuck like animals. I didn't cry and run out of the room with pink cheeks from embarrassment.

Taking a deep breath, I compose myself, open the door, and walk over to my cubicle. Dropping into my seat, I stare at my reflection. My eyes well with tears again. This is worse than when I realized I needed to become Miss Sunshine to survive. That I needed to strip my way through university. No one except Nicole and my colleagues here knew what I was doing, knew about my alter ego who took her clothes off and danced for money. Nicole wasn't going to tell anyone because she was in the same boat as me but now that I've been exposed, it suddenly feels dirty and cheap.

I startle when my phone pings. Without even picking it up, I know it's from him and when I glance at the screen, I'm right. I have a new message from Mr. H.

Holding my phone in my hand, I stare at the screen, not knowing what to do. I know we need to talk but I just can't, not right now. I'm mortified beyond belief so I throw it into my bag and do the mature thing, I ignore it and the problem I now find myself in.

Miss Rhi comes into the dressing room and as soon as she sees me, she opens her arms to me. Jumping up, I race over, and she envelops me in the hug that I need right now. Closing my eyes, I let the tears fall and I blubber into her shoulder.

Eventually, I lift my head and stare at her. "You knew him, didn't you?"

Nodding, I wipe at my tear-stained cheeks. "He's my dad's best friend."

"You know, in all the years I've worked here, no one has ever described a girl to a T like he did with you. For what it's worth, he didn't look angry just now."

"You saw him?"

She nods. "Yep, he was at the bar, looking for you."

"He texted; he wants to talk."

"Darling, I think he wants more than to just talk. He wants you."

"He's my dad's best friend," I plead. She shrugs and waits for me to continue. Sighing, I tell her our story. "I've had a crush on Mr. H since forever but nothing can happen."

"Who says nothing can happen?"

"Society. My dad, everyone," I dejectedly reply with a frustrated sigh.

"Screw society, your dad, and everyone else." She pauses. "Put the guy out of his misery and talk to him. You never know what might transpire but most of all, don't let anyone dictate what you want. Your happiness matters too. Why don't you head on home? It's been a big night for you," Miss Rhi offers after I sigh for the millionth time.

"I don't want to let you down."

"You'll let me down if you go out there. Your head isn't in the game and you, girl, mean more to me than anything else."

That's one of the things I love about Miss Rhi, she cares for each and every one of 'her' girls. She doesn't tolerate any bullshit, from us or the paying clients. She wouldn't care if the world's richest man was out there, if he was acting like a douche-hole, she'd kick him out without a second thought.

"Thanks, Miss Rhi, I think I will head home."

"Good, but I'm secretly hoping you'll go and see that bearded hunk instead of heading home."

A laugh escapes me at her description of Mr. H. "Bearded hunk, eh?"

"I call it as I see it, and personally, I think you need to see what happens. Life's too short to worry when it comes to love."

"But it's so complicated."

"When is love not complicated?"

"Touché," I reply. "But—"

Miss Rhi presses her finger to my lips, shushing me. "Nope, no buts. Before you make any rash decisions, talk to him, you might be surprised."

Nodding, I process her words. "That's for tomorrow Cali to worry about. Tonight, I'm going to go home and eat my weight in chocolate chip cookie dough ice cream."

"I'm more of a vanilla girl," Miss Rhi says, shocking me with her ice cream flavor choice.

"Vanilla, really?"

"When it comes to ice cream yes, but behind closed doors I'll try all thirty-one flavors on offer and sometimes I'll mix them together too." She winks and walks out, leaving me laughing. Even if from this day forward, I'll never be able to walk into a Baskin Robbins without thinking about this conversation with Miss Rhi.

Shaking my head at what I just discovered about Miss Rhi, I walk back to my cubicle, grab my phone, and text Mr. H. We text back and forth for a little while and he tells me he isn't leaving New York until we chat. Can I hide from him forever? *New York is a big city ... but not big enough because he found you,* I berate myself.

Twenty minutes later, I'm walking out the staff entrance and I decide to put on my big girl panties and face Mr. H tonight, rip off the Band-Aid as they say. Before I chicken out, I shoot off a text.

CALI: If you're still awake, I'd like to talk

Climbing into a taxi, I give the driver my address and sit back. Staring at the roof of the car, my mind plays the evening over and I can't believe what happened. My phone pings in my hand with a text, I jump in fright and drop it. Leaning forward, I pick it up and notice the driver looking back at me, he's staring down the front of my top. "Eyes on the road, buddy," I tell him as I swipe into my message.

Mr. H: I'm awake and ready to talk. Where did you want to meet?

CALI: I'm in a taxi, I'll come to you at the hotel

Mr. H: Okay

Leaning forward, I clear my throat. "Excuse me, can we change the destination?" The driver nods. "Can you now take me to Hotel Q on Fifth?"

"Sure can." He changes lanes, taking me to Mr. H and a conversation that is going to be awkward.

CALI: On my way, be there in 15

Mr. H: Meet me in the bar.

I'm kind of relieved that he offered to meet in the bar because I'm not sure I want to be alone with him right now.

CALI: Okay. See you soon

Mr. H: See you soon **wink emoji**

Sitting back in my seat, my nerves begin to fester, wondering how this is going to play out.

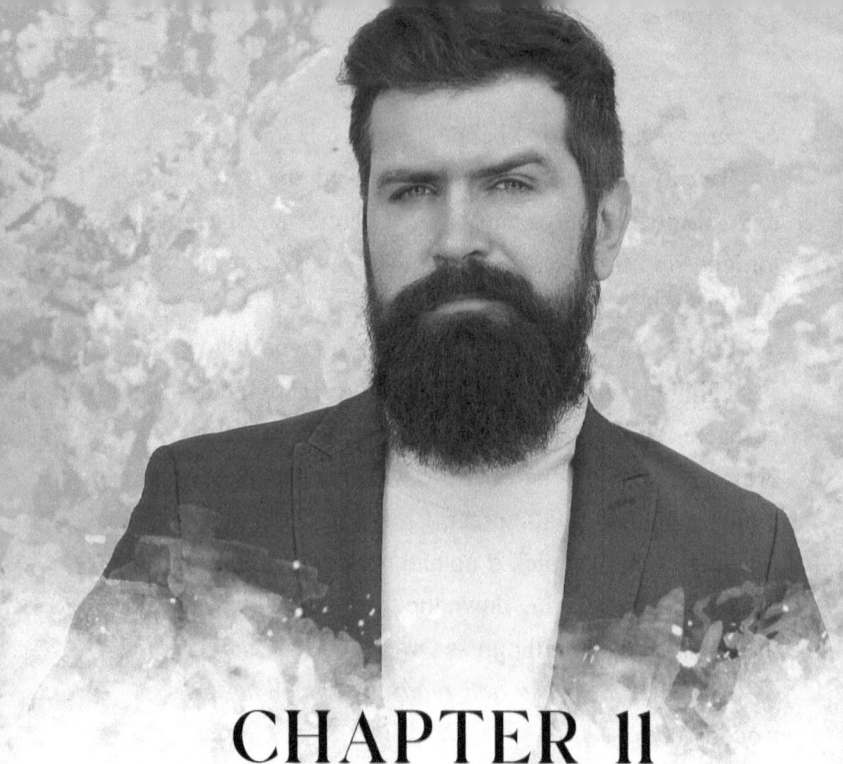

CHAPTER 11

Kane

Sitting on the bed in my suite in nothing but my pants, I drink straight from the bottle of scotch I grabbed on my way back here. Calliope or Miss Sunshine as I now know her to be, is at the forefront of my mind. I cannot get the image of her out of my head. Her tits covered in pale pink lace is a memory that will be seared into my brain forever. My cock likes it too because right now, I'm harder than fucking steel. I don't think I have ever been this hard in my entire life.

Placing the bottle on the side table, I free my aching, throbbing cock from the confines of my pants, grip it in my palm, and begin to stroke. The tip is leaking like a geyser, allowing my hand to effortlessly slide up and down the shaft. I'm imagining sliding my dick between Calliope's tits, in reality they aren't big enough for that. They'd be nothing more than a handful but that's more than enough.

Focusing on the task at hand—pun intended—I continue to pump my cock. Back and forth I stroke, and all too soon, I come harder than ever before. Streams of white coat my hand and chest but my dick is still hard.

My phone lights up beside me and I smile when I see Calliope's text on the screen. Wiping my hand on my pants, I pick up my phone, and my contented smile widens when I read she wants to chat. We agree to meet in the bar soon, so I jump off the bed and race into the shower. I need to clean myself up, I can't have this conversation with her covered in cum.

Ten minutes later, I'm sitting at the bar waiting for her. Like last time, I order her a plate of buffalo mozzarella sticks, a glass of red, and a scotch for me. Bringing the glass to my lips, I take a sip and then I feel the hairs on my neck stand on end; she's here.

When I spin around, there at the entrance to the bar is Calliope. She's wearing jeans and a low-cut top that showcases her stunning tits. Tits that up until this evening, I have never fully appreciated before. She looks just as sexy fully dressed as she did earlier in next to nothing and as she walks closer to me, I realize I'm screwed.

So

Fucking

Screwed.

CHAPTER 12

Cali

As soon as I enter the bar, I immediately spot Mr. H, it's hard to miss the sexy as hell silver fox. From where I'm standing, he looks calm, cool, and collected. The complete opposite to me, I'm on edge, jumpy, embarrassed, scared … the list goes on.

Taking a deep breath, I put one foot in front of the other and I make my way over to him. With each step I take, my heart races faster and faster. *Is it possible to have a heart attack at twenty-three?*

Obviously feeling my presence, he turns to face me and

all the air is knocked out of my lungs at how handsome he looks in this light. "Hello, Calliope," he croons, all proper and Mr. Heatherington-like. He kisses my cheek and holds out the chair next to him for me.

"Hi, Mr. Heatherington," I murmur as I take a seat, nervous and unsure of what to say or do. I've never before been in the situation where my dad's best friend was the next client I was to give a strip tease/lap dance to.

"I think you can call me Kane now … especially after tonight."

My head snaps up and over toward him. "How … how are you so okay with this?"

He laughs and for some unknown reason, that chuckle puts me at ease. He's running his fingers through his beard like he does when he's anxious. "Sunshine, I'm far from okay right now. I'm the complete opposite of that but at the same time I'm …" He drifts off, leaving me hanging.

"You're what?"

"Thinking things I shouldn't be thinking." He stares at me as he says this, his gaze heated. Something I have never seen directed at me before, and then I process his words. My eyes pop open in shock when what he just said hits me— he's been thinking about me how I've been thinking about him.

"Ohh," I utter.

"Yeah, ohh," he says with a nod. "If you were any other woman, I would have let happen what was meant to happen, but your dad is my best friend. I can't be wanting those things from you."

"Ohh," I dejectedly reply, looking down at my lap again.

Swallowing back the lump building in my throat, I close my eyes but the first tear falls and splatters on my hand, much like my heart is right now.

"Sunshine, no," he protests, "please don't cry." He reaches over and cups my cheek, brushing away the falling droplets. Lifting my gaze toward him, we stare at one another as I silently cry. The air around us thickening and pinging with electricity. The tears continue to fall as we watch each other. "This is so messed up," he finally says.

"Just another messed-up thing in my life," I tearfully reply.

His thumb brushes away another stray tear. "Wanna tell me what happened? How you ended up there?"

"How long you got?"

"For you? As long as you need me."

Can this man be any more perfect? His words mean everything to me and they cause the floodgates to open farther. I'm now sobbing uncontrollably. Mr. H pulls me into his arms and whispers sweet nothings to me as I break down in his embrace in the middle of the bar. I'm a tear-stained snot monster at the moment and now that the tears are flowing, I can't stop them.

Finally, they stop falling but I don't pull away. I like being held like this. Mr. H's hand gently runs up and down my back. Reluctantly, I pull away and wipe under my eyes. Noticing my wine, I pick up the glass of red and take a sip, the fruity liquid calming my nerves slightly. "Thank you," I finally whisper.

"Why are you thanking me?"

"For letting me breakdown like that. The last few years

have been so freakin' hard."

"How so?" he questions, but I ignore him. I take another sip that turns into a gulp and before long, the glass is empty. "Please, Sunshine, talk to me. What happened that you needed to turn to stripping? We all thought everything here in New York was good."

Running the tip of my finger around the rim of the glass, I stare into the emptiness and it hits me. Just like this glass, I'm empty—emotionally, physically, and mentally. Even though I'm bringing in the big bucks, I'm empty inside. No longer do I have any joy in my life. I'm not doing what I want to be doing. I mean, who grows up and says, "Mom. Dad. I'm gonna be a stripper when I grow up?" No one does that, well maybe Miss Rhi, she was born for this.

I'm snapped away from my wallowing when I feel a hand on my arm. His touch is electric, it brings me to life and I feel like the old Calliope, the Calliope who had a future and a plan. Turning my head toward him, I see nothing but concern etched on his face. "I'm fine—" He gives me 'that' look that says, 'I'm not stupid' and he waits. "Okay, fine. Fine probably isn't the best word to describe my life right now."

"Ya think?" he sasses.

"I don't think, I know. Life here got expensive and hard, and I didn't want to let anyone down. So I did what I had to do to survive. And then I graduated. I thought things would turn around after that, but I haven't had any luck landing my dream job, or any marketing job for that matter."

"Okay, I get that, but stripping?"

"I had no choice," I snap at him. "It was either that or

admit I was a failure, and I couldn't do that. I couldn't let everyone back home down. My roommate got me the job there. She was raking it in and paying off her debt while studying and living life to the fullest. I wanted my life back, so I gave it a go. Turns out, I'm pretty good at it and it's fun. I juggled that part-time and my studies for the last year of my degree. When I couldn't find a marketing position, I went full-time."

"I would have hired you."

"And I would have felt like shit, you just handing me a job. I want to get the job 'cause I'm the best candidate, not because my dad's your best friend."

He nods. "I get that, I do, but stripping?"

Shrugging at him, I sigh. "A girl's gotta do what a girl's gotta do."

"The father in me wants to take you over my knee." My eyes widen at that scenario. My heartrate increases at the thought of Mr. H smacking me on the ass, massaging my peachy globe to ease the sting before smacking it again and again. I'm snapped back to reality from that kinky scene when I hear him say "… your father."

"No!" I shout. "He cannot find out about this. It will crush him."

"You want me to lie to him?"

"Just don't tell him."

"That's lying by omission."

We stare at one another, neither one of us wanting to give in, and then I play a trump card. "If you tell him, you then have to admit to Dad that you were in a strip club, and then you also have to admit that you saw me in nothing but—"

He presses his finger to my lips. "Okay. Okay, you win. Your father would kill me if he found out I saw you like that, so your secret is safe with me."

"Thank you, I appreciate it."

"What are you going to do now?"

"Keep doing what I'm doing until I get a marketing job." He goes to open his mouth but it's my turn to press my finger to his lips. "And no, I'm not taking a job that you create for me. If and when a job becomes available, I will apply … under an alias … so I know I got the job based on my skills and not because you're Daddy's best friend."

"But you are still looking for a marketing gig?"

"Every day, Mr. H, I promise. I don't want to strip forever. I may be good at it, and it's the best freakin' cardio work out there is, but I've always wanted to be a marketing manager. I know, one of these days, the right job will come along. I just need to bide my time until then."

He eyes me, and then nods. "I admire your tenacity, and in a way, I'm proud of you for looking after yourself. You really are an amazing young woman."

"Thanks, Mr. H, I appreciate that."

We stare at one another. I feel relieved that it's out in the open and Mr. H seems okay with it all, and he's agreed not to tell Mom and Dad, so that's a plus. The evening takes a turn when he looks intently at me and says, "Sooo, are you still wearing that sexy AF pink number?"

"Did you just say sexy AF?"

He shrugs at me and I shake my head with a grin, this man continually surprises me. "You are something else,

Kane Heatherington."

"As are you, Calliope 'Miss Sunshine' Fischer." My eyes widen when he uses my stage name. "And don't worry, Sunshine, your secret alter ego is safe with me because there's no way in hell I'm telling your dad about your banging body."

My eyes widen farther and I shake my head. "Please don't ever use banging body and refer to my dad in the same sentence together ever again."

"Deal." He offers me his hand and I shake it. That electric jolt when we touch is still there but this time it feels different, and I don't know how to process that.

"Sooo," he asks again, "are you?"

Just like that, all the angst, unease, and mortification from earlier dissipates, and moments later, the evening takes another unexpected turn with what transpires next.

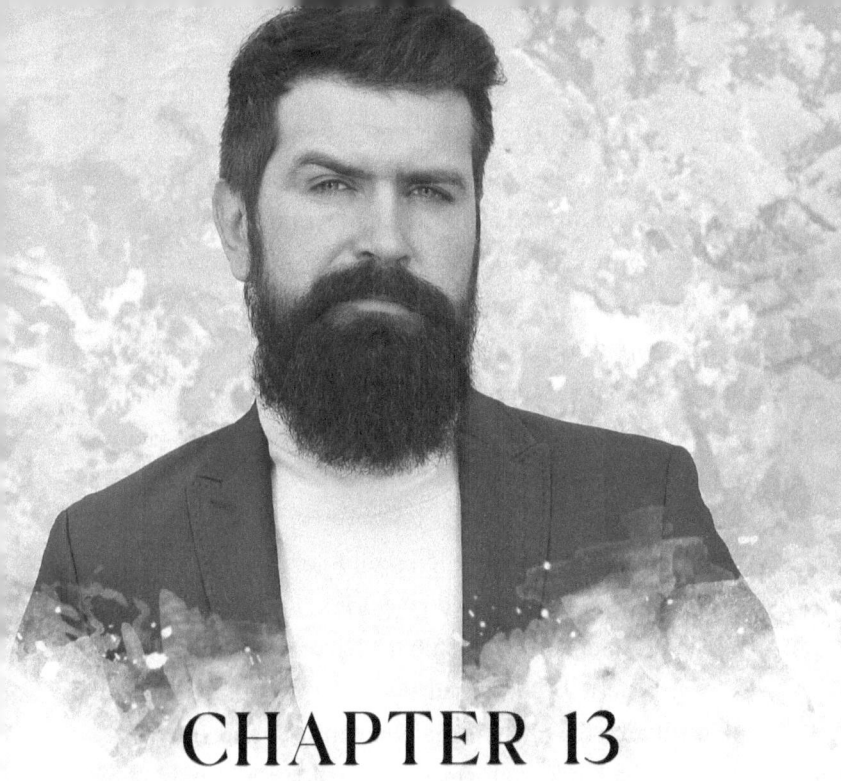

CHAPTER 13

Kane

Today is one for the memory books and the spank bank … but I will never admit that to anyone. It's a secret I will take to the grave. Calliope Fischer is the last woman on Earth I should be jerking off to or spending time alone with. However, I was never one for rules, hence, why I'm sitting in a bar with a woman I should not be sitting in a bar with. But when she told me her story, my heart broke for her and I was so glad to have broken the rules. If I'm honest, I was amazed at what she did to survive. Making the decision she did couldn't have been easy but somehow, she managed to get through university on her own. That's no easy feat, especially in New York. This city isn't cheap and that's reaffirmed as I order another thirty-dollar glass of scotch for myself.

Once Calliope and I clear the air, we grab a booth in the back and I cross a few more lines. May as well obliterate them, I'm already going to hell. Over copious amounts of scotch, red wine, and buffalo mozzarella sticks, Calliope and I have an amazing night together.

We laugh.

We reminisce about Silverbell Shore.

We drink, boy-o-boy do we drink. I can't remember the last time I drank this much but I have to say, after how my evening started, it's turned out to be pretty awesome and that's due to the phenomenal woman sitting next to me.

The bartender announces last call and I'm not ready to end the evening, so I do something stupid, again. I open my mouth with a proposal that I hope she agrees to. "Calliope, do you want to continue this up in my room?"

Without missing a beat, she nods. "I'd love that."

We order a bottle of red for her and since I have my scotch upstairs, I just grab a clean glass. With our drinks in hand, we make our way up to my floor and the forbidden.

Entering the room, she walks over to the window and pulls the curtains back. "Oh. My. God, you can see the park and The Plaza from here. I've always wanted to stay at The Plaza."

"You have?" I ask, smiling at her excitement.

"Yep, ever since I saw *Home Alone 2* when I was little I've wanted to stay there."

"You should treat yourself one weekend."

"Maybe I will. Just need to find someone to spend a weekend there with. It's not like I need to sightsee, and it would be a waste to have a huge bed like that to myself."

Her words stir something inside of me and I get the urge to growl 'me' but I know I can't. She's Garrick's daughter and as it is, if he ever found out about The Nirvana Lounge and this booze-filled evening, he'd kill me.

Needing to change this topic of conversation, I focus on getting us another round of drinks. Picking up the bottle from before, I pour myself a glass. Walking over to Calliope, who's still gazing out of the window, I take the wine bottle from her grasp. My fingers brush hers and her breath hitches. Surely, she didn't feel what I felt but from the way she's looking at me now, I know for a fact she did.

"Mr. H," she breathlessly purrs.

"Calliope," I whisper back.

We stare at one another and for once in my life, I want to let loose. I want to do something reckless. Something for me. I know what I'm about to do is wrong and crosses so many lines, but fuck the consequences. Before my brain can catch up, I think with my dick and step toward her. I grip her cheeks in my palms and press my lips to hers.

CHAPTER 14

Cali

Kane Heatherington is kissing me.

His tongue is in my mouth.

His hand is on my ass.

My boobs are squished against his chest.

Holy

Fucking

Shit

I'm kissing Kane Heatherington.

I must be in a coma and I'm dreaming because this isn't reality, it can't be, but it's true. His lips are pressed against mine and our tongues are tangoing in each other's mouths. This is wrong. So wrong. The mistake of all mistakes but I've already made many mistakes in my life, why not add to the list?

To be honest, I don't care because kissing him feels like home. I know I won't regret this come morning. So I give myself over to him and this amazing as hell kiss, secretly hoping that it will turn into more since we're now in the privacy of his room. We're already in the danger zone, we may as well smash through it now, but as quick as the kiss starts, it ends.

Mr. H pulls away from me.

Regret is written all over his beautiful, bearded face. He rests his forehead against mine and sighs heavily. When he dejectedly whispers my name, "Calliope," my heart drops and shatters into a million pieces.

The urge to flee overwhelms me, pushing him away from me, I murmur, "I ... I have to go." Stepping around him, I grab my purse off the bed and leave. "Stupid, Cali, stupid, stupid, Cali," I mumble to myself as I hurriedly walk to the elevator.

Thankfully, as soon as I push the call button the doors open. Stepping in, I turn around and when I look up, I see Mr. H standing in the hallway. We stare at one another, both of us look like shit and are breathing heavily. He steps forward but fate is on my side and the doors begin to close. With our eyes locked on one another, he runs his fingers through his hair and pulls, in frustration? Anger? Sadness? I'm not sure but what I do know is that he mouths the word "Fuck," clearly upset. Well, me too, buddy, me fucking too.

The first tear falls after the doors close. Standing in the elevator car, I fall against the back wall and my shoulders start to shake as I cry. Alone and feeling rejected, I let the tears fall as I process what just happened. I went from the highest of highs, and with one breathy whisper of my name, to the lowest of lows.

Realizing I'm not moving, I look to the panel and realize I didn't push any buttons. With a shaking hand, I reach out and press the button for the ground floor. Wiping at my eyes, I try and compose myself. Digging deep, I put on my brave face and with my head held high, I exit the elevator and make my way outside.

The concierge hails a taxi for me and opens the back door when it comes to a stop. Nodding my thanks, I climb in and give the driver my address. The door slams closed and I sit back in my seat. As we pull away and out into the early-hours morning traffic, I begin to cry again. The tears stream down my cheeks like a waterfall as I fall apart.

The driver keeps checking on me in the rearview mirror. Sadly, I smile back at him and before long, we pull up at my apartment. Paying the driver, I go to climb out when he says, "I hope it all works out for you."

How does he know? I nod and smile but it doesn't reach my eyes. Closing the door, I watch him pull away. Turning around, I walk toward the building. Letting myself inside, I step into the waiting elevator and it whisks me up to my floor.

Entering the apartment, I'm happy to find that Nicole isn't home. I don't want to people right now. Grabbing a bottle of water from the refrigerator, I head to my bedroom.

Taking a sip, I place it on my bedside table and then strip off my jeans and shirt. When I remove my bra, I begin to cry harder when I see the pink, thinking back to *him* seeing me in this earlier. Ripping my panties down my legs, I grab the offending garments and throw them in the trash can. I don't ever want to wear them, or pink, ever again. It will only remind me of this heartache.

Naked as the day I was born, I walk into the en suite and turn the shower on. Climbing in, I slide down the cold tile wall and pull my knees up. Wrapping my arms around my legs, I rest my forehead on top. The water beats down on me as I cry my broken heart out.

Crushes are meant to stay that, they aren't meant to evolve because when they do, it's nothing but heartbreak when they eventually reject you. I know Mr. H and I can never be but when he kissed me, fuck me sideways, I thought all my Christmases had come at once … only for it to come crashing down. I never want to hear my name pass through his lips again, I'm done with Mr. H. He can eat a fat chocolate dick.

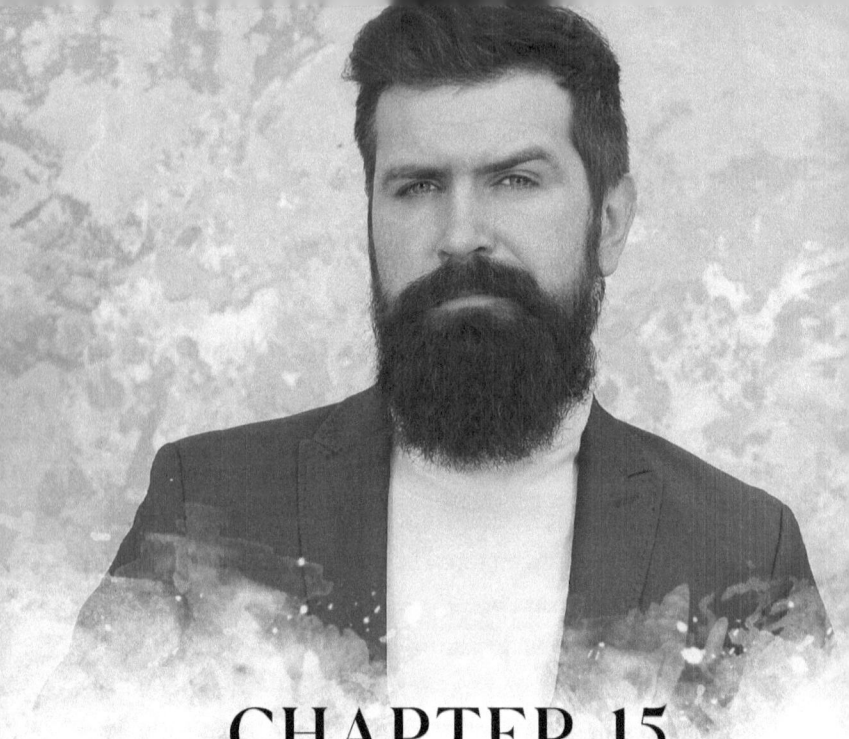

CHAPTER 15

Kane

I know earlier I thought fuck the consequences, but I didn't imagine the immediate 'ohh fuck, what have I done' feeling to smash into me when I came to my senses after the best fucking kiss of my life … with my best friend's daughter. And that 'ohh fuck' moment hit me again when I saw how broken and hurt Calliope was. I was more upset seeing that than when my wife left me. This, right now, is so much harder to bear. I never should have crossed that line, I'm an asshole. Plain and simple.

I'm

An

Asshole

But we can't do this, there's too much at stake. There's also the fact that she's twenty-three. Twenty-fucking-three years old and I'm forty-five, that's twenty-fucking-two years older than her. Plus, her father is my best friend. How can I do that to him?

I'm an asshole, that's all there is to it.

Calliope may hate me now but in the long run, it'll be for the best … even if it was the best fucking kiss of my life, but there's also a teeny tiny part of me that thinks it was a mistake. I shouldn't have pushed her away but it's done now, I can't change that fact. I need to focus on the future … without Calliope.

Falling to the mattress, I stare up at the hotel ceiling, wondering if I have completely fucked up my relationship with Calliope.

The next morning I'm woken when the sun rises because I fell asleep with the curtains open. It's a beautiful day outside and I need to clear my head, so I change into sweats and a shirt, grab my running shoes, and head out to the park.

An hour later, I'm all sweaty but still feel like shit. I can't get that heartbroken look on Calliope's face out of my head. Picking up my phone, I send her a text.

KANE: *Morning, Sunshine. Hope you got home safely. I'm sorry about what happened last night.*

With the text sent, I strip off and climb into the shower. My phone pings and knowing it will be Calliope, I climb out. With my towel around my waist, I pick up my phone and my eyes widen when I see it's not from Calliope but her dad.

GARRICK: *Kane, any chance you can check on my princess for me before you come home?*

Yes, I think to myself. I'd love to but she doesn't want to see me ever again, so for the first time in our friendship, I lie to my best friend.

KANE: *Will see what I can do but it's not looking good*

GARRICK: *Bitchifer giving you hell?*

KANE: *Actually no, for once. I'm waiting to sign the official divorce papers.*

GARRICK: *About fucking time. So happy for you*

KANE: *I'll be happy once they are signed off by the judge and it's official official*

GARRICK: *Dinner and drinks to celebrate when you get back?*

KANE: *Deal*

Staring at my phone, I will a text to come from Calliope but nothing comes through. Placing it down, I return to the bathroom and finish getting ready for the day ahead. As I'm brushing my teeth, another text comes in. My heart begins to race and I know, I just know it's from Calliope. I feel like a thirteen-year-old girl right now, excited 'cause her crush texted her, but that excitement dies when I see her message.

CALLIOPE: *Lose this number*

"Fuuuuck," I groan, tugging on my beard in frustration. I knew I'd hurt her, but I didn't realize just how much.

KANE: *Please, Calliope, don't cut me out. I'm sorry for taking advantage of you last night. I'm the adult here and totally in the wrong. Don't beat yourself up for my mistake.*

Her reply comes immediately and like moments ago, I deflate when I read it.

CALLIOPE: I'm not beating myself up, I'm crushed and defeated. Do you know how long I've wanted to kiss you like that? I feel everything you feel, felt, whatever, and I have since I was thirteen. To be rejected like that hurt more than when Sean Masters humped and dumped me when I was sixteen <— do not tell Daddy that. To go from the highest of highs to the lowest of lows was gut-wrenching.

CALLIOPE: I need to forget you exist and move on

CALLIOPE: Please, leave me alone.

"Fuuuuck," I groan and again tug on my beard. I never knew any of this and now I feel like even more of a jackass. I need to fix this.

KANE: I'm so sorry, Calliope. Please meet me for coffee before I fly out so I can fix this. I didn't mean to hurt you.

CALLIOPE: I can't, Mr. H

CALLIOPE: I'm sorry

KANE: You don't need to be sorry, Calliope. I'm the one who should be sorry and I am.

I'm so fucking sorry and I need to fix this, but how?

CHAPTER 16

Cali

Lying on my bed, I reread his last text message and the tears start to fall again. All I've done since I got home last night is cry. I have never been so mortified in my entire life … and I'm a stripper. I went from being blissfully happy when Mr. H kissed me, to absolutely gutted when he rejected me.

He and I have been walking a fine line for a few years now, and I can't believe I'm saying this, we never should have crossed it. I would have rather kept him in the crush zone than to be in the crushED zone I'm currently in.

My phone pings again and when I pick it up, the tears

fall harder when I read his latest message.

Mr. H: *I never meant to hurt you*

Mr. H: *Please don't shut me out*

Mr. H: *I'm so sorry, Sunshine, please don't hate me*

I don't know what to do. On one hand, I don't want to give up the friendship we have, but on the other, he broke my heart when he pushed me away. Knowing that he will keep blowing my phone up until he hears from me, I text him back.

CALI: *I need time*

Three words, that's all I have in me.

Mr. H: *OK*

One word is all I get back. Then it pings again.

Mr. H: *Just know I'm sorry and I hate that you hate me right now*

CALI: *I don't hate you*

CALI: *I just ...*

Mr. H: *need time*

Mr. H: *I'll be right here waiting for you*

I hate that he knows what I want because it shows he really does know me. If he was any other man, I would jump up and down and fight for this, for us, but I can't. He's my dad's best friend and my sister's best friend's dad. There's just too much at stake. Man-o-man, would the rumor mill back home eat this up.

Sighing, I take a deep breath and come to the conclusion that I need to forget all about Mr. H and his delectable lips and move on. And I can do that right after my shift. Hopefully, I can lose myself on stage as Miss Sunshine.

Well, that was the shift from hell.

The patrons tonight were all handsy-handsy and the tips were shit. Nicole and I are in the dressing room, changing back into our everyday clothes. "I need a bottle of wine and an orgasm," she dramatically informs me as she pulls up her jeans.

"That sounds wonderful. Know where I can get an orgasm?"

"Speaking of orgasms, what happened with the delicious man who requested you last night?"

"Ohh, ummm, nothing," I quickly reply. Turning my back on her, I pull my locks up into a messy bun.

"I call bullshit," Nicole teases. "I think you finally came over to the big O side of stripping and you're just embarrassed about it."

"Embarrassed definitely, but I'm still the big O virgin of The Nirvana Lounge."

"Why are you embarrassed then?" She looks at me confused and if it was any other situation, the look on her face would be hilarious.

"Just, ugh, never mind." I shake my head and close my eyes, willing the events of last night away, but alas, I cannot. Those events are the headline act in my brain at the moment. "I really just want to forget that this week ever existed."

"Cali," she says, her voice laced with concern. She walks over and takes my hand. "Did he do something that he shouldn't have?"

Closing my eyes, I think about last night. His lips on mine. Him pushing me away. The heartbreak of said pushing away. Swallowing back the hurt, the first tear falls.

"Cali, babe, do we need to call the police?" She pulls me in for a hug and it causes me to cry harder. She's squeezing in the way only a best friend can, it reminds me of Fern. I really need Fern. I wish she was here for me to cry my heart out to.

Shaking my head side to side, the tears continue to fall. "No, it's nothing like that," I blubber through my tears into her shoulder. Lifting my head, I stare at her. "I … I knew him."

"Wow, that's kind of embarrassing."

"Yeah, well, I ended up back at his hotel and um …"

"Are you sure we don't need to call the police?"

Shaking my head, I swipe the tears off my cheeks. "I'm sure. We kissed and then, he pushed me away."

"Fucking asshole, why would he do that?"

"Because he's my dad's best friend."

"Holy fucking shit, seriously? You got it on with your dad's bestie?"

"Yep." I let the p pop. "I've had a crush on him for as long as I can remember, and I thought that maybe this was my chance, but instead, after the best kiss of my life, he pulled away, rejecting me."

"Okay, we are going home for wine, ice cream, and a debrief. I need all the deets and then we can come up with a game plan for you to get your man."

"Yes to the wine, ice cream, and chat 'cause it's been forever since we've done that, but no to the game plan to win him back. I just want to forget that I ever kissed him so I can pop him back into the crush zone and move on."

"I'll work on you … mark my words, lady, you and him will be a thing. I feel it in my clit."

"I think the phrase is 'feel it in my bones' not 'feel it in my clit.'" Even if my clit is buzzing at the thought of Mr. H and me as a couple.

"That is true, but a clit has more feelings than bones do and that's how confident I am that you and he will end up together. My clit's buzzing over it."

"Please don't mention your clit, buzzing, and me in the same sentence ever again." I pause. "Or him. I never want to think of him again."

"Come on, Miss Clit Buzzer, let's get you home."

Nicole and I head home and we do as she said. We drink wine, eat ice cream and I tell her all about Mr. H. At stupid o'clock I fall into bed, feeling a little less heartbroken and majorly horny. Damn Mr. H, getting my clit buzzing.

CHAPTER 17

Cali

... three months later

The last three months have been hell, literally. After rejection night as I now refer to it, Mr. H never gave up on messaging me. I've received a message from him daily. They started with him begging me to forgive him. Wanting me to pardon him for kissing me and then pushing me away. To quote Cher from *Clueless*, "As if" it's that easy. As if I can just forgive and forget the best fucking kiss of my life. When I didn't heed to him, he stopped with the begging and started sending random facts and silly memes. And now, ninety days later, yes, I'm counting, sue me, we are on simple pleasantries texts morning and night.

Mr. H: *Morning, Sunshine*

Mr. H: *Good night. Sleep tight, Sunshine.*

Why does he have to be so fucking sweet? Just be an asshole about it and let me move on, but noooo, Kane-fucking-Heatherington is a kindhearted soul who will keep persisting until I forgive him. And I'm close to giving in because Mr. H is the kindest man I know, well, apart from my dad. But I can't let it go, I'm still hurt so I'm doing the mature thing, I'm ignoring him. To date, I have not replied to any one of his text messages.

The gifts he's sent, however, are a different story. I've drunk the wine he sent, hello, it was the good stuff. I gave the flowers to Nic or Miss Rhi. I shared the chocolates with Nic but I returned the lingerie. That was just too much, especially when it was pink, like what I was wearing that night.

But the biggest change, stripping is no longer enjoyable but I need to pay the bills so I continue to work at The Nirvana Lounge. I did up my efforts to get a marketing job but three months later, still no success.

Every time I'm on that stage, I still imagine *him* and as soon as the song is over, I'm once again hit with the pain of his rejection. Night after night, I relive that rejection. And night after night, that pain still hurts. *When will I be over it?*

Nicole and Fern were my saving grace. The two of them kept me going when the hurt became too much. They cheered me up when I was down, laughed when I laughed.

Cried when I cried and when Fern visited me in New York, we danced—with my clothes on—the hurt away 'til the wee hours of the morning in Chelsea and did all of the above in person rather than via FaceTime.

Hell, I even went on a few Tinder dates, but it never went further than kissing because each time I'd imagine *him,* and then everything I felt for my date dissipated and I ran away with my tail between my legs. Plus, none of them could kiss like Mr. H. If kissing was an Olympic sport, he'd be the gold medalist. Mr. H has ruined me for all other kisses.

Right now, I'm on my way to La Guardia, I'm heading home to Silverbell for Mom and Dad's anniversary party. I want to be there for my folks on their special anniversary, but I also don't want to be there because it will be the first time I've seen *him* in the flesh since rejection night.

My phone pings just as the airport comes into view.

Mr. H: *Have a safe flight, Sunshine*

Of course he knows I'm coming home, Dad would be singing it from the clifftop that his princess is coming home for the weekend. My finger hovers over the screen. For the first time in months, I want to reply but the taxi comes to a stop outside the terminal. Is this fate's way of telling me not to reply? Fate can be a bitch, but I think I'll listen to the bitch this time.

Throwing my phone into my bag, I pay the driver and climb out. Since it's just a weekend trip, I don't have any checked luggage, plus Fern and I are planning on hitting up the shops before the party. Normally when I'm home, I'd stay at Mom and Dad's, but this time I'm staying with Fern. *He* is not likely to pop in for a visit if I'm at my bestie's and

I want as little time with *him* as I can get.

Fern is now back living in Silverbell. Like me, her big Hollywood plan didn't quite work out. Her dream of making it big in Hollywood came to a crashing end, literally, when she was involved in a serious car crash. She's lucky to be alive and after weeks and weeks in rehab, she returned home. I think there's more to the reason for her return. She's hiding something from me but I know my bestie, she'll talk when she wants to talk.

She fell into a job back home at The Clifton. Mr. H being the caring and amazing person he is, aside from the 'giving me the best kiss of my life before ripping my heart out' part, he helped Fern out with a job at the hotel at the check-in desk. In the twelve short months she's been there, she's worked her way up the ranks and now is the head concierge. She's kick ass at it and I'm so happy she found her happiness after it all came crashing down around her.

Lucky for me, Fern has a two-bedroom apartment on Main Street. When she found out I was coming home for the weekend, she offered, well demanded, that I stay in her spare room, and I jumped at the chance to hide away at her place. Daddy wasn't too happy I wasn't staying at home, but Mom reminded him that I'm a grown woman now. I love when Mom puts Dad in his place, it doesn't happen often but I was glad she snuck a win in this time.

The flight was uneventful—thankfully—and when I disembark, I make my way toward the exit. Digging in my bag, looking for my phone, I'm not watching where I'm going and I bump into someone and begin to fall backward. Before gravity takes hold of me and I end up on my ass by the baggage carousel, a hand reaches out and grabs me. As soon as their hand touches me, a spark ignites every nerve ending in my body and when I look up at my rescuer, my eyes widen.

"Mr. H," I breathlessly whisper, while at the same time he drawls out my nickname, "Sunshine."

He pulls me upright and takes my hand in his. Our fingers entwine, his thumb strokes the back of my hand, my skin buzzing from his touch. In the middle of the busy terminal, we stare at one another, holding hands. *Has he gotten hotter in the last three months?* His beard is longer and a little grayer than I remember. I want to reach out, pull him to me, and kiss him again. I want to see if what I remember about that kiss is correct or if I'm embellishing how amazing our kiss was.

A voice from behind me yelling "Dad" pulls us apart. He drops my hand and instantly I mourn the loss. Mr. H smiles at someone behind me. "Konrad," he says, stepping around me and toward his son. Turning around, I see them embrace. Konrad notices me and smiles.

"Cali," he questions, "what are you doing here?"

"Just flew in for Mom and Dad's anniversary party this weekend."

"Of course." He nods.

"You're coming, right?"

He nods. "Yeah, I am, but I'm here early to check on Dad. To make sure he's okay."

Mr. H rolls his eyes. "I told you I'm fine."

"What's wrong?" I ask, my voice high-pitched and I worry that something is wrong with him. If Konrad is here and worried, then something must be amiss.

"Nothing," Mr. H snaps, "I'm—"

"Nothing my ass, Dad," Konrad growls. "You've been miserable for months now." My eyes widen at that revelation. "None of us believe that you're fine, but I had to see it for my own eyes, hence my early arrival."

The overhead speakers crackle to life and the lady says which carousel the just arrived flight's luggage can be collected from. Konrad slaps Mr. H on the back and walks over to collect his bag. I step toward him and when he looks at me, I notice sadness reflecting in his eyes.

"What's going on, Mr. H? Are you really okay?"

"I'm fine, Calliope. My children are just overreacting." I eye him suspiciously. "Really, I'm fine."

Nodding, I open my mouth to tell him I'm here for him when my name is screeched from behind me. A smile graces my face and when I spin around, I see Fern running toward me. Without thought, I drop my bag and race toward her. She reaches out and pulls me in for a hug. "You're here," she coos into my ear.

"I'm here," I reply, hugging her back harder than ever before.

Her body stiffens in my arms and she whispers, "Is he here for you?"

Shaking my head, I go to tell her no when she starts to nod. "Ohh, I see Konrad's here."

Nodding, I turn and see Mr. H and Konrad walking toward us. Mr. H has my bag in his hand.

"Fern Halstead," Konrad purrs, yes, he purrs. "Looking good."

My best friend blushes, she actually blushes. We will definitely be discussing this as soon as we get into her car, especially when she says his name back in a seductive manner. "Konrad Heatherington." She then looks to Mr. H. "Kane." It's so weird hearing her call him Kane, but he is her boss and we aren't kids anymore. "You must be happy to have your son home early for the weekend?"

"You knew?" he questions her.

"Maaaaybe," she coyly replies with a shoulder shrug. "But we have to get going, Cali and I have big plans before the big party tomorrow night."

Before we can say our goodbyes, she grabs my bag from Mr. H's hand and takes my hand, dragging me away. "Later, fellas," she throws over her shoulder and then she's pulling me toward the exit.

"What? Why? Fern, have you lost your mind?"

"Maaaaybe," she replies with a shrug. "But I had to get you out of there before you two started banging."

"Please," I scoff. "Mr. H and I will never bang. If he was turned off by a kiss, I can only imagine what he'd think if we, you know."

"Fucked like rabbits?" she offers, clicking the button on her key fob, unlocking her car.

"You're inner Raven is showing," I tell her as I bend to climb into the passenger seat, but before I do, I look at her over the roof of her car. "And I freakin' missed it."

"I've missed you too."

She starts the engine and backs out of her spot. "So, what's new with you?"

"I'm seeing this guy, Tucker."

"What happened to the other guy?"

"Francis?"

"No, Bobby?"

"It didn't work out. Seems I was missing a penis."

"No way?"

"Yes, way. I caught him getting a BJ from his roommate, Steve."

"You really know how to pick them."

Something flickers on her face but as quick as it appeared, it's gone again. "Says the woman lusting after her dad's best friend."

"Touché, lady. "Touché. So, what's new around here?"

"It's Silverbell, there's always something going on but I haven't heard of anything so scandalous since you became Miss Sunshine."

"I find that hard to believe, to quote you, 'It's Silverbell.'"

"Speaking of your alter ego, when are you going to give up being Miss Sunshine?"

"When I get a new job."

"And how's that going?"

"Well, I'm still Miss Sunshine so …." I shrug.

"Come home then?"

"I can't."

"Can't or won't?"

"What do you mean?"

"I don't think you want to give up stripping. You graduated forever ago, but you're still swinging around a pole and from swinging around the pole, you came face-to-face with he who shall not be named—"

"He's not Voldemort, he's—"

"May as well be, but as I was saying before you rudely interrupted me, stripping was what started you on the path of 'oops daddy's BFF caught me and then we kissed and then everything imploded' drama you currently find yourself in. If you had a marketing job ..."

"I had no choice," I snap at her, angry that we're having this argument, again. "You know that."

"We always have a choice, Cal." She pauses. "Please come home?"

"I can't, I can't live here when he's here. Seeing him is just too painful."

"I still find it hard to believe he's that good of a kisser."

"Fern, you have no idea. It was the best fucking kiss ever."

"I'm so jealous. Not many people get to make out with their childhood crush."

"Trust me, it doesn't live up to the hype because now I've been rejected and cast aside, and that hurts more than anything."

"I'm sorry, babe, I really wish it turned out differently."

"Me too, Fern. Me too." I sadly look over at her and she squeezes my hand. "I propose we put stripping, crushes, and best kisses ever aside and have a fantabulous weekend."

"I like the sound of that. Let's party like rock stars." She turns up the stereo and when we come to a set of traffic lights, she looks over at me. "Babe, we are going to have so much fun this weekend." She winks and when the light changes, she puts her foot down on the gas.

There was only one problem with her suggestion. Her definition of fun and mine are two very different definitions.

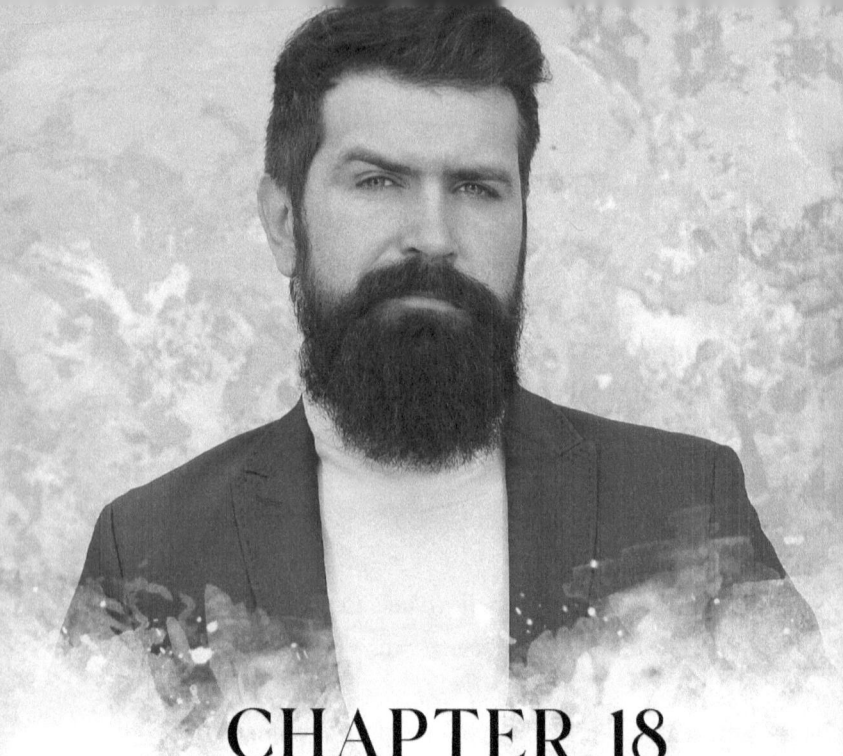

CHAPTER 18

Kane

It's been three months since our previous encounter and it's been three months of radio silence from her. Every day, I sent her a text and every day she read said text but not once did she reply. That was a kick to the nuts but seeing her just now, that was a kick to the dick.

Somehow, she's gotten even sexier in the last three months. Speaking of my dick, it definitely liked what we saw—jeans that should be illegal, a black tank that showcases her gorgeous tits, and if I'm not mistaken, a pink bra.

A

pink

fucking

bra.

I can't see the color without getting hard because my mind drifts back to that room at The Nirvana Lounge and My Sunshine in her sexy pink get up.

I'm snapped back from watching Calliope and Fern leave when Konrad says, "How badly would Mr. Fischer kill me if I went after Cali? She's gotten H-O-T, hot."

"Probably the same as if anyone went after your sister."

"Riiiight," he says nodding. "Speaking of the she-devil, how is my little sister?"

"How I'm not gray yet, I will never know."

"Umm, dude, you looked in a mirror lately? I'm seeing a few silver sprinkles in the beard and hair."

"Okay, fully gray, better?" Konrad chuckles at my answer. "But your sister is doing well."

"And you thought Michael was the degenerate of the family," he teases.

"That's a bit harsh, even for you, but you and I both know your brother has been through a lot. Someone once pointed that out to me and when I started seeing things from his point of view, everything changed. With effort from both of us, he's really turned his life around."

"And who knew Michael had a love of cooking?"

"He just needed to find his passion, not everyone knows what they want to be when they're nine years old."

"Touché, Dad, touché. What do you say we go have a beer?"

"I'd say let's go."

Half an hour later, Konrad and I enter The Irish Giant and we take a seat at the bar. "Mr. Heatherington. Dr. Heatherington," Rosie says in greeting, "what can I get ya?"

"Two beers, please," I order and I notice Konrad grinning. "What's got you grinning?"

"I still get a kick out of it when people call me Doctor. There were so many times I wanted to quit, when it got so hard I felt like I was drowning, but something pushed me on and I did it. I'm a real doctor now."

"And I couldn't be prouder of you, son."

"Thanks, Dad."

Over a few beers, Konrad and I catch up and it's been great. He even asks me about dating but I quickly change the topic, that's not something I want to discuss with my son. Especially since the only person I actually want to date is forbidden fruit. I may have only had a little taste but I have a new addiction and it's one I need to conquer. No good can come from Calliope Fischer and I doing anything more than we already have.

Later that afternoon, Michael and Finley arrive and the four of us enjoy a family dinner at the pub, just like old times, and it's perfect. We laugh. We eat. We're a family again. Looking at my three kids, I smile, I haven't felt contentment like this in a long time, but I'm snapped back to the present when I realize all three of my children are staring expectantly at me. "What?" I ask them, unsure as to why all three of them are looking intently at me.

"Daddy," Finley says in the sweet tone that I have come

to know is anything but sweet. "When are you going to start dating again? Mom's been gone for years now. That bitch ain't coming back and I, well, we think it's time you put yourself out there again."

"My love life, or lack thereof, is none of your concern. I'm happy—"

The three of them scoff. "Happy, you? Really, Dad?" Finley says. "For the last three months in particular, you've not been happy. I get this divorce shit with Mom is hard but don't let her win."

The divorce shit my daughter mentioned, Bitchifer refused to sign the divorce papers. She reneged on the agreement that we settled three months ago. Alex was livid when she called me to tell me that they were returned with the words 'how about no' where she was meant to sign. Alex was ready to take it to court there and then but I told her to leave it. I'm not emotionally ready to deal with it, that's a fight for another time. And really, it's not like I'm wanting to get married anytime soon. It's just a piece of paper. Right now, I just don't have it in me to fight her. I need a clear head because when I face off with Bitchifer, she will not win. I refuse to go down when it comes to her.

"You know, Dad," Michael adds, tipping his beer bottle toward me. Whatever he's about to say he clearly means business if he's tipping his beer bottle toward me. "The best way to get over someone is to get under someone else."

My eyes widen at his comment because I'm now imagining a certain green-eyed blonde underneath me. Shaking my head, I focus on the present because I need to: A. Not have a boner at dinner with my kids. And B. It can never happen.

"Like you've ever been under someone," Konrad teases his brother, playfully smacking him in the arm. "You and Mrs. Palmer are very well acquainted and you two have been since you were thirteen."

"Says the one who told me all about Mrs. Palmer when I was thirteen."

Finley covers her ears and sings, "La lalalalalallalaa." She uncovers her ears and adds, "I don't need to hear about you guys and Mrs. Palmer, and I definitely don't what to think about you two bumping uglies with anyone. Ugh!" She shudders, then schools her features and if I know my daughter, she's about to shock her brothers, and me. "Just like I'm sure you don't want to think of Dad and Mrs. Palmer." Hmmm, that was tame … and then she adds, "Or me flicking the bean."

I'd just taken a sip of beer when she adds that last part and beer sprays across the table, covering Konrad and Michael. "Finley Heatherington," I growl.

"Ooo, you just got full-named," Michael teases.

Wiping my mouth, I shake my head. "I was just thinking that this was a great evening and now we're in the gutter."

"Dad," Konrad laments, "it's not a family dinner if we don't end up off the beaten—pun intended—conversation path."

"This is true," I nod, "but there are some things a father doesn't want to think about. Loosely talking about that topic is okay but when it's directed at specific family members, no, just no."

"Someone's gone soft in their old age," Konrad whispers

not so quietly to Michael.

"Maybe he can't get it up anymore and that's why he's not dating. They do say it's all downhill after forty."

"My dick is just fine," I tell them.

"Daaaaaaad," Finley screeches, shaking her head. "Okay, new rule, no more dick and bean talk at the dinner table."

"Deal," Konrad and Michael shout. Then all eyes are on me.

"Hey, I didn't start it but yes, I agree." I pause. "But it might be HARD for your brothers though."

My boys laugh and my daughter, well once again, she screeches my name. I can't help it and I laugh, but that laugh quickly stops when I look over at the bar and see Calliope, Fern, and a gentleman. The gentleman is standing precariously close to My Sunshine. I clench my teeth in anger, I know I have no right to be angry but I can't help it. It seems Calliope Fischer is going to be the death of me.

CHAPTER 19

Cali

Fern dragged me to The Irish Giant for a few sneaky drinks before she meets up with her current fuck buddy, Tucker. Why I need to be here too, I don't know. It's not like the three of us are going to have a ménage, I love my bestie but not like that. I'm a one dick girl and the one dick I want is currently sitting at a table nearby having dinner with his family.

Tucker has just gone to the restroom again for what seems like the millionth time. "What's up with his bladder?" I ask Fern, just as Rosie places another glass of wine in front of me.

"I don't know," Fern replies with a shrug. "Maybe you make him nervous?"

"Me?" I screech. "What the hell?"

"Your reaction just now was priceless, babe."

"Eat a dick, bitch."

"I plan to later." She winks at me and I shake my head.

"Please don't ever change, Fern. You are the one constant in my life."

"I don't ever plan on it. You're stuck with me until we are old and senile in the old folks' home and then when we forget each other, we will become best friends all over again."

"Fern, that's the nicest thing you've ever said to me, and for the record," I reach over and squeeze her shoulder, "I can't wait to forget you to meet you again too."

She pulls me in for a hug and while she's hugging me, my gaze connects with *him*. How am I ever going to get over Mr. H? I've had a taste and after just one hit, I'm addicted. Maybe I need to listen to Nicole and Fern and get under someone else, but how can that happen when I can't even get past kissing?

"Question," I ask Fern when she pulls back.

"Does the Pee Man have a friend?"

"Are you asking what I think you're asking?"

"Maaaaaaaybe." I bring my glass to my lips and drink, hoping to calm my nerves now that I've voiced my request. However, the crisp wine does nothing to ease my worries about my love life, well, lack thereof due to a certain sexy silver fox who is currently staring intently at me.

"He does." Fern nods but then she makes a face. "But no, just no. Pee Man, or Tucker as I call him, has shit taste in friends."

Nodding, I then ask, "Another question, why are you with him?"

"His tongue," she nonchalantly replies with a shrug.

"His tongue," I repeat. "Explain?"

"I have never climaxed the way I do when he goes down on me. Like I will seriously take his tongue over his dick, that's how talented his tongue is."

"Wow."

When I look up, Tucker is walking back toward us. He licks his lip, and somehow, he makes that look seductive and I think I can see the appeal. Fern smacks me in the shoulder. "Back off, that tongue is mine."

How she knew what I was thinking I will never know. "A good friend would help me get over you know who."

"And I am the bestest friend you have ever and will ever have, but that tongue is mine and mine alone. Do not make me kill you, I don't have time to find a new bestie."

"Man, I missed you," I tell her, nudging her shoulder with mine.

"And I missed you too. When are you moving back here?"

"Half past never. My time in Silverbell is over. I have a job—"

"As a stripper," Fern whisper-snarls. "Which I still can't believe you are but, babe, what about your degree?"

"I told you, I'm looking," I hiss through my teeth. "You can lose that look because believe me, I am. I can't be at the club anymore without thinking of *him,* but a girl needs to eat and live. I have no choice right now."

"But—"

"No," I shout. "I'm not having this conversation with you again." I don't mean to yell at her but it's my life. I know she doesn't agree with the choices I made but I had, and still have, no choice in how I make a living. I made a shit situation manageable and now I have to suffer the consequences of the decisions I made. Needing a moment to breathe, I jump off my chair. "I'll be back."

With my head down, I race to the corridor where the restrooms are located. Turning the corner, I bump into a hard body and from the scent enveloping me, I know exactly who it is. "Mr. H," I breathlessly whisper when I lift my gaze to his.

"Sunshine." My name sounds so sexy passing through his lips and it causes every single nerve ending to light up in my body. He takes my hand and drags me down the corridor and into the family restroom.

"Mr. H, what are you doing?"

"We need to talk," he says, closing the door behind him and flicking the lock.

"In a family restroom?"

He shrugs. "I ... I ..."

"You what, Mr. H?"

"I can't stop thinking about you," he whispers.

My eyes widen at his statement. "What? You can't ... what?" I stammer.

"You heard me, Sunshine, and ... and, I think you've been thinking about me too."

Swallowing deeply, I stare up at him. My breathing becomes labored. My heart is racing. My hands are clammy and my panties, well, they're soaked. He steps toward me and I back up but when my ass hits the counter behind me, I have nowhere to go. He crowds me in, resting his palms on the countertop, trapping me. "Mr. H, what are you doing?"

"Sunshine, I can't stop thinking about you." He reaches up and cups my cheek gently running his thumb along my jawline. "You've been on my mind constantly for the last three months. You're my first thought when I wake up and you're my last thought before I go to sleep."

Holy shit, this must be a dream. This can't be real, but if it is, it's the best fucking dream of my life. "Is this real?" I whisper.

"Is what real, Sunshine?"

"You. This. Now." I tilt my head into his hand.

"It's real," he whispers. "I've missed you so much, Calliope."

"I've missed you too but you hurt me."

"I know I did and I'm so sorry about that. Kissing you was the best thing I have ever done. Pushing you away was the stupidest thing I've ever done."

Blinking rapidly, I process his words. He regrets it but still, he's made no move to indicate he wants more but truth be told, I don't know what we can do. We stare at one another, his hand still cupping my cheek. The heat from his palm radiates through my body and even though we're in a public restroom, I want him to kiss me deeply before spinning me around and fucking me from behind. Each of us intently watching one another in the mirror as his dick slides in and out of me. My dirty video is interrupted when he murmurs, "I really want to kiss you, Sunshine."

"Do it," I purr. "Kiss me, Mr. H." Pausing, I cover his hand on my cheek. Leaning into him, I whisper into his ear, "I dare you."

Pulling back, I raise my eyebrows at him. He reaches his other hand up, grips both my cheeks in his palms, and ever so slowly, our heads start moving toward each other. We're a hair's breadth apart when there's a knock on the door.

Both of us freeze but the person knocks again. "Just a minute," he growls. Dropping his hands from my face, he pulls away and takes a step back. The moment is broken and I instantly feel the loss. "I need to see you," he demands and the roughness in his voice soaks my panties further.

"You're seeing me now," I joke.

He laughs. "Don't be a smart-ass, I need to see you. I think, we need to, umm, talk."

Nodding, I stare at him, biting my lip while I think about what to say. He reaches up and pulls my lip free. "I really want to bite your lip."

"I'm not okay with that," I murmur, "and yes, I do think we need to talk, but I don't want to talk in a public restroom."

"When then?"

"Tomorrow?"

He nods. "Come by the hotel at ten, and we can chat in private then."

"Okay." I nod. It feels like a weight has lifted but we still have so much to discuss. I don't want to get my hopes up but it's hard not to. Not after what almost transpired just now, stupid person knocking on the door.

"Okay," he confirms. Stepping to me, he cups my cheeks again and like before, I tilt my head into it. As quickly as he cups my face, he pulls away and I immediately miss the contact. That is until he leans forward and presses his lips to my forehead.

Closing my eyes, I focus on the connection of his lips on my skin.

All too soon, his lips are gone. He stares at me, I can feel his gaze deep in my soul. "See you tomorrow, Sunshine." And without another word, he steps around me and exits the restroom. Leaving me alone with my jumbled thoughts.

Flipping the lock behind him, I lean against the wood. Closing my eyes, I take a deep breath and sigh, quietly I mumble, "What the fuck just happened?"

CHAPTER 20

Kane

What did I just do?

What the fuck did I just do?

Calliope Fischer causes me to lose my ever-loving mind. I feel like a clueless teenage boy when I'm around her and not the responsible forty-plus-year-old father of three and business owner that I am.

If someone hadn't knocked on that door, who knows what I would have done to her in that bathroom.

Walking back to the table, I stop and smile as I watch my three kids laughing together. Their mom may have abandoned them, but I think I did a pretty good job at raising them into the well-adjusted adults they are. I'm especially happy that Michael has found his calling. I was extremely worried about him for a while, but he's finally found his feet and place in life.

A small voice that has my cock twitching says, "Excuse me." When I look over my shoulder, I see Calliope trying to get past. And like most times I see her, my throat dries up at her beauty. She's stunning and she doesn't even know it.

"Sorry," I offer, stepping to the side and letting her pass. Her scent invades my nose and it, like her angelic voice, heads straight to my cock. Subtly, I adjust myself and follow behind her, my eyes dropping to her ass. *I'm so going to hell,* I think to myself as she turns right and I make my way back to my family

"Took long enough, Dad, you having prostate issues?" Konrad teases.

"Wait 'til you're my age and we'll see how quickly you use the restrooms."

"Better book him into the old folks' home now, he's forty-five and already about to start pissing himself."

"And once again, we're back in the gutter. How about we forget about my bladder and take this home? We can have a family movie night, just like we used to."

The three of them nod in agreement. Then Finley stares us all down. "But no fucking clowns and, yes, Dad, I'm aware that I swore. But after *Beavis* and *Butthead* over there," she flicks her thumb at her brothers, "made me watch *IT* and *IT Chapter Two*, clowns can fuck right off."

"Aww, come on, sis," Konrad coos, draping his arms

over her shoulder, "what's not to love about a clown who drags you into the sewer?"

She glowers at him and then turns to me, giving me the sweetest of sweet faces. "Please, Daddy, no clowns."

"That sweet daughterness right now won't work on me." She goes to interrupt but I raise my hand and stop her. "But I'm not in the mood for scary tonight, we need something funny. I want to see which one of you three snorts first."

"Michael," Konrad and Finley both say at the same time, earning themselves a bird flip from their brother.

From the corner of my eye, I see Calliope watching us and I'd love nothing more than to have her join us. But is that possible? Starting something with her has so many obstacles in the way. Her father. Her current profession. The fact she lives in New York. Maybe we aren't destined to be, it's not like I have a good track record. I'm an almost divorced man with three grown children. I'm not really a catch. She's young and still has her whole life ahead of her, do I want to trap her? Will she become unhappy like Danica and run off, leaving me once again alone?

"You okay, Daddy?" Finley asks. "You're a million miles away."

"I'm fine, Munchkin. Just got a lot on my mind."

"You work too hard. You really need to take a break. What's one thing you've always wanted to do?"

Calliope immediately comes to mind but I can't tell my daughter that. I can't tell anyone that. So, I tell her the PG version. "Drive Route 66 in a gunmetal gray Shelby Cobra."

"That's very specific and I can totally see you doing that." She pauses. "So when's the big trip?"

"Considering I told you twenty seconds ago, I'd say in a few years."

"Daddy, you need to start living. Time to get back on the dating horse."

"Have you been chatting to your brother?"

"No, but if we need to gang up on you for you to start living, I'm happy to start a group chat."

"No more group chats, please. I'm still scandalized over the last one." A few years ago, we had a family chat to help keep us organized and my oldest son shared more than I ever wanted to know about him when he sent a message to the wrong chat. Let's just say, I will never look at whipped cream and chocolate sauce the same again. I was thankful he was away at school because if I had to look at him across the dinner table, I would have died.

The movie—sans clowns—has finished and my stomach still hurts from all the snort-laughing. Finley was the first to snort and before long, all of us were laughing … and maybe snorting too. Snort-laughing is a vicious cycle in the Heatherington household. But seriously, what is it about someone snorting? Their one innocent snort sets off a chain reaction of snorts and then everyone is snorting and laughing.

Saying goodnight to the kids, who are staying up to watch the second *Grown Ups* movie, I head on up to my room. After brushing my teeth, I slip into my boxers and climb into bed. Nothing beats freshly laundered sheets. Snuggling down, I drift off to sleep and like most nights, I dream of Calliope but tonight's dream is a very sexual

Calliope dream …

… Calliope and I are in a gunmetal gray Shelby Cobra and we're cruising along Route 66. Her hair flies in the wind as I put my foot down on the accelerator. Pulling off the highway, we find a secluded picnic spot and stop for lunch. Grabbing the picnic basket from the back, I walk around to her side of the car and open her door. Offering her my hand, she places hers in mine and I pull her out. Pressing a kiss to her forehead, I smile down at her as I lace our fingers together. We walk a few feet from the car and stop. I place the woven basket on the ground and pick up the picnic blanket and spread it out.

Dropping down, Calliope sits next to me and she begins to pull out the sandwiches and a bottle of red. She hands me the bottle and I uncork it while she arranges the food.

Handing her a glass, she smiles at me over the top and takes a sip. She moans and my cock loves the sound. "You keep moaning like that, Sunshine, and I'll be eating you for lunch."

She stares at me, bites her bottom lip, and moans. She places her glass down next to her and traces her fingertip along the neckline of her halter dress. Leaning forward, she tugs at the material and gives me an unobstructed view of her gorgeous breasts.

Sitting back up, she raises her eyebrows at me. I beckon her to me with my index finger. Lifting to her knees, she shuffles over and straddles my legs. Draping her arms over my shoulders, she stares into my eyes as I slide my hands up her thighs. My eyes widen when I reach between her legs and my finger effortlessly slides between her wet folds.

"Oops," she innocently purrs, "I forgot my panties this morning."

"Oops, indeed," I reply as I sink my digit deep inside her. Her head drops back and she moans at the intrusion. Hooking my finger inside her, I rub over that magical spot. She cups her breasts, squeezing them as I continue to thrust my finger in and out.

Her walls clench around my finger as she comes. She rides my hand, drawing every ounce of pleasure from my finger and hand. She opens her eyes and I withdraw my hand. With her eyes fused to mine, I lick her juices off my fingers.

Leaning forward, I capture her lips with mine and kiss her deeply. Pulling back, she rests her forehead against mine. "Fuck me," she demands, and who am I to deny her?

Quickly I free my cock, and she lifts up and slides down my shaft. Both of us moaning as she seats herself completely on me. She begins to rock her hips back and forth. Gripping my shoulders for support, she gains speed and out of nowhere she screams, "I'm coming," and she sets me off ...

... my eyes fly open as I feel the first spray of cum hit my stomach. My hand is clenched around my hard cock as I squeeze my release out. After the final spurt, I shake my head, it was just a dream. An erotic fucking dream. I'm forty-five and just had a wet dream, I haven't done this since I was thirteen.

Climbing out of bed, I walk into the en suite and turn the faucet on. No need to strip off since I removed my boxers in my sleep. When the water's hot, I climb in. The water beats down on my shoulders, relieving some of the tension that built from realizing I had a wet dream.

Tilting my head back, the water cascades over me, washing away the remnants of my erotic dream. Pumping some soap into my hand, I wash myself. I'm disgusted with myself that I did that but that dream, it felt so real.

Once I'm clean, I climb out and dry off. Slipping back into my boxers, I climb into bed and close my eyes. My phone vibrates with a text, who could possibly be texting me a one in the morning? Picking up my phone, I smile when I see it's from *her*.

Opening her message, I smile.

CALLIOPE: *I know it's late, but I need to apologize. I'm sorry if I was rude earlier tonight. You surprised me and then we were interrupted*

KANE: *You have nothing to apologize for. If anything, I should apologize to you, I'm sorry for cornering you like that.*

CALLIOPE: *I really wanted to kiss you*

CALLIOPE: *Shit, I shouldn't have sent that last message*

KANE: *You know you can always be honest with me, Sunshine*

KANE: *And for the record, I really wanted to kiss you too but ...*

While I wait for her reply, I update her name to Sunshine in my phone and I grin like a fool when I see the name on my phone screen when she replies.

SUNSHINE: *but ...*

SUNSHINE: *So many buts*

SUNSHINE: *What are we going to do?*

KANE: *Sleep now and we can discuss it tomorrow.*

SUNSHINE: *OK*

KANE: *Sleep tight, Sunshine ... till tomorrow*

SUNSHINE: *See you tomorrow*

One text session with My Sunshine and I'm hard again. I'm so fucked when it comes to this woman.

CHAPTER 21

Cali

Sleep eludes me tonight. Ever since I climbed under the covers after my shower, I've tossed and turned like a fish out of water. I was hoping after I texted *him* I'd be able to sleep, but then he replied and now I'm even more wide awake … and horny.

I'm so fucked when it comes to this man. I think I'm at the point where I don't care about the consequences. I want to be selfish and follow my heart, I want to take a leap with him. We will either nail the landing or break everything. Never have I felt a connection with anyone like I do with

Kane Heatherington, but there are so many things against us.

His age.

My dad.

My age.

His kids.

His marriage, technically.

Our living arrangements: he's here in Silverbell, I'm in New York.

Is it selfish of me to pursue this? But there's also him, what does he want? I could be misreading everything. Maybe tomorrow he wants to tell me to cease all contact with him. I'd be crushed if that happens. This unease is obviously why you should always leave your crush as just that, a crush. But what I feel for Mr. H is more than a schoolgirl crush.

Ever since he helped me after the Seth incident, I've seen him in a different light and then there's the kiss. That one kiss set my body alight like never before. It jumped-started my heart and turned what I felt for him into more. I'm pretty sure he feels it too. There are just too many factors against us, but love isn't easy so maybe these are just tests being thrown at us to see if it's worth it.

"Gah," I growl into the darkness of my room as I punch the mattress in frustration. Where's my fairy godmother right now? I could do with a wave of her magic wand and bippity-boppity-boo, all my worries are sorted.

Climbing out of bed, I quietly make my way into Fern's kitchen and turn on the light. Looking around, I can't decide between tea or tequila, so I choose both. While I make myself a cup of green tea with jasmine, I'll have a shot of tequila. The tequila burns—it's the cheap shit—but it does relax me a little so I take another shot while I wait for my tea to brew.

With my tea in hand, I shuffle back to my room and climb into bed. Resting against the headboard, I think on what to do. I don't get far into thinking because Fern appears in the doorway. "I can hear you thinking from my room. What's got you braining so loud at stupid o'clock in the morning?"

She climbs in next to me, grabs my tea, and takes a sip. "You should be drinking tequila."

"Had two shots while I was making this." I pause. "Two things. One, the tequila didn't magically make everything better. And two, that was some nasty cheap shit."

"Tucker bought it but I'll be sure to let him know he has shit tequila taste."

"You do that. The next time I have a midnight meltdown, I want the good stuff to commiserate with."

"Why are you breaking down alone with tequila in the middle of the night?"

Looking anywhere but at Fern, I think over what to tell her.

"Calliope Victoria Fischer, what are you hiding from me?"

"Ohh, you full-full-named me."

"And I will vagina punch you if you don't spill the beans. I know something happened when you went to the bathroom at the pub, now tell me."

It's crazy how well my bestie knows me and I know if I don't give her something, she'll keep harping on it until

I relent. "Fine," I hiss. "Mr. H pulled me into the family restroom and we …"

"You fucked him in the family restroom?" she screeches, digging her nails into my arm and nearly causing me to spill hot tea all over myself.

"No," I scoff. "And remove your freakin' talons from my arm."

"Sorry," she replies, releasing her grip on my arm. "So, did you?" she asks again, as she crosses her legs and leans her elbows into her knees.

"Have I ever been known to fuck in a restroom?" I throw back at her.

"No, but I also never pegged you to be a stripper and …." She shrugs.

Sticking my tongue out at her, I continue, "We spoke, for the first time since the kiss and all the memories of that kiss came flooding back. We were, ummm, about to kiss again but someone knocked and we jumped apart."

"Kissblocked by some fucker."

"Yep, and then I agreed to meet him at The Clifton tomorrow to chat."

"Where you will finally fuck him."

"I'm not fucking him at his workplace. Nor will there be any fucking. Nothing good can come from he and I being together."

"Says who?" I open my mouth to protest but she raises her hand and gives me the 'shut your pie hole, I'm not finished yet' look. Rolling my eyes at her, she pinches my arm and continues, "The va-jay-jay wants what the va-jay-jay wants, Cali, and yours has wanted Kane Heatherington for as long as I can remember. Sure, there's a bit of an age gap, and sure, he's your dad's BFF—and your sister is best friends with his youngest daughter—and you are currently a stripper living in NYC, and he's a hotel owner here in Silverbell, but, babe, what about what you want? What you both want? Personally, I think everyone else can shove a pineapple up their ass, pointy end first. Follow your va-jay-jay … and heart."

"They both want Mr. H," I honestly tell her.

"Then that's all you need to focus on. I know your dad, after the initial shock, he'll come around."

"I don't know about that; he still hates Raven after he caught the two of us practicing to kiss when we were eleven."

"Most people hate Raven 'cause, well, he's Raven." I nod and smile because she's right. Raven is an acquired taste but when you get to know him, he's the bestest. "You're now twenty-three and a responsible stripper. Maybe you should tell him you're stripping, that might soften the blow before telling him you're in love with his BFF."

"He can NEVER find out about that. He'd be more pissed at that than me and Mr. H being together."

"With Garrick Fischer, anything is possible, but in all honesty, chat with Kane tomorrow and go from there."

"Mr. H and I have sooo much to chat about."

"Just try keeping your tongue out of his mouth, that might help you iron things out." She pauses, and then says, "You do realize that if you two start dating, you will have to start calling him Kane?"

"That's future Calliope's problem. Current Calliope is

going to finish her tea and then Calliope is going to go back to sleep. Also, Calliope likes referring to herself in third person. Calliope thinks Fern should try it."

"Fern thinks Calliope is losing it and is going to go back to bed to have some middle of the night nookie, so Calliope might want to turn some music on or get to sleep quickly."

"Calliope thanks Fern for the warning. Calliope also reminds Fern that if it's not on …"

In unison we repeat, "… it's not on."

"Thanks for the midnight pep talk, Fern, Calliope appreciates it."

She pulls me in for a hug. "Anytime, lady, anytime but stop with the third person referencing, Fern does not want to punch her bestie." And with that statement, she kisses my forehead and exits my room, leaving me to ponder her words.

Finishing my tea, I place the empty cup on the side table and lie back. I stare at the ceiling, playing out every scenario I can think of. I've come to the conclusion that no matter what happens, someone is going to be pissed and/or hurt.

Flicking off the light, I decide that future Calliope can worry about that. Current Calliope is going to try to get some shut-eye. I'm just about to drift off to Neverland when I hear Fern. "Tongue my ass, Tucker, tongue it good and then fuck it. Fuck it harder than you ever have before."

Groaning, I pull my pillow over my head and scream into it, "Fuck my life." Looking out the window from under my pillow, I see that the sun is starting to rise so I change into a pair of shorts and a tank, pull my hair up into a pony, grab my shoes, and head out for a run. Sitting on the bottom step, I lace my sneakers and take off on my run.

The hill up to The Clifton is a killer but it's good for the glutes, so I push myself forward. Reaching the top, I stop at the hotel's rhododendron-lined driveway. The pebbled driveway crunches under my feet as I walk back and forth, taking deep breaths, staring through the woodlands and up to the hotel building. I smile when I see the hotel's chimneys peeking over the treetops. The Clifton sits on the bluff, overlooking the white sandy beach and Silverbell below. It has a slate roof with dormer windows, white shingle siding, and a wraparound porch on the ground floor. It was all brought back to its former glory when Mr. H restored the hotel after he purchased it all those years ago. The changes he made stayed true to the original design of the home, which he turned into a hotel. I'm glad he kept it all original, it really adds to its beauty.

A marketing job here would be amazing, the packages I could put together staying here would be endless, but Kerrie is the current MD. She recently took over from Hannah when she quit to enjoy retirement with her husband. It occurs to me just now that he never offered the position to me, something he promised Dad he would do one day, but I guess, he doesn't want me back here after all and I know I said I didn't want him to hand me a job but it still would have been nice to have been offered it. That thought hurts. It would have been great to work here … with him, but it's moot so I may as well forget about it.

Shaking my head, I spin on my heel and race back down the hill and toward the beach. My feet sink into the sand when I reach the bottom of the hill. I'm huffing and puffing, so I drop to the sand and pull my legs up. I stare out at the ocean, the sound of the waves crashing into the shore calms me.

It's so peaceful here this time of morning but my peace is broken when I see a lone figure running along the shoreline and as they get closer, my eyes widen when I realize who it is. I take the moment to appreciate the fine specimen running toward me. Even all covered in sweat he looks amazing. He's a few feet away when he looks up and our gazes meet. He smiles and with that one little lift of his lips, I know exactly what I want to do.

I just hope *he* wants it to.

CHAPTER 22

Kane

After my wet dream and text conversation with Calliope, I can't get back to sleep. I lie here, staring at the ceiling, wondering what's going to happen later today when we meet up. Now that I'm staring down the barrel of discussing everything with her, I don't know what the hell I want to do. Well, I'm ninety-nine percent sure what I want but the consequences of it are massive. However, it's Calliope we are talking about. I've never met anyone like her in my life.

When I'm around her, my heart beats like never before.

Right now, I feel that this is the calm before the storm because if we do this, it's going to cause waves. Big tsunami-sized waves. If she were any other woman, I'd jump in with both feet but she's my best friend's princess. His eldest daughter. Garrick has hated every boy she has ever dated and I really don't want my best friend to hate me, but Calliope Fischer is perfect in every way. She's a bright beacon of light in the darkest of nights. She's worth his wrath but does she feel the same way? That's the million-dollar question right now.

Climbing out of bed, I decide to go for a run to clear my head. Running along the beach has always reset my mind and calms my soul. I really hope this morning will be no different. Walking down the front steps of the house, I see the sky is just beginning to lighten, the sun will rise soon, shedding light on a day that will change my life forever.

Putting one foot in front of the other, I take the long way to the beach and I find myself jogging down Main Street. When I pass Fern's apartment, I look up and smile, knowing that one flight of stairs away Calliope is sound asleep, possibly dreaming of me.

Picking up the pace, I head toward the beach. Before I hit the sand, I look to the clifftop and take a moment to admire my hotel. The Clifton was old and run-down when I purchased it. Everyone told me I was crazy when I bought it, but I ignored their concerns and followed my heart. The Clifton is now a popular getaway location and most seasons we're fully booked before the end of the current season for the upcoming one. We are busy year-round and I have to say, Christmas at The Clifton is my favorite. We spare no expense on the decorations and the chefs really step it up, creating some of the most delicious foods I have ever tasted. I'm hoping to entice Michael to come and work for me when he finishes his apprenticeship. Under the guidance of Pierre, my current head chef, Michael could become amazing, well, more amazing than he already is.

Turning away from the hotel, I jog down to the harder sand at the shoreline and start my run. Once I'm at the opposite end of the beach, I turn around and slowly make my way home. The fresh air has cleared my mind and given me the clarity of what I need to do today. As much as I want Calliope, I'm going to leave the decision up to her. Will I be gutted if she chooses not to explore an us? Hell-fucking-yes I will be, but I don't want her to do anything she doesn't feel comfortable with. I've already hurt her once when I pushed her away after kissing her in New York, and I vow never to hurt her again.

A lone figure is sitting in the sand and when they look up, my breath hitches and I almost stumble when I realize it's Calliope. She looks amazing in her running gear, my eyes roam over her as I walk toward her.

"Good morning, Calliope," I offer by way of greeting.

"Morning, Mr. H," she replies with a nod and a shy smile.

"Mind if I join you?" *Please say yes. Please say yes.*

She nods. "Of course, it's a free country … and I wouldn't mind the company."

Dropping down next to her, I pull my legs up like hers and silently we stare out at the ocean. The silence isn't awkward, if anything it's calming. A smile appears on my face at that thought.

"Mr. H." The sound of her soft voice pulls me from the view and I turn to face her. "What's got you grinning like that?"

"You," I honestly tell her. Her cheeks tinge pink at my honesty. "That color suits you." Her cheeks darken further and I'm sure she's remembering exactly what I'm referring to. "I haven't been able to get that image of you in the private room out of my head."

"I haven't been able to stop thinking about what happened in your hotel room." She pauses and then adds, "Well, I've tried to forget the end part but up 'til that bit, it was the best moment of my life."

"I'm so sorry I treated you how I did, Sunshine. It's not every day that I make out with my best friend's daughter, it … it took me by surprise."

"I think it took both of us by surprise but really, are we surprised it happened? We've been dancing around each other since that first night in New York. I … I've had—"

Reaching over, I place my finger on her lips, shushing her. "No, Calliope, don't tell me what you want because I know we both want the same thing. And … and I don't think I can hold myself back anymore. I wanted so much to fuck you in that restroom last night, but you deserve more than a quickie in a family restroom. You deserve everything, Calliope, but I just don't know if I'm the right man to do it."

She grips my wrist and removes my hand from her lips. "Can I tell you what I think?"

"Of course, you can tell me anything."

"I think we've had years and years of foreplay, and I think it's time we took that final step. I want you, Mr. H."

Silently I stare at her and process her words. This conversation is going much smoother than I thought. It seems we are both on the same page, but there's one factor I'm not sure I can get past. "What about your dad?"

"What about him?" she nonchalantly says with a shrug. "This is between you and me. Everyone else can take a flying leap off the clifftop. Mr. H—"

"Mr. H, really? If we do this, I need you to call me by my first name."

She laughs. "Okay, Mr. H." I eye her and she giggles. "My bad." She shimmies around to face me. "Okay, Kane, what do you say, do you wanna leap with me?"

CHAPTER 23

Cali

Holy shit, I can't believe we are considering this. Never have I been so glad for insomnia to take hold of me and bring me to the beach so we could chat. I don't think we would have been as honest with one another in his office. Anyone could have overheard us but here on the beach, it's just the two of us, it's perfect.

"Okay, Kane, what do you say, do you wanna leap with me?" Waiting for his answer is killing me and thankfully, he doesn't make me wait too long.

"I'll leap with you, Calliope. I'd leap into the depths of

hell for you."

Before I can register what's happening, he pushes me back to the sand, covers my body with his, and presses his lips to mine. I slide my hands into his luscious locks and he moans into my mouth when I gently pull on them. My body is buzzing right now, if I thought the kiss in New York was perfect, this kiss trumps that one tenfold. This is the kiss of all kisses and it's cementing a new journey for me … for us.

He pulls back and immediately I feel the loss. I begin to think he's going to run just like he did last time, but he shakes his head. "I'm not going anywhere, Sunshine." *How did he know?* "But we need to stop. Otherwise, I'm going to fuck you here in the sand and now that the sun is up, people will be here soon, and you deserve more than a quick sandy fuck. You deserve to be treated like a princess." Both our eyes widen at the use of princess—Dad's pet name for me. "I … umm, shit, I promise never to call you princess again."

"Thank you. I don't want to be thinking of Dad when we're, you know …"

"I know and neither do I. I want my sole focus to be on you, and all the pleasure I'm going to pull from your body when we finally take that leap. Sunshine, when I finally get my hands on you, you won't be able to walk for a week without people knowing you've been fucked ten ways from Sunday."

Nodding, I bite my bottom lip. I want him to do everything he just said and more. "When?"

"When what?"

"When can we, you know? Do all that you just said."

"Ohh, umm, I don't know. We have your parents' party

tonight."

Shaking my head, I push him away. He sits on his heels and watches me intently. I want nothing more than to shout this from the clifftop. There's a chance this will all implode because of who we are to each other, but I can't risk ruining tonight for Mom and Dad. "Not tonight, Kane." I shake my head. "I can't ruin this for them. We need to keep it just us, for a little while at least. No point in imploding everyone's life if we don't work out."

He doesn't say anything and I begin to doubt that we have a future and then he grins. "What are you grinning at?"

"You called me Kane."

"You told me to."

"I know I did, but hearing you say it, it's music to my ears."

Now it's my turn to grin up at him. "Kane," I whisper, causing his smile to widen. "I need you to kiss me again so I know that this is real and not a dream."

"Sunshine, I'll kiss you anytime you want."

To prove his point, he grabs me by my shoulders and pulls me into his chest. He leans forward, grips my cheeks in his hands, and presses his lips to mine. My tongue pushes between his lips and into his mouth, there's not an inch of space between us as we kiss in the morning sunlight. He pulls back and rests his forehead against mine, both of us breathing heavily. "That real enough for you?"

"Very." I nod. "But just to be safe, you better kiss me again … Kane."

He pulls me into his lap so I'm straddling him and we kiss in the morning light. Wrapping my arms around his neck, I give myself over to the man I've lusted over for as long as I can remember. We hold on to each other tightly, afraid to let one another go. Afraid that if we let go, this will all disappear. I don't know who, but one of us pulls away, breaking the physical connection but the emotional ethereal one, it's buzzing around us. Breathlessly, we stare at one another. The only sounds are the waves crashing on the shore, our hurried breathing, and the pounding of my heart.

"Why did we wait so long to accept what this was?" he asks, cupping my cheek in the Kane way.

"'Cause we're idiots," I reply with a shrug, "but I don't think we were ready then. I think we needed time to process all of this."

"You are very wise, Calliope Fischer."

"Thank you, Kane Heatherington."

"Fuck, I love hearing you say my name."

Smirking, I look deep into his eyes and huskily purr his name, "Kane." But it totally backfires on me because, before I know it, he flips me onto my back, his body cocooning mine, and once again we make out like teenagers on a Saturday night at the drive-in.

"I will never tire of kissing you, Calliope."

"Just kissing?" I taunt him.

"For now," he growls and the deep timbre of those two words vibrate through my body. My clit buzzes to life at the thought of more than kissing this man. Then my panties combust when he leans in and whispers, "Calliope, you deserve to be pampered and worshipped. Devoured. When we finally get to that, you won't be coming up for air until I've had my fill, and when it comes to you, I have a voracious appetite. We've had years of foreplay, that's a lot of orgasms to make up for in a weekend."

Fuck me, who knew Mr. H, I mean Kane, was so dirty?

Seems sassy and playful Cali is at the beach because I lean into him and whisper, "Only a weekend?" Then I nip his earlobe. "I thought a silver fox like you would have more stamina than that." He growls and it turns me on, I can't wait to hear him growl like that when we are naked and covered in sweat.

"Don't test me, Calliope."

"Maybe I want to … Kane."

The sound of a car driving past causes Kane to jump off me quicker than the Flash. He towers above me and looks around, seeing if anyone is nearby, but it's still just the two of us. He looks back down at me and offers me his hand. Placing my hand in his, he pulls me into a standing position. "I guess we better go before someone finds us."

Nodding, I smile but it's not as vibrant as moments ago. The thought of parting ways hurts. "Do you still want me to come by today?"

"I'd love nothing more but if you do, once that office door closes, I cannot be held accountable for what I do to you."

"Mr. Heatherington, behave."

"It's Kane to you from now on."

"Kane … behave."

"Man, I love hearing you say that," he playfully says.

"Well, then, Kane," I emphasize his name, "I guess I'll see you later then."

"I guess so."

Stepping to him, I kiss his cheek and start walking away from him. I can feel his gaze on me so I add a swagger to my step, swishing my ass from side to side. When I reach the street, I look both ways before I cross the road and just as I step out, I feel a hand at my lower back. Looking to the side, I see Kane escorting me across the road. "Looks like we're both going the same way."

"Looks like it … or you might just be stalking me."

"You call it stalking, I call it escorting a beautiful lady across the road."

A smile graces my face and we silently fall into step, making our way to Main Street and Fern's apartment. Just as we reach her place, the door opens and she steps out. "Morning, hussy, where did you ru—"

"Ohh, good morning, Kane."

"Good morning, Fern. Lovely morning, isn't it?"

"Yep," she says, letting the 'p' pop. Her eyes dart between Kane and me, and if I know my bestie, I'm about to face the Spanish Inquisition.

"I will see you later this morning, Calliope."

"Sure thing, Kane."

Fern's eyes widen when I say his name and I know the mistake I just made.

"About time you started using my first name. I've only been saying it for years."

"My dad told me to respect my elders."

"Hey, enough with the elder talk, I'm not that old." A silence falls between us and then he says, "I'll leave you to it, ladies." He nods at us, steps around Fern, and continues down Main Street.

He's not even out of earshot when Fern starts. "Oh. My. Fucking. God, girl, you and I need to debrief now. Is it too early for wine?"

"Wine, yes … but maybe a mimosa, it—"

"is a brunch drink after all," we finish that sentence in unison.

Over brunch, I fill Fern in on my adventures this morning. I can't remember the last time I felt this relaxed but a few hours later, that feeling dissipates with one text message.

CHAPTER 24

Kane

I'm on a high after leaving Calliope and Fern, nothing, and I mean nothing, can bring me down. However, those are famous last words because when I enter my office later that morning, I come face-to-face with Bitchifer herself. "Danica, what the hell are you doing in here?" I growl from the doorway to my office.

"It's nice to see you too, husband." She accentuates the word husband, and I can't help but roll my eyes at her.

"Ex," I snarl, "ex-husband."

"Not yet, dear husband," she sasses, once again focusing

on the husband part while I focus on not throttling her. I remind myself orange doesn't look good on me … or if I'm locked up, I won't be with Calliope.

"What do you want, Danica? I have a meeting soon."

"Cancel it, we need to talk."

"We can talk through our lawyers. I have nothing to say to you."

"Don't be like that, we have a good thing going."

"The only good thing is you being far far away from Silverbell. The town and me are certainly better without you in it."

"That's not a very nice thing to say."

"Just stating the truth, now, get the fuck out. I have work to do."

Surprising me, she stands up and marches out of my office. I let out the breath I was holding but before I can take a seat at my desk, she stomps back in and stops next to me. She gives me a look that I think is meant to be seductive but it has no effect on me whatsoever. Lifting her hand, she traces her finger down my chest toward my dick. Grabbing her wrist, I stop her from touching the goods.

"You can't stay away forever, Kane, you know you want me."

Sighing, I roll my eyes and ignore her. It pisses her off because she shoves me in the chest. She storms out, barging into Kerrie, who was walking past, causing her to fall to the floor and drop the papers in her hand.

"Shit, Kerrie, are you okay?" I race over to make sure she's okay.

"Who the hell was that?" Kerrie snaps as I bend down

to help her collect the papers she dropped.

"Bitchifer," her nickname slips out before I can think, then I quickly add, "Danica, my soon-to-be ex."

"What I just saw seems awfully friendly for a couple getting divorced."

"Trust me, it's anything but friendly. That woman will be the death of me, I've been trying to officially divorce her for years now, but she refuses to sign the papers."

"Divorce is a sin in the eyes of God, Mr. Heatherington."

"Trust me, he'll give me a free pass for this one."

She purses her lips. "I was just coming to hand you my—" Before she can finish, there's a commotion in the lobby. Racing toward the loud voices, I come to a halt when I see Danica with Konrad, Finley, and Michael. My three children look pissed. I don't blame them really. Danica is all fake smiles and trying to butter up the kids, but my kids are smarter than that. From the look on her face, I think she's finally starting to realize they want nothing to do with her.

"I'm your mother," she screeches.

"If you were indeed our mother, you wouldn't have ditched us like you did."

"That wasn't my fault."

"It wasn't your fault that you packed a bag and left, never to make contact again?" Michael sneers at his mother. "You left us, Mom, and for what? So you can be a selfish bitch. Well, congrats-u-fucking-lations, you're a selfish bitch and we want nothing to do with you."

The sound of a hand slapping a cheek echoes through the lobby.

"Enough," I bellow and march over to them, putting

myself between the kids and her. "You will never raise a hand to my children again, you hear me?"

"Did you hear the way he spoke to me? He deserved it."

"No child ever deserves to be treated like that, much less mine. Now, I suggest you leave right now before I call the police department and have you arrested for trespassing and assault."

Her eyes widen and she gasps in shock. "You wouldn't?"

"Try me."

"Mom, just go," Konrad pleads.

"And don't come back," Finley adds, confirming our solidarity.

She shakes her head. "I don't need this. Fuck you all." She flips the bird at us, spins on her heel, and exits the hotel. We stand here and watch her climb into her car and spin the wheels as she takes off.

Turning to face the kids, my gaze flicks between the three of them before landing on Michael. "You okay, son?"

"She's never hit me before."

"And she never will again." Reaching out, I pull him into me. He's stiff at first but then he relaxes and hugs me back. Finley and Konrad join us and the four of us hug it out in the middle of the lobby.

Over Michael's shoulder, I see Kerrie and she's scowling at me. I really miss Hannah, she had been with me since the beginning and the reopening was a success due to her marketing and genius ideas. Don't get me wrong, Kerrie is efficient but she's no Hannah.

"I think we should have a movie afternoon before the party tonight. Forget all about her and watch some people blow shit up. I'm thinking *Battleship*."

"You just wanna perve on Skarsgård."

"No, I like it for the storyline."

"Bullshit, sis, but I'm down for that one," Michael says, smiling for the first time since Danica hit him.

"I'll get popcorn on my way home," I say and without another word, the three of them head out to Michael's car to head home for our impromptu movie session. Then I remember I was meant to be meeting with Calliope in an hour. Reluctantly, I pull my phone out and send her a text.

KANE: *Something's come up and I need to cancel.*

Walking back to my office, I grab my things to head home. I've just climbed into my car when my phone pings again.

SUNSHINE: *Ohh ok … hope everything is ok*

KANE: *It will be … I hope*

KANE: *See you tonight.*

SUNSHINE: *Yeah, sure, OK*

Fuck. Fuck. Fuck. She's upset and I hate knowing she's upset, but even more so, I fucking hate the woman who caused me to miss my catch-up with Calliope. I can still feel her lips on mine … and I want to feel them elsewhere. My cock hardens just thinking about her dainty lips wrapped around my dick. As I drive to the store, my cock gets harder and harder. I have to think about fat naked men to get it to deflate.

With popcorn in hand, I make it home just as the movie is starting but I can't focus. I keep thinking about Calliope and what the future will hold for us; a happily ever after? Or my death when Garrick finds out?

CHAPTER 25

Cali

It's amazing how one text message. Eight words. Thirty-three—yes, I counted them—letters can take a girl from the happiest of highs to the lowest of lows. When Kane canceled on me, it felt like the beginning of the end. I'm probably being overly dramatic but after this morning, I was hoping for … well, I'm not sure exactly what I was hoping for but, whatever the case, I'm left feeling upset. Abandoned. Alone and majorly pissed off.

Fern points out that I'm being a miserable bitch several times throughout the afternoon, while we're helping Mom set up the party at the country club in the outdoor gazebo. Each time, I flip her the bird and stick my tongue out before getting back to the task Mom has given me. Mature, I know, but I'm hurting right now.

"Mom, this looks amazing," I tell her once we're done. The gazebo is adorned with fairy lights crisscrossing their way along the ceiling. The tables are covered in white linen with vases of lilies, the flowers Mom walked down the aisle with when she married Daddy, and tea light candles to create a romantic vibe. The dance floor in the middle is shiny and ready for people to get down and boogie. Two bars are set up on either side and a covered walkway leads into the country club where just inside we have a room set aside that is currently housing the cake, thank-you gifts, and a makeup stand to touch ourselves up should we need it.

A waiter joins us and hands us each a glass of champagne. "Compliments of Mr. Fischer, to be handed to you three ladies when everything is set and ready."

The three of us all coo. "Daddy is so sweet," I tell Mom.

"He sure is. I was lucky to find my Romeo all those years ago."

Smiling, I wonder if Kane and I will ever get to celebrate a milestone like this, but then I remember he canceled on me earlier today and my smile deflates. *Why did he cancel?* I have asked myself that question a million times today. Maybe I need to give him the benefit of the doubt before I go jumping to conclusions, but I'm a woman. When it comes to matters of the heart, we don't think clearly. I always did have an overactive imagination, hence why I'm good at marketing. Well, I think I am, but the fact I'm a stripper and not working in marketing may suggest that I do in fact suck at marketing.

"So, Cali, honey, are you seeing anyone?" Mom asks, just as Fern takes a sip. Said sip sprays everywhere when she starts to cough and splutter. Me being me, I laugh while Mom, goes into mom mode. "Fern, sweetheart, are you okay?"

"I'm fine, Momma J, just went down the wrong way."

"That's what she said," I mumble under my breath, causing Fern to choke on her laugh.

"You'll pay for that, Fischer."

"Bring it on, Halstead."

Mom shakes her head and smiles at us. "Please never change, girls."

"Not a chance," Fern and I say in unison. She drapes her arm around me, pulling me in for a side hug.

"She's my Cal, Momma J, and she's stuck with me forever."

"More like you're stuck with me, babe." We smile at each other and then I look to Mom. "Well, we all better get home and make ourselves beautiful."

"I'm already gorgeous," Mom sasses just as Dad slides his arms around her waist.

"Hell yeah, you are." He kisses her cheek and Mom's smile widens.

"My parents are too cute," I say to Fern just as we hear Mom and Dad agree to a 'quickie' before the evening's festivities. "And on that note, Fern and I are going to go. We'll see you both back here later."

"After their quickie," Fern mumbles under her breath,

earning herself a jab in the ribs from me.

"Bye, girls," Mom sings out, thankfully not hearing what Fern just said, she'd be mortified to know we heard her. "Thank you again for all your help, I couldn't have done it without you."

"Anytime, Mom." Kissing my parents on the cheek, we say our goodbyes and then Fern and I quickly get out of here. Mom and Dad are being all lovey-dovey and gross, I don't need to see that. And to add more unease to the situation, Fern starts singing, "Boom-chicca-wow-wow," as we exit the country club.

"I hate you," I say, play smacking her in the arm.

"No, you love me. Now let's get home and make ourselves beautiful."

A few hours later, I'm almost ready to go when there's a knock at the door. "Can you get that?" Fern shouts out from her bedroom.

"Sure." Dropping my shoes by the sofa, I answer the door and when I swing it open, I'm met with a huuuuuge bouquet of sunflowers. I smile because sunflowers are my favorite. I start to get excited that they are for me when they say, "Delivery for a Fern Halstead."

"Ohh," I mutter, sadness hits that they aren't for me. "That's my friend."

"That's good enough for me." They hand me the flowers and walk away. Turning around, I head back upstairs and place them on the kitchen counter just as Fern walks out. Her eyes widen when she sees them and they widen farther when I say, "These are for you."

She walks over, grabs the card, quickly reads it, and then throws the card into the trash.

"Everything okay?" I hesitantly ask.

"Fine," she snaps. Before I can probe her on her delivery, she turns and walks back into her bedroom, slamming the door behind her. This reaction to flowers confirms my theory that she's hiding something from me, but what? And right now, I feel like a shit friend because while I'm going through my drama, seems she too has something going on. From secret calls, random flower deliveries, and her wanting to make it work with every man she sleeps with, I'm guessing she too has man troubles. I wish we didn't have to go tonight. I wish we could stay home and debrief, but then again, she won't open up until she's ready.

With a sigh, I drop to the sofa and slip my heels on. Standing up, I brush my hands down my dress when Fern walks out. My eyes widen when I see her. She's changed into a different dress and she looks hot. H-O-T-T hot. "Fuck me, babe, you look hot." She's now wearing a simple, little black dress that stops just above her knees. It has a deep V in the front—hope she has tit tape in place—and a killer pair of sparkly heels.

"Ummm, says the hot one." Since I'm standing, I do a spin, causing my blush pink dress to flair out at the bottom. "Kane is totally going to be sporting a woodie all night long when he sees you in this."

"Doubt it," I snap, still pissed he ditched me earlier.

"Who pissed in your Cheerios?"

"No one," I screech, but we both know I'm full of shit. When I look over at her, the look on her face confirms my 'full of shit' analysis. "Fine," I harrumph, "he canceled our date, catch-up, what-ever-the-fuck it was earlier, and it hurt. This morning at the beach it was perfect and then he cancels. Is he having second thoughts? Is he just another douche leading a girl on?"

"Why did he cancel?"

"He said something came up."

"Yeah, his dick," she teases. I roll my eyes. "Seriously, talk to him. Something probably did come up."

"But—"

"Nope, no buts. Give him a chance to explain. From what I know, he has never done anything to lead you on. Maybe he got scared and that's okay, I mean he wants to bang his bestie's daughter, that's big—pun intended—and entitles him to a freakout."

Shaking my head, I smile at her because with one sentence, she makes me realize I'm overanalyzing this. I need to give him a chance to explain and if he has changed his mind, THEN I can wallow and pout. "Thank you for pulling me off the ledge. I just …"

"I know what you just want." She winks at me. "Now let's get to this party so you can put your mind at ease and see your man."

"It's not like we can shout to the world that we are whatever we are. We agreed to keep it quiet."

"You know that's not going to end well, right? Secrets are always exposed."

"I know, but what if we don't work out? Why implode Daddy and his friendship if he and I go boom?"

"You two will definitely go boom boom." She wriggles

her eyebrows at me. "Your dad too, possibly, but when he sees how Kane treats you, he'll come around." She pauses and then adds, "Cal, babe, that man has it bad for you. Anyone with eyes can see you two have a connection. Follow your heart."

"But what—"

She presses her finger to my lip and shakes her head, "Nope, but buts, unless you're into that," *After last night, I know she is.* "Just see what happens. Stop trying to make everyone happy. As long as you're happy, that's all that matters. Now, let's go celebrate the love of your parents, WHO I might remind you, got together against your nanna's wishes and now look at them."

Nodding, I realize she's right—not that I will ever admit it to her—I need to follow my heart and right now, my heart wants Kane. As selfish as it is, I'm going to go for it with him, I'm going to take a leap … I just hope I survive the fall if it all goes wrong.

Fern and I pull up at the country club and she parks in the lot. Lady Luck is on our side and we get to park close to the building. Arm in arm we walk inside and head out to the gazebo. In the dark it looks even more stunning. The fairy lights really add to the ambiance and I find myself smiling.

"This looks amazing," Fern says as if reading my mind just now. "We did a fucking fantabulous job."

"We really did." I spin around and take it all in. It's a magical wonderland and it's perfect for Mom and Dad's party. "I'm going to find Mom and Dad."

"I'll get us drinks."

Fern and I split up and I find Mom and Dad off to the side and make my way over to them. Mom's face lights up when she sees me. "Cali, honey, you look stunning. That shade of pink really suits you."

"Thanks, Mom, you look beautiful too."

"Doesn't she?" Dad says, pulling her into his side, pressing a kiss to her head. After all these years, Mom and Dad are still ridiculously in love. If I can find a love half as intense as theirs, I will be one lucky gal. I deserve to be treated how Dad treats Mom, maybe Kane is that for me. Who knows, but what I do know is I won't settle for second best.

CHAPTER 26

Kane

The kids and I pull up to the country club and I smile when I see Fern's car already here because that means Calliope is too. I hope I get a moment to chat with her, to apologize for canceling today. As much as I want something with Calliope, the welfare of my kids will always be my number one priority.

The four of us exit my car and head inside. My steps falter when I see Danica sitting alone at the bar. Not wanting another confrontation, I speed up, ushering the kids quickly past and hoping like hell she doesn't see us. Passing the entrance to the bar, I let out the breath I was holding when we make it past without incident. Inhaling deeply, I follow the kids who are now in front of me.

We enter the gazebo and Finley veers to the left, making a beeline for Cari. Konrad and Michael head to the bar while I look around, looking for Calliope. I don't see her but I do see Jayne and Garrick, so I make my way over to them. The breath is knocked out of me when I'm a few steps away from them. Jayne has stepped to the side and I see Calliope. She's in a pink strapless dress that flares at her hips before stopping just below her knees. My gaze lifts and I see a hint of cleavage and I realize I'm screwed when it comes to this woman.

"Evening, Fischers," I say in greeting as I stop before them. Leaning over, I kiss Jayne on the cheek before offering my hand to Garrick. "Happy anniversary, you two." Then I look to Calliope, I try to school the smile trying to break free. "Calliope, good to see you again."

"Hi, Mr. H," she timidly replies. "It's good to see you again too." I don't like her tone and I want nothing more than to sweep her into my arms and kiss her hello, but we agreed to keep it quiet. If we were able to meet today, we would have set some official ground rules, but Bitchifer ruined that for me.

"Please, Calliope, you're an adult now, call me Kane."

She goes to reply but Garrick beats her to the punch. "She's respecting her elders, just like I taught her to."

"Daddy, be nice. Kane," she emphasizes my name and like earlier today, my heart skips a beat when she utters those four letters, "is older than you, if my memory serves me correctly, so really, Daddy, you need to respect your elders."

Garrick laughs. "I just got schooled by my daughter. Lucky I love you, Princess."

She sweetly smiles at her dad but when she looks over at me, that smile dims and I don't like it.

"As much as I love the defense, Calliope, maybe we ease up on the elders talk. Forty-five isn't that old."

"I'll leave you old folks to it," Calliope teases. "I'm heading to the bar."

"I'll come with you." I look to Jayne and Garrick. "Again, happy anniversary, guys. You two really are perfect for one another."

"Thanks, Kane," Jayne says, looking to her husband with hearts in her eyes. "I hope you find love again one day."

Calliope's eyes widen and I don't miss the hitch in her breath when I say, "I hope so too, you never know what's around the corner." Looking to Calliope, I offer her my arm. "Shall we head to the bar?"

She nods but doesn't take my arm, she turns and walks toward the bar, leaving me standing here. Her refusal hurts. I thought she would have jumped at the chance to be close to me. Racing to catch up to her, I place my hand on her lower back. "Have I done something to upset you?"

"You canceled on me," she hisses through clenched teeth. "I thought … well it doesn't matter what I thought because you canceled … without explanation."

"My kids needed me," I snap, I didn't mean to be so harsh but her anger isn't warranted right now, and to be honest, she's pissing me off.

"Ohh," she whispers, "is everything okay?" Her voice sounds remorseful and the look on her face confirms that.

"Yes. No. I don't know." We reach the bar and I notice the bartender checking her out. I can't help it and I growl. He doesn't hear but Calliope does. She turns toward me, her eyebrows raised. "Did you just growl at that man?"

"Yes, that asshole was checking you out. And he's not a man, he's a boy."

"Jealous?" she teases me.

"Yes. No one checks out what's mine except for me."

Her eyes widen and a smile graces her face. "I'm yours, am I?"

"Well, after this morning I thought so, but now I'm not so sure."

"Weeelll, he does have a nice … pour." She picks up the drink he placed in front of her and takes a sip.

"What can I get you, sir?" he asks me, but his eyes are once again locked on Calliope and her lips wrapped around the rim of her wine glass.

"Scotch. Neat." He doesn't move so I clear my throat. That snaps him to attention and he gets my drink.

"That kid just shit his pants," Calliope whispers with a smile from behind her glass.

Shrugging at her, I turn around and lean against the bar. From the corner of my eye I watch Calliope. She has no idea just how beautiful she is. "You look beautiful this evening, Calliope."

"Thanks, you look pretty spiffy yourself."

"Spiffy, eh?"

"Yep." The bartender places my drink down. Picking it up, I raise it. "To us," I whisper.

"To us." She clinks her glass with mine, just as Fern joins us.

"Cal, babe, sorry to interrupt, but your mom needs you for a family photo."

"Of course," she looks to me, "I'll umm, see you soon."

Nodding, she links arms with Fern and I watch the two of them whisper and giggle as they walk away. No doubt talking about me as they make their way over to Garrick, Jayne, and Cari. Standing here, I watch them and think about the future. This could be Calliope and me, well, not the twenty-five years married part, but I can see us, well me, being old and gray … er, celebrating our love together.

"What's got you grinning like a loon, Dad?" Konrad asks before ordering himself a beer and me another scotch.

"Nothing in particular. Just happy for my best friend and his wife."

"Ever think you'll get married again?"

"Haven't really thought about it," I tell him, but that's a lie because moments ago I was picturing Calliope and me, old and gray together, celebrating a major anniversary. "How about you? Got a lady friend back at school?"

"Lady friend, really, Dad?" Shrugging at him, I take a sip of my drink. "If you must know, I'm seeing a lovely nurse, Kate. I met her in the cafeteria after a grueling night shift. It's just starting to get serious, Dad, but I really like her."

"I'm happy for you, son."

He leaves me to join Michael, and I find a table in

the corner to hide out. Parties aren't really my thing but when your best friend celebrates his twenty-fifth wedding anniversary with the love of his life, you put aside your unease and you man up.

The evening is well under way now, the meal is over and people are up dancing. I'm still sitting in the corner but my eyes are glued to Calliope as she and Fern dance up a storm. She starts to dirty dance with Fern and I have to say, it's the hottest thing I've seen since I saw her in the pink number in the VIP room at The Nirvana Lounge. Seems working in the strip club has its benefits, and I really hope that one of these days she will dance for me like that.

Pulling my phone out, I tell her exactly that.

KANE: *I hope you dance for me like that one day.*

She and Fern exit the dance floor and take a seat after grabbing a glass of champagne from the asshole who has been staring at her all night long. She pulls her phone out and when she sees my name on her screen, her face lights up. That smile widens when she reads my message.

SUNSHINE: *I think that can be arranged **wink wink***

From my vantage point, I can see her but she can't see me. She really is a vision. If we can't physically be together, I guess we can text together.

KANE: *You look ravishing in that dress*
KANE: *The things I want to do to you in that dress*
SUNSHINE: *I'm wearing pink*
KANE: *I can see. I have eyes and as I said, ravishing*

She looks up and across the gazebo, our gaze meets. She smiles at me and I feel it deep in my bones. Something passes over her face and then she quickly types out a text.

SUNSHINE: *I'm not referring to my dress **wink wink***

Faaark, she cannot say stuff like that to me when her mom and dad are at the table next to me.

KANE: *You'll pay for that*

SUNSHINE: *How so K A N E????*

KANE: *I'll spank your sexy ass*

SUNSHINE: *Looks like I'm in for a spanking*

KANE: *Your ass does look fine in that dress but I think it would look better tinged pink ... it is the best color on you after all.*

And the minx she is, she stands up, spins around, and points her ass to me, flicking her hips side-to-side as she makes her way over to the bar. The bar that I notice is empty of other people except for the bartenders. Pocketing my phone, I stalk over to the bar and stop beside her. I stand much closer than is appropriate, but she's mine so I can do what I want.

Leaning into her, I whisper-growl, "You are testing my patience, Sunshine."

"Who me?" she playfully replies, shoving me in the shoulder with hers before placing her hand on her chest, just above her tits. Tits that are begging for me to bury my face in between.

"Yes, you. The things I want to do to you in that dress."

The barman places Calliope's champagne in front of her, again checking her out. He looks to me and I glare at the motherfucker. "Scotch, neat." Then I tack on, "please." Don't want the asshole spitting in my drink.

He nods and I turn my attention back to Calliope. We quietly stare at one another, our eyes roaming over each other. She bites her lip and I nearly lift my hand and pull the plump mound free from her teeth, but then I remember that we can't do that in public. "It's so hard to hold myself back right now," I honestly tell her.

She steps into me and whispers into my ear, "Meet me in the room just inside the door in ten, and maybe I'll let you do some of the things that you want to do to me."

"We can't just take over another room."

"We're not. We rented it too, in case we needed a time out." She pauses. "And I think I've been a bad girl and need a time out."

I can't believe I'm about to say this but before I can hold the words back, I growl, "Ten minutes and not a second later."

Picking up my drink, I walk away from her. I can feel her gaze on me as I exit the gazebo, not quite believing what I'm about to do.

CHAPTER 27

Cali

Standing here with my heart racing for what's about to happen, I watch Kane walk across the room, out of the gazebo, and into the country club. I have ten minutes until I need to join him so I race over to Fern. Grabbing her arm, I pull her to me and whisper into her ear, "Cover for me, I'm meeting you know who."

Her eyes widen and a cheeky smile graces her face. "EEEEK, are you two gonna get your boom-chicca-wow-wow on?"

"Noooo," I scoff, "well, I don't think so."

"But you totally want to."

"Well, yeah, but not here."

"Pffft, I say, just go for it."

Of course she would say that, but if I'm honest, I do want more than a few sneaky kisses with Kane, maybe even a spanking. Ever since that text, I haven't been able to stop thinking about him doing that to me. Shaking away that sexy thought, I grab my clutch, kiss her cheek, and head to the restroom to freshen up.

After using the facilities, I wash my hands and slap some gloss on my lips. I'm reaching for the door handle when it swings open and I come face-to-face with Danica Heard. "Mrs. H, what are you doing here?"

"My invite to your parents' party must have gotten lost in the mail," she sneers.

"You'd have to take that up with them, I'm only home for the weekend."

"Law, right?"

"No, marketing."

"Why you want to study and work when you can just hook yourself a rich man, I will never know. A girl with your looks could sink her claws into any sap she bats her eyelashes at."

WOW, what a vapid woman. No wonder Kane and the kids want nothing to do with her. "Oooookay, well, it was nice to see you."

"You haven't seen my husband, have you?"

My eyes widen at her question. "And why would I know where he is?"

"Because he's your father's best friend."

"Exactly, my father. Now, if you'll excuse me, I have a party to get back too."

Stepping around her, I race to the room where I'm meeting Kane and when I step in, I'm relieved to see it's empty. I need a few moments to compose myself. Of all people to run into, it had to be Bitchifer herself. I guess she was the something that came up today, also explains the aloofness of Michael earlier and Kane needing to spend time with the family.

I'm so lost in my head, I don't hear him enter. He slides his hands around my waist and I scream in fright. I rear back and accidentally headbutt him. "Fuuuuck," he groans, covering his nose.

"Shit, Kane, you scared me. Are you okay?"

"Mmmhmpf," he utters from behind his cupped hands.

"I'm so sorry. I didn't hear you come in and then you scared the shit out of me when you touched me." *But you also set my body alight.*

"And I felt the brunt of that scare."

"Let me go grab some ice." I go to step around him but he grips my wrist. He shakes his head. "No, I don't need ice, Calliope, I just need this." He lets go of my wrist, cups my cheeks, and presses his lips to mine. Our kiss starts out slow, our tongues languidly sliding in and out of each other's mouths. Covering his hands with mine, I press myself into him, deepening our connection and kiss. Pulling apart, we rest out foreheads together, each of us breathing heavily from the intense make out session just now. "All better," he whispers and I can't help but laugh.

Pulling back, I lift my hand and gently rub his nose.

"Are you sure you're okay?"

Nodding, he smiles. "I promise but where were you when I entered? You were a million miles away."

"I ran into Danica in the restrooms before I came here. I'm guessing she was the something that came up earlier today with the kids?"

He nods and I hate the sadness reflecting back at me. "Yeah, she really is a piece of work. The way she spoke to the kids today was unacceptable and then they wanted a family movie afternoon, and they will always come first."

"Do not apologize, I understand. We're still new. We'r—"

"You still want this after what happened?"

"Kane, I want you for you." I place my hand over his heart. "For what's in here. The love you have for your children is one of the many things that makes you amazing."

"What about my crazy ex?"

"What about her? We all have a past and she can't be helped, but one of these days she'll be irrelevant so really, she's moot."

"You truly are amazing, Calliope." We stare at one another, the air around us buzzing. "Well, now that we've discovered that we're both amazing, what should we do?"

Shrugging at him, I bite my bottom lip. "I think my ass was mentioned." His eyes widen. "I don't mean like that, you perve. I meant, I'm due a spanking for being sassy."

"That's right, you were taunting me about wearing pink."

"Ohh yes, that." Feeling brazen, I take a step back and grab the zipper at my side. With my eyes locked on his, I begin to lower it down.

"Calliope," he growls my name, "what are you doing?"

"Showing you all the pink I'm wearing."

My dress begins to loosen and when the zipper is at my waist, I wriggle my hips side to side and my dress falls to the floor. Leaving me in nothing but a matching blush-pink strapless bra and G-string set and my heels. Stepping out of the dress, I place my hands on my waist and cock my hip to the side.

"Fuck, Calliope. You were stunning in the dress but out of it, you're a vision." He spins his finger. "Turn around for me, Sunshine. Let me see you from the back."

Spinning around, I turn my back to him. My heart is racing. My breathing is hurried and then there's a crack in the air and my ass cheek is burning. "Told you I was going to spank you," he whispers into my ear. His hand massages away the sting and then he spanks me again and again. A moan slips out of my lips. "You like that, huh?"

Nodding, I swallow, waiting for the next slap to come but it never does. Looking over my shoulder, I see Kane's gaze roaming over me. He adjusts himself and I giggle. Turning to face him, we stare at one another. "Kane," I breathlessly pant.

"Yes, Calliope."

"I—" I don't get to finish because there's a hurried knock on the door followed by Fern whisper-yelling, "Psssst. Cal, your mom's looking for you and she's coming this way."

My eyes widen but I'm frozen on the spot. I know I need to get dressed and Kane needs to get out of here, but I can't move. I'm cemented to the spot. Kane grips my shoulders and gently shakes me, snapping me back to the present. "Calliope, snap out of it. You need to get dressed. Now."

"We are so screwed and not in the good way. Fuck. Fuck. Fuck." I stand here staring at the door, waiting for Mom to come in and bust Kane and me.

"Calliope," he shouts my name and my gaze slowly turns to his. "Get. Dressed. Now."

He drops to his knees and holds my dress open for me. Stepping into it, he pulls it up and snickers. "I wanted to take this off you, not put it back on." For some reason, I find that hilarious and I begin to laugh and laugh. With nimble fingers, he pulls his zipper up just as the door flies open and Mom enters. "Cali. Kane, what's going on?"

"I ... I ..." I stammer, unsure of what to say.

"I came to make sure Calliope was okay, she had a run in with Danica."

"She's here?" Mom screeches, pulling the door closed behind her.

"Yes." Kane nods. "She stopped by the hotel earlier today, caused a scene, and then accosted Calliope in the restrooms just now. I saw her upset and wanted to make sure she was okay."

"You're a good friend, Kane, thank you for looking after my baby girl." Mom takes my hand and squeezes. I squeeze back. "You okay, honey?"

Nodding, I smile. "Yeah, Kane comforted me." *And by comforted me, I mean spanked me and I want him to spank me again ... and more.*

He shuffles on his feet. "I'll, umm, ahh, leave you with

your mom now, Calliope. I'm sorry and I'll ahh, see you soon."

"Thanks for coming to my rescue, Kane." Letting go of Mom's hand, I go over to him and hug him. He hugs me back and I whisper, "And thank you for the spanking, maybe we can do that again."

"Behave," he whisper-growls and the tone of his voice has my clit buzzing for more.

He breaks the hug. "I'll leave you two ladies, and I'll get Fern to bring in a drink for you both."

"So thoughtful," Mom says and then in unison we both say, "Thank you, Kane."

"We sounded like schoolgirls then." Mom giggles and I can tell she's had a few drinks. She looks to Kane and finger waves before adding, "Bye, Mr. Heatherington." Giggling once again.

"Bye, Jayne. Calliope."

With that, he walks to the door, leaving me with a tipsy Mom, a sore ass, and a thrumming vagina. Just before he steps out, he winks at me and I can't help but smile and with that one wink, I can see myself falling deeply in love with that man.

CHAPTER 28

Cali

After Kane leaves, Fern returns with a bottle of bubbly and three glasses, just what I need to calm my frayed nerves.

"You sure you're okay, honey?" Mom asks for the millionth time. "You look a little flushed."

"I'm fine, Mom, I'm just …"

"Horny," Fern says under her breath so only I can hear her. My eyes widen but I'm not surprised my bestie would say something like that, it is Fern after all.

Mom and I finish the whole bottle with Fern before we decide to head back to the party. My nerves have calmed somewhat from almost being busted, but I'm still horny as a goat. Nothing can be done about that right now so I have another drink instead; alcohol is the next best thing to an orgasm.

"Okay, let's get back out there," I say to Fern and Mom, linking arms with them and heading toward the door. With each step I take, excitement builds at the prospect of seeing Kane again when we rejoin the party.

Before finding Dad, we stop at the bar and with fresh drinks in hand, we make our way over to Dad, where Fern and I listen to my parents tell stories from their many years together. I find myself grinning and hoping that I too one day will have a love like them and stories to tell.

I'm disappointed not to see Kane again but after being interrupted by Mom, I think it's for the best because I don't want to ruin their night.

Before I know it, Daddy is driving Mom, Fern, and me home. The three of us sit in the back and sing along to "Wannabe" by the Spice Girls. Mom is past tipsy right now, she's so fun when she gets like this. That is until she regales Fern and me with stories that a daughter and her friend should never hear about her parents. It's like you KNOW that happens but you don't want to HEAR about those things happening.

"Your mom is a hoot when she's tipsy," Fern says, grabbing a bottle of wine from the fridge after we arrive home. I'm on the sofa, flicking through Netflix to find a movie to watch.

"She is," I agree as I bring up our all-time fav movie, *Clueless*. "But I did NOT need to know about them doing all that dirty stuff. I need to bleach those thoughts from my mind."

"Maybe you and Kane could take notes," Fern unhelpfully offers.

"Eeeeew, no. Now shut up and watch the movie."

We snuggle together, drink wine, and mimic the lines since we know the movie word for word. At some point we both drift off because I wake at stupid o'clock with a kinked neck and Fern drooling on my shoulder.

Waking her up, we each shuffle to our rooms. I strip off my dress and underwear and fall naked into bed, snuggling under the covers. I'm pretty sure I'm once again asleep before my head hits the pillow.

A few hours later, I wake up with my fingers inside me after having the sexiest dream involving Kane. He's bending me over his desk and he's spanking my ass. Once my ass is glowing, he spins me around and fucks me senseless. After bringing myself to orgasm in real life, I happily drift back to sleep with a grin on my face.

The next morning, I wake late and miss brunch with Mom, Dad, and Cari. I literally have enough time to shower and get to the airport for my flight back to New York. I don't get to see Kane again. That sucks donkey dick but we do text back and forth, garnering myself an evil eye from the flight attendant before we take off.

Kane and I have made arrangements for him to visit next weekend and I can't wait. I'm super excited because he and I can go out like a normal couple. We won't have to hide us because in a city of eight million people, the likelihood of seeing anyone we know is slim to none.

The flight home is uneventful—but the traffic back to my apartment is shit … and I love it. I sit back and while the driver honks on the horn and yells for the traffic to "Moooove," I text Kane.

CALI: *Made it back to the Big Apple.*

Bringing up Facebook, I scroll through absentmindedly, nothing really catching my attention, thankfully Kane texts me back so I have something to focus on.

KANE: *Glad you arrived safely in NYC. Silverbell misses you*

CALI: *Just Silverbell?*

KANE: *Maybe I do too*

CALI: *Only maybe?*

KANE: *There's no maybe about it, Sunshine. I miss you like crazy*

CALI: *I miss you too … how can I miss you when I really haven't had you?*

KANE: *The heart knows what it wants and mine wants you, Calliope Fischer. It beats only for you*

Holy fucking swoon, Batman.

CALI: *You sure know how to make a girl's heart skip a beat*

CALI: *… and for what it's worth, mine beats only for you too*

CALI: *Can't wait to see you on the weekend*

Staring at my phone, I wait for a reply but nothing comes. I start to wonder if I came on too strong but when I read back through our messages, he was the one to start the deep stuff. Shaking my head, I throw my phone into my bag, sit back, and stare out the window.

Why am I being so insecure? I'm not one to wait around by the phone. I wonder if it's because it's *him*, I've had a crush on Kane for as long as I can remember. This is a dream come fucking true and after this weekend, I will be sleeping with my crush. I feel like a giddy teenager again and I'm going to focus on that feeling. No more insecure Cali, falling in love Cali is the only version of Cali that is allowed.

My phone pings from within my bag but before I can answer, we pull up at my apartment. I pay the driver and he helps me with my carry-on bag and by help, I mean he gets it out of the trunk and throws it onto the sidewalk. "Asshole," I mutter to myself as I pick it up and head inside.

Entering the apartment, I call out to Nicole but she doesn't answer. "Welcome home, Cal," I mumble as I head to my room. Exhaustion overtakes me and as soon as I lie down, I drift off to sleep.

I'm woken later when my phone rings. It's muffled and it takes me a few moments to realize it's still in my handbag. Pulling it out, I smile when I see it's a FaceTime request from Kane. "Well, hello," I sleepily say in greeting when I see his beautiful, bearded face on my screen.

"You didn't text me back, I was worried."

"Sorry, I conked out when I got home."

"I thought I scared you off with what I said."

An unladylike snort bursts free. "I was thinking the same thing." He smiles at my revelation. "I'm normally so confident in a relationship but with us, I'm nervous and a little scared."

"Why are you scared?"

"Kane, I've had a crush on you for years. It's not often your crush becomes more. I'm scared that this is all a dream and then there's also the fact that your best friend is my dad. What if us being an us ruins that?"

"What if us being an us brings us all closer together?"

"You really think that's possible? You don't think Daddy will kill you?"

"Well, I didn't until you brought it up just now, but you know what?"

"What?"

"You are worth any wrath that may come our way, and no matter what, I'll be by your side. Calliope, since running into you on the beach yesterday morning, I've been the happiest I've been in a very long time. This might be selfish but fuck everyone else. All that matters is you and me. This coming weekend, I'm going to make you the happiest woman ever. You and I both deserve it."

"Are you real? This doesn't happen in real life."

"I'm very real and, Calliope …" He stares intently at me through the phone screen. "You and I are going to continue what we started in that room before your mom interrupted us. This time, no one is going to stop me from spanking your ass raw. Once it's my favorite shade of pink, I'm going to devour you with my tongue and then I'm going to make sweet, sweet love to you."

My eyes are wide as saucers as I process his words. My mouth opens and closes. "If you keep doing that with your mouth, Sunshine, I'll have to fill it with my cock."

"I'd be okay with that," I whisper. "And I'm totally okay with the rest of your ideas too … I hope Nicole is out this weekend."

He shakes his head. "Uh- uh, no interruptions and to make that happen, I've booked us a suite at The Plaza."

"You remembered."

"I remember everything you've said, Sunshine."

This man is something else, I always knew he was amazing but seeing it firsthand, it's something else entirely. He really is perfect. "I wish we weren't so far apart."

"I do too, Sunshine, and in a few short days, we will have a glorious long weekend together."

"I like the sound of that." A yawn slips free. "Sorry."

"I'll let you get back to sleep, I just wanted to see your beautiful face before I went to sleep. Good night, Sunshine."

"Good night, Kane." He blows me a kiss and disconnects the call. Flopping back to the mattress, I stare at the ceiling, smiling. All the fears I had earlier have evaporated and now I'm excited for the weekend ahead. Why is Friday so far away?

Four days later, I'm back at work. I've just finished my set and am sitting in front of the mirror, I stare at my reflection and for the first time since starting at The Nirvana Lounge, I feel icky. "You've been requested in VIP 3," Miss Rhi says, popping her head into the dressing room.

Turning to face her, I nod and smile but it's fake. "You okay, hun?"

Widening my fake smile, I nod again. "Yeah, just tired."

"Okay, well, why don't you call it a night after this? It's kind of slow for a Thursday."

"You're a gem, thank you."

"You know I'd do anything for my girls." Before I can say anything else, she sashays away.

Taking a deep breath, I grab a corset and quickly change for my last dance of the night. With my waist cinched where I can just breathe, I slip on my dressing gown, and make my way to VIP 3.

CHAPTER 29

Kane

I've flown in a day early to surprise My Sunshine. After checking into the hotel and dropping off my bags, I climb into a taxi and head to The Nirvana Lounge to see her. Exiting the taxi, I pay the cover charge and head inside. As I step over the threshold, my nervousness ramps up to Mach speed. As soon as I enter, Miss Rhi sees me and her face lights up like a Christmas tree. She waltzes over to greet me. "I knew I'd be seeing you again." She leans in and air kisses my cheeks, just like the first time we met. "You hurt her and I hurt you," she warns me and then smiles brightly and nods to the right.

"Head on back to three. I'll send Miss Sunshine in. She's just finished her set."

Reaching into my pocket, I pull out my wallet but she covers my hand and shakes her head. "Uh-uh, you don't need to pay to see your girl."

"You sure?"

"Positive," she replies with a nod, "besides, this isn't a brothel. I can't be seen taking money from a paying customer who is going to bang one of my girls in one of my VIP rooms."

"I never alluded to or said anything about banging."

"Yeah, and Elvis ain't dead. Just treat her right, that's all I ask of you. I'm very protective of my girls."

"I promise, I'm not going to hurt her." I smile at the protectiveness from this woman for her 'girls' as she puts it. "From that statement, I can tell you really care about them."

"What can I say, everyone loves me." I laugh at her cockiness but it's cocky in an endearing loving way. "Just remember my warning … Tiny over there …" She points behind me and when I turn around, I see an almost seven-foot monster of a man watching the room. He has muscles on muscles and with one punch, I'd be knocked out for a week. "He knows how to make it hurt. Any hurt you inflict will be returned tenfold."

"Not planning on hurting her."

"Good." She taps my cheek, nods, and turns around, heading down the hallway that I presume leads to the dressing rooms. Nodding at Tiny on my way past, I make my way into the room to wait for Calliope.

While I sit here and wait, I realize that I'm not overly

comfortable with her doing this, but do I have a right to tell her to quit? She's only doing this because she had no other choice and while I understand the why, I don't like it. At a time like this, I'd love to talk to my best friend about it but I can't because my best friend is her father. Before I can stew on this further, "Closer" by Nine Inch Nails begins to play, the lights dim, and the door opens behind me. Without even turning around, I know it's her. Miss Rhi assured me that she'd send her in, but there was a part of me wondering if she'd send someone else. Turning around, I notice that, just like last time, she's staring at the floor. Her shoulders rise as if she's taking a deep breath and when she lifts her head, she stares at me for a few beats before her face breaks out in a massive smile. "You're here," she coos.

"I'm here, Sunshine."

We stand here, staring at one another and then suddenly, we're both moving. When she's in leaping distance, she does exactly that and launches herself through the air. I catch her and spin us around as she wraps her legs around my waist. We hold each other tightly as our lips slam together. Her tongue pushes into my mouth and in the middle of the private VIP room, we kiss our hello to one another.

Stepping backward, my legs hit the couch and I drop down. She's straddling me but not once do our lips part. She pulls back and stares into my eyes. "You're here."

"We've established that."

"But you're not meant to be here 'til tomorrow."

"Surprise."

"Best surprise ever, Kane."

"Fuck, I love hearing you say my name. Say it again."

She leans into me and breathlessly whispers my name, "Kane." The huskiness of her voice heads straight to my dick and it twitches between us. "I want nothing more than to take this further but not here. I don't want our first time to be in a seedy club."

"As much as my cock is going to hate me, I agree. Plus, with the things I want to do to you, I don't want us to be interrupted because my time's up. What time do you get off?"

"I'd like to say right now." She winks and rubs herself against me. "But I need to see Miss Rhi when I'm finished."

"I can wait for you, if you like?"

She nods quickly. "I'd like that very much." Leaning forward, she presses her lips to mine and begins to grind herself on me.

"Again, it pains me to say this," I murmur against her lips, "please stop doing that." She giggles and it's music to my fucking cock. "I fucking love when you laugh like that, but can you laugh while not rubbing yourself on me? It's taking everything I have not to take this further but as I said, our first time together is going to be something to remember."

She cups my cheek. "Is this really real?"

"It's very real, Sunshine. It may have taken us a while to get here, but we are definitely real. I regret hurting you the way I did the last time we met in this room, but I think the wait was worth it. Now, give me another kiss and then get back to work."

"Did you just tell me to go back to stripping?"

"I guess I did." *Fuck, don't encourage her. She's a*

stripper, you're not okay with that and deep down, you know she's not okay with it either. Dammit, I really need to talk to her about this.

"Well, lucky for you, mister, you were my last dance for the night."

"But you didn't dance for me."

"Do you really want me to dance for you here? Or would you rather a super special dance when we leave here?"

"I'll take option three please?"

"And what's option three?"

"A dance now and a dance later. For months I've imagined what you'd be like dancing here."

"I'm sure that can be arranged but you need to remember, no touching."

"But—"

She presses her finger to my lips. "House rules BUT if you're lucky …"

"Lucky how?"

She nonchalantly shrugs at me before she slides off my lap. Her hips begin to sway side to side as she steps away from me. She grabs the tie on her dressing gown and begins to spin it around. Turning her back to me, she drops the gown off one shoulder and then the other. It's hanging down her back, showcasing her shoulder blades and giving me a hint of her pert ass. She leans forward and the satin gown slides up, exposing her mesh—pink by the way—covered ass. Pink will forever be associated with My Sunshine.

She stands back up and turns to face me, her gown is now open at the front and if it wasn't for her arms, she'd be standing before me in the sexiest pink and black mesh corset. "Fuck me, Sunshine, you are the sexiest woman I have ever seen. The things I want to do to you."

Lifting my arm, I reach out but she steps back and shakes her index finger side to side, "Uh-uh. Sir, no touching."

Hearing her call me sir has my already aching cock painfully pressing into the zipper of my slacks. If she keeps this up, there will be a zipper imprint on my dick. "Fine." I huff. Leaning forward, I rest my elbows on my knees and keenly watch her dance in front of me.

Her body moves in sync with the music. It's sensual. It's erotic. It will forever be seared in my mind … like my zipper on my dick.

She steps closer to me. I clench my fists tight so I don't reach out. She notices and smirks at me. *She'll pay for that,* I think as she rests her palms on my shoulders and pushes me back into the sofa. She straddles me and moves forward, her tits in my face, she must see the anguish in my eyes and whispers, "Go for it."

Halla-fucking-lujah, I slide my arms around her back and pull her into me. Pressing my face into her tits, I open my mouth and suck on her nipple when there's a knock on the door. "Time's up," a deep rough voice booms through the door.

"Noooooo," I whine, "two more minutes."

She laughs but makes no move to hop off my lap. My sexy little minx leans in and purrs, "To be continued." Standing up, she reaches down, picks up her robe, and slips it back on. "Meet me by the staff exit in twenty minutes."

"Mmmhmpf." I think I'll need that long to calm my cock down before I can leave this room.

"You okay?" she asks, her voice laced with concern.

Nodding, I reply, "Mmmhmpf," again.

Calliope giggles. She leans down and presses a kiss to my cheek. "That was the best dance I have ever given. Thank you, Kane."

"Mmmhmpf," I mumble, I don't think I've ever been this turned on. One word answers are all I'm capable of right now. Finally, the sexy fog clears and I realize I'm alone. "Huh, when did she leave?" I mutter to myself as I stand up and exit the VIP room.

Walking through the club, I make my way to where Calliope said to meet her. I'm so glad I decided to surprise her because that was the perfect way to start our weekend together.

CHAPTER 30

Cali

Leaving Kane in the VIP room, I head back to the dressing room and change into my normal clothes. After changing, I make my way to Miss Rhi's office. I need to speak with her before I leave and if I don't do it now, I'll never do it.

Raising my hand, I knock and wait for her to welcome me in. I made the mistake once of just waltzing in and I caught Miss Rhi on her sofa being eaten out by someone. That is a sight I never want to relive.

"Come in," she singsongs.

Opening the door, I step in and close it behind me. Taking a deep breath, I open my mouth but she raises her hand in a stop motion. "I accept your resignation."

"How did you know?"

"Tonight when you were up on that stage, that *je ne sais quoi*, that sparkle that usually radiates off of you was missing. Then when I saw that fine man return, I knew."

"I'm sorry, Miss Rhi—"

"Don't be, sweetie, I always knew you weren't a lifer and that's okay. Your time here is done, but promise me you won't be a stranger. Anytime you want a spin, you're always welcome here. Now go." She shoos me with her hand and stands up. "Go have wild monkey sex with that man and name your firstborn after me."

Shaking my head, I laugh and walk over to Miss Rhi. We hug each other tightly and then when I make my way back to the dressing room and quickly pack up my things, I find myself grinning. I'm happy I have no job, but even happier that my last dance at The Nirvana Lounge was for Kane.

With my belongings in hand, I make my way to the staff exit. When I step out, I see Zed guarding the door but over his shoulder I see Kane and I smile. Zed thinks I'm smiling at him and he returns the smile, that is until he hears Kane approaching behind him. He looks over his shoulder and quickly spins around, placing himself between Kane and me in a protective manner. "Entrance is that way, buddy," Zed growls.

"Oooookay," Kane says, "but I was—"

"Turning around and going the other way. This is the

staff entrance."

"I know, and I'm—"

"Zed, stop," I snarl.

He glares at me over his shoulder. "Shut up and let me do my job."

"Hey," Kane shouts, "don't speak to her like that."

"Fuck off, pretty boy."

"Zed," I screech. "Stand down now, that's my boyfriend."

"Your what?" he bellows, spinning to face me, his eyes scrunched in anger. "You're dating that old guy?" He flicks his thumb over his shoulder at Kane.

"He's not old, and yes, I'm dating him." Stepping around Zed, I walk over to Kane. When I'm in front of him, he reaches out, slides his arm around my waist, pulls me into him, and slams his mouth to mine. Dipping me backward, he claims me as his in the alphaiest of alpha ways and it's the hottest fucking thing ever. "Alpha much?" I pant when he breaks the kiss and pulls me back upright.

He shrugs at me and then over my shoulder glares at Zed. He laces our fingers together and without another word, pulls me back toward the street. "Night, Zed," I throw over my shoulder as Kane and I walk away. He hails a taxi and when the car stops at the curb, he opens the door for me. "Such a gentleman," I sweetly state before bending down to climb in. Kane slaps my ass before shuffling in after me. "Such a caveman."

"Just you wait." He winks at me and pulls the door closed. He tells the driver to take us to The Plaza, and suddenly I'm nervous for the night ahead.

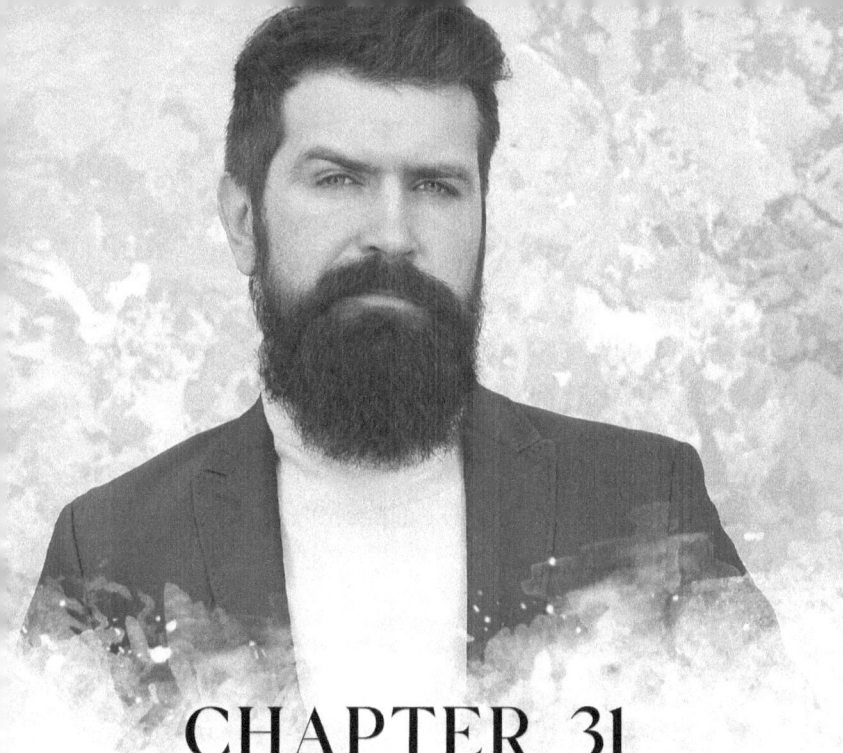

CHAPTER 31

Kane

"Who the hell was that asshole?" I ask Calliope as we pull away from the curb.

"He's no one." She rests her hand on my thigh but it does little to ease the raging jealousy coursing through me over that douche-nozzle... ohh hell, I sound like Finley right now. Douche-nozzle, I don't use words like that.

"No one would go all growly like that."

"Says the growly one," she throws back at me.

"He started it." I huff.

"Aww, you're cute when you're all jealous."

"I'm not jealous," I snap. She stares at me with a 'really' expression on her face. "I wasn't jealous per se, I was just worried about you."

"I'm a big girl, Kane, I know how to look after myself, but for what it's worth, thank you for looking out for me."

"I'll always look out for you, Sunshine."

She smiles at my response before shuffling closer to me. She lifts her hand from my leg and begins to trace her fingertip up my arm. "How can I ever thank you for looking out for me?"

"I have a few ideas."

"I bet you do … but they'll have to wait, because we're here."

Looking up, I smile when I see the taxi has come to a stop at the hotel. Pulling out my wallet, I hand the driver the fare and climb out. Turning, I offer Calliope my hand. She places hers in mine and hand in hand we enter the hotel, cross the lobby to the elevators, and we wait. There's a ding then the doors open. "After you," Calliope says, ushering me in.

"Shouldn't I be letting you go first?"

"Probably," she replies with a shrug, "but I wanna check your ass out."

"What the lady wants, the lady gets." Turning around, I step into the elevator and lift my jacket up so she can see my denim-clad ass. Looking over my shoulder, I ask, "To your liking, madam?"

"Very much so." She nods with a smile.

"You're turn," I playfully reply.

"I'll save my ass for upstairs … I have a treat in store for you, Mr. Heatherington."

"Well, hurry up and get into this elevator, Ms. Fischer."

She salutes me and steps in. Walking straight over to me, she pushes me against the elevator wall, and presses her lips to mine. Sliding my hand up her back, we kiss. Devouring each other's mouths. The clearing of a throat has us pulling apart. Calliope lowers her head to my shoulder in embarrassment while I smile at the elderly couple in the entrance to the elevator.

"We'll get the next one, George," the lady sneers, and if looks could kill we'd be dead. Her husband on the other hand is grinning like a fool and giving me the 'go you' look. His wife notices and she whacks him in the stomach, he grunts from the force of the hit.

"Have a good evening, folks," I offer with a nod, leaning around Calliope to press the button for our floor.

Once the doors have closed, Calliope lifts her head, mortification written all over her gorgeous, flushed face. "Oh. My. Fucking. God, that was mortifying."

"I found it hilarious." That comment earns me a smack to the stomach like George only moments ago. "Come on, Sunshine, it's funny."

"I hate you right now," she growls. Stepping around me, she crosses her arms and leans against the back of the elevator. The way she holds her arms causes her breasts to lift up. My gaze focuses on them but when I feel her glaring at me, I lift my gaze to hers. "You seriously are not checking me out right now?"

"Well, umm, yeah I am, your tits are always amazing

and holding them up like that makes me want to bury myself in between them again, like I did at the club earlier."

"You're such a perv."

"Only for you, Sunshine, only for you."

"Whatever," she sasses. "Maybe I won't tell you my news now."

"News? What news?"

"I'm not telling you." She sticks her tongue out and nods her head side to side and sneers at me.

"Sunshine," I growl. "Don't make me spank you."

"I think, after last weekend, we both know that isn't a threat but I'm happy for you to spank me again, just to make sure."

The elevator comes to a stop at our floor, Calliope steps out into the hallway and turns to face me. "Coming to spank me?"

"That and more," I tell her. Stepping out of the elevator, I scoop her over my shoulder, slap her on the ass, and head toward my room.

"Put me down, you brute." She giggles. "I have two legs, you know."

"I know." Ignoring her, I slap her ass for good measure and stop outside my door. Digging in my pocket, I remove the room key and unlock the door. Stepping into the room, I walk to the end of the bed and throw Calliope down. She playfully squeals as she flies through the air, giggling as she bounces on the mattress but as soon as our gazes meet she stops laughing. The air, and my dick, thicken at the intensity building by the second.

Everything between us is about to change and I'm

nervously excited for what lies ahead.

CHAPTER 32

Cali

The moment I land on the bed, I know that after this—after we cross this line—there will be no going back. I'm nervous but not because I'm worried about the fallout, I'm nervous to take this step with Kane because it's Kane. This step is always huge in a relationship and suddenly, it feels massive. "I'm nervous all of a sudden," I honestly tell him.

"I kinda am too," he admits, staring down at me and from the intensity of his gaze, I suddenly feel okay. "We don't need to do anything, Calliope. I just want to be with you. Sex can wait, I—"

"No, I want this. I want this more than anything, Kane. I've never wanted anything more in my life."

"We can take it slow … we do have a few days together."

"But not too slow, I think we've danced around enough."

"I do like your dancing."

He throws me a wink and I laugh, instantly relaxing further and now wanting this more than I need my next breath. "How do you do that?"

"Do what?"

"Relax me with a few words."

"No clue, but I do know that I'm about to wear you out, Sunshine. You ready for that?"

Nodding, I beckon him forward with my finger. "I'm definitely ready, Kane. Now come here and fuck me."

"I might need to spank you again for the filthy mouth of yours but because I really, really want to fuck you, that will have to wait." He grips my ankles and drags me down the bed, my dress sliding up and exposing my pink panties to him. He drops to his knees and opens my legs. He stares intently at my panty-covered pussy and licks his lips. Watching him watch me is turning me on, I feel myself becoming wet and apart from gripping my ankles, he hasn't even touched me. "Touch yourself, Sunshine," he demands, "show me what you like."

I've never touched myself in front of anyone before, I'm a little nervous to do it but my hand lifts on its own and runs a fingertip over the material. Pushing it to the side, I slip my finger between my folds. It effortlessly slides through, I push my finger inside, hooking it to reach that pleasure spot. A moan slips out and I press my digit in and out. The material of my panties is in the way, I pull my finger out and bring it to my lips. Sucking my juices off, I stare at Kane. His eyes are fused to mine and they are full of hunger.

"Why'd you stop, Sunshine?"

"My panties were in the way."

"Take them off," he commands. Hooking my finger into the band, I lift my ass up and slowly pull them down. He reaches out and continues to pull them down my legs. He bunches the material in his hand and slips them into his pants pocket. "As you were," he growls.

Slipping my hand between my legs, I repeat my earlier actions. Now that I'm pantyless, I slide my hand up to my clit and circle the bundle of nerves before pushing two fingers back into me. With my other hand, I squeeze my bra-covered breast, wishing I was naked so I could tweak my nipples. Closing my eyes, I give myself over to the pleasure I'm giving myself.

Opening my eyes, I see Kane has his pants open, his cock out and he's gripping himself. Squeezing his shaft in time to my fingers pressing in and out of me. That tingly feeling begins to develop low in my pelvis, I don't think I've ever come this quick before. "I'm… I'm going to come."

"Come for me, Sunshine, let go. I want to see you writhing in pleasure as you fuck yourself with your fingers."

Who knew Kane was such a dirty talker? But his words spur me on and when I slide my hand down my stomach, I pinch my clit and the pressure is just what I needed. I explode like a volcano. "Faaaaaark," I screech as pleasure ricochets throughout my body. When my body stops moving, I pull my fingers out, and Kane grips my wrist and brings my hand to his lips. He sucks my fingers into his mouth, licking me clean.

"You taste divine, Sunshine. I can't wait to bring you to climax with my tongue but first, I need to fuck you."

"Please," I pant, "fuck me, Kane."

He removes his pants and briefs and kneels on the bed. Leaning over, he presses his lips to mine, I can taste myself on his lips and it turns me on once again. He slides his rock-hard dick between my folds. Running his shaft up and down my slit, he finally presses himself inside me. "Yes," I mewl against his lips as he fills me completely.

He breaks our kiss and stares at me as he begins to thrust his hips back and forth. I meet him thrust for thrust, a light sheen of sweat covering our bodies as we pick up the pace. Sliding his hand down my body, he grabs my calf and lifts my leg up, resting it on his shoulder. He's so much deeper in this position and the sensations coursing through me are in overdrive now.

This is the best sex of my life, it's so much better than I ever imagined it could be. "Yes. Yes. Yes," I groan, as he hits that magic spot deep inside.

My eyes drift closed. "Eyes on me, Sunshine," he growls, and I immediately open them. Staring up at him, we watch each other. "I want to see you come apart."

With our eyes locked on one another, we watch and wait. Waiting for that moment when we reach the point of no return. I'm teetering on the edge, ready to tumble, but I can't quite get there. As if he's reading my mind, he grunts, "Play with your tits."

Lifting my hands, I squeeze my boobs. Closing my

eyes, I focus on the building pleasure. Kane once again demands I open my eyes and when I do, I see nothing but ecstasy written all over his face. He bites his lip and starts to really thrust into me.

Pinching my nipple through my bra, I moan, biting my own lip as the orgasm of all orgasms detonates. "Kaaaaaaaaaaane," I squeal as I crash into orgasmic ecstasy. My climax sets him off and he grunts my name as he comes inside me.

Collapsing to the bed beside me, we both lie here, breathlessly panting. Completely sated, I close my eyes, then they fly wide open. "We didn't use protection."

"Shit, Calliope, I'm so sorry. I got lost in the moment but I assure you, I haven't been with anyone and I'm clean."

"I … I'm … I'm on the pill and I haven't been with anyone in a long time, and I've always, always used protection before. What if …"

Turning my head, I roll to my side, giving him my back but he doesn't like that. He rolls me to my back and grips my chin in his hand. "We will deal with it if it happens. I'm not going anywhere, Calliope."

"I … but—"

"Not going anywhere, Sunshine. You're stuck with me cause I'm gonna need some more of that. That was the best sex of my life."

"Mine too, Kane, mine too."

He places a gentle kiss on my nose and I know that no matter what, we'll be okay.

"Now that we agree it was fucking amazing, should we do it again to make sure?"

"Dude, how are you ready to go again? I'm going to need at least an hour before I'm ready to go again."

"Fine, but in exactly sixty minutes, I'm going to fuck you again but this time, no clothes. I want to feel and see all of you, Sunshine."

And fifty-nine minutes later, he fucks me for a second time and it's just as amazing as the first. I'm totally addicted to this man and in all the sexual, dirty-talking excitement, I forgot to tell him that I quit The Nirvana Lounge. I can tell him tomorrow because right now, I'm too tired to talk. Kane has worn me out but he can wear me out like this anytime he wants.

CHAPTER 33

Kane

Waking up with Calliope's lips wrapped around my cock is a pleasant surprise, and one I hope to have happen again and again and again. After one fan-fucking-tastic evening with her, I'm addicted and so fucking happy to have the next few days with her.

After coming down her throat, after the best morning blow job ever, she climbs back up the mattress and snuggles into my side. Draping her arm across my body, she kisses just above my heart. "Good morning," she whispers.

"Very good morning, indeed, but I need a good morning

kiss."

She mumbles into my side, "Eeeeew, no, I have cum breath."

"Don't care," I reply. Placing my finger under her chin, I lift her head up but she pulls away, shaking hers and covering her mouth. She pushes away from me and jumps up off the bed, racing into the bathroom. Climbing off the bed, I walk to the bathroom and lean against the doorframe, watching her brush her teeth. She watches me watching her in the mirror. Her hair is disheveled and she's never looked more beautiful. "You are stunning," I tell her.

She spits and turns to face me, her toothbrush hanging in her mouth. "And you need your eyes checked. I look like a sleepyhead."

Stalking over to her, I slide my arms around her waist and remove the toothbrush from her mouth and drop it into the sink behind her. She drapes her arms over my shoulders, leans forward, and presses her lips to mine. My tongue seeks access to her mouth and she willingly opens, she pulls me into her, deepening the kiss and our connection.

Pulling back, I rest my forehead against hers. "Good morning, Kane."

"We've already discovered it was a good morning but I think it's time for breakfast." She begins to nod as I slide my hands down to her ass, lifting her onto the vanity and dropping to my knees. Pushing her legs apart, I lean forward and lick her from taint to clit. Swirling my tongue around before sliding it back down, pushing between her folds and inside her.

"Kane," she mewls, pulling on my hair and pushing my

face farther into her. Her hips rock forward and meet me as I devour her. Her thighs clench around my head and then she comes. Drenching my face with her climax and letting out the sexiest groan as I lick and suck every last drop of her release.

Dropping back to my heels, I look up at her. "Breakfast of champions."

"Kane," she berates, "that's gross."

Shrugging, I stand up and stare at her. "You look well sated," I tell her, cupping her cheek in my hand, running my fingertip over her plump bottom lip.

"And you are a mess, we better get you cleaned up but first, kiss me."

"No, I have cum breath … and face."

"Shut up." She playfully slaps my stomach. Reaching up, I grab her wrist and hold it to my chest. Stepping between her thighs, I push her back against the mirror. Leaning forward, I stop, mere millimeters from her lips, our heated breaths mingling together.

"Kiss me," I demand.

She slides her hand around my neck and pulls me into her. Her mouth covers mine, our tongues seductively sliding together, in and out of each other's mouths. She wraps her legs around my waist, my cock nudges at her entrance and she swivels her hips in that enticing 'please fuck me' way. My thought is confirmed when she begs, "Please."

Breaking the kiss, I pull back and we both lower our gaze to where our bodies join. We watch as my cock sinks inside of her. We both groan at the intrusion and we watch as I slip in and out of her. She reaches between us and begins to circle her clit. A growl forms in the back of my throat and I push her hand out of the way and take over massaging her tight bundle of nerves. Cupping her breasts, she massages them and pulls on her nipples as I grip her hips in my hands and increase my thrusts. Her head drops back, elongating her neck. Leaning forward, I lick up the column of her neck and she moans. Sucking on her jaw, I nibble my way to her lips and slam mine against hers. Pressing my lips to hers, we kiss and fuck like two starved people.

"I'm coming," she pants against my lips. I feel her walls tighten around me as she begins to climax. The tightness of her clenching my shaft sets me off, pulling out of her, I grip my shaft in my palm and spray my release over her stomach and pussy. She wipes her finger through the mess I just made on her skin and lifts her finger to her lips and licks it clean.

"That was unexpected," I tell her. Wrapping her hand in mine, I pull her up into a more comfortable position on the vanity. She drops her legs from around my waist and uses her hand for support. "I think we need a shower now."

She nods at me. "Mmmhmpf."

Reaching up, I cup her cheek in my palm. "You are full of surprises, Calliope Fischer."

"And I have one more."

"Ohh, yeah, and what might surprise number two be?"

"I quit."

"You quit," I repeat and she nods. My eyes widen when I realize what she means. "You quit, quit?"

Nodding, she bites her lip. "I told Miss Rhi last night before I left."

"What are you going to do now?"

She shrugs at me. "Get a job at Starbucks?"

"Come work for me?"

Shaking her head, she rests her hand on my naked chest. "I don't want a job out of charity, I want a job because I earned it."

"But—"

"Nope." She shakes her head. "No buts. The future is future Cali's problem. Current Cali is going to have a shower and current Cali would love it if you joined her. And then she's going to eat some food because she's famished. She worked up quite the appetite this morning. Then, she's going to come back to her hotel room, order an ice cream sundae from room service, and she's going to watch a movie and again, feel free to join her on that."

"Do clothes need to be worn at this movie session?"

She shakes her head. "Nope, but clothes will be required for brunch because no one but me gets to see you and your cock in all its naked glory."

"Same goes for your sexy as fuck body. Can I just say, I wasn't concerned with you working at The Nirvana Lounge but hearing you quit, it made me the happiest man ever."

"Maybe we should celebrate?"

"And how might we celebrate you no longer working there?"

"With a sexy shower and if you play your cards right, I might be persuaded to give you an all-access private show."

"All access?"

"Yep. All access." She winks. "Now, let's start the celebrations with our sexy shower."

"After you." I help her off the vanity and into the shower for one that I will never ever forget.

Calliope and I have the most amazing weekend together. We fuck. We talk. We explore the city and we fuck some more. Before we know it, it's time for me to head back to Silverbell. She travels to the airport with me. The car trip is quiet. "When will I see you next?" she quietly asks, her tone sad and aloof.

"I don't know."

"Ohh," she whispers. I hate seeing and hearing her so down.

"Look at me, Sunshine." She turns her gaze to me. "We may not be together, together but you are always in here." I cover my heart with my hand and tap. "We have FaceTime and I'll do my best to come and visit you again as soon as I can."

"I wish I could come home and see you but …"

"I know, I want that too but you know, if we don't hide this, we can. We can shout it from the clifftop, I just want to be with you, Sunshine."

"I want that too but … but I'm just not ready. I don't want you to think I'm ashamed of you, I just don't want to ruin your relationship with Daddy if we don't pan out."

"Sweetheart, you don't need to defend yourself to me. I understand completely where you're coming from. This is new territory for me too."

"So you don't bang all your best friend's daughters?"

"Nope. Don't get me wrong, Cari is nice but she's not you."

"Thanks, I think," she playfully replies, shuffling across the back seat to snuggle into my side.

Draping my arm around her, I pull her closer and press a kiss to her hair and cup her head. "You are the only daughter of my best friend that I want."

"I know, Kane, and for the record, you are the only friend of my dad's that I want too. I've had a crush on you since I was a little girl and I can say, it was worth the wait. I've had the time of my life with you this weekend, Kane, and I look forward to many more."

"You can be my sexy dirty little secret for now, but I won't hide us forever, Calliope."

CHAPTER 34

Cali

... two weeks later

I t's official, I'm returning to Silverbell. After quitting The Nirvana Lounge and having the most amazing weekend with Kane, I started job hunting but fate was on my side, I got a job immediately. You are now looking at the new MD—marketing director— at The Clifton. I have my first real adult job, not the stripping kind of adult but a real nine-to-five adult job.

While Kane and I were sexing it all up in New York, Kerrie, his current marketing director, quit leaving him in the lurch. It seems, she was not happy living in a 'Podunk secret-and-rumor-filled hick town with more scandals than Hollywood' and she's better than that. The rumors were buzzing as to what rumors she was referring to.

Dad being Dad, he manipulated Kane into offering me the job, not that it took much convincing. After our amazing weekend together and my currently being unemployed, it was a no-brainer when Kane called with his predicament and offer. Not only do I now have a job in the field I studied in, but it also means I will now be in the same town as Kane too. It will be hard to keep us hush-hush but as soon as I know what we have is more than just my crush coming to life, we will come clean. I have to admit, the thrill of sneaking around is adding to the fun of our relationship.

Kane is everything I imagined him to be and more. He's attentive, funny, and ohh so dirty in the most deliciously sexy way. I always thought phone sex was sleazy and cheap but in actual fact, it's really really fucking hot. There's something about watching a man fall apart just from your words.

The only downside to returning, the rumors. The rumor mill is currently in overdrive—hello, it's Silverbell— nothing new there. At the moment, Kane is front and center of the gossip mill. Rumors are rife that Kerrie and he were having an affair, and when he wouldn't have a baby with her, she lost her shit and that's why she quit and left town. Don't know how either can have an affair when both are single, but I guess technically he's still married because Danica still refuses to sign the divorce papers. Scandal aside, I have a marketing job, just like I always wanted, and I'm excited for the new venture ahead. Plus, I'll be living with Fern.

When she found out I was returning, she offered me her spare room and I jumped at the chance to live with my bestie. All we need now is for Raven to return and our trio will be whole again, but I can't see that happening anytime soon, or ever, actually. Rave is happy and in love in Chicago. He's a teaching assistant at the U of C—University of Chicago. He happened to find love with the professor he TAs for, and a girl. Yep, Raven Mitchell, the loudmouth goofball from Silverbell Shore is living as part of a throuple and I could not be happier for him, James, and Abi.

Saying goodbye to Nicole was hard but we promised to keep in touch. Miss Rhi, being the amazing lady that she is, threw a surprise going away party at the club for me. She closed for the afternoon, something she has never done before, and the girls and I had one last hurrah together on the stage. Dancing and drinking the afternoon away.

Now, I'm walking into the country club with Cari, Mom, and Dad for my welcome home dinner. We are seated and I notice that the table is set for seven. "Are we expecting company?"

"Kane, Finley, and Michael are joining us. We have dinner with them the first Friday of every month and tonight just so happens to be that night. Hope that's okay?" Mom says, picking up the menu. I don't know why she does because she gets the same thing every time we come here.

"She better get used to seeing Kane, he's her boss now," Dad states like I'm not aware who Kane is.

And more than that, I think to myself. "Yeah, it's fine I was just asking, thought it was just a family thing."

"Ohh," Mom says, dropping her menu. "I never thought that you might want just a family thing, I'm sure we can cancel."

"No, Mom," I say, shaking my head, "it's fine. Just got to get used to the swing of things and if I'd have known, I would have invited Fern too."

"Next time, we'll invite her. Just family for tonight," Mom says.

"With the Heatheringtons."

"Princess, they ARE pretty much family," Dad offers, and I smile at that because maybe one day, our families will be combined.

Picking up my menu, I look it over when, suddenly, the hairs on the back of my neck prickle and my lip lifts into a smile. He's here. Looking over my shoulder, I stifle the moan wanting to break free when I see Kane walking in with Finley. He looks divine tonight in jeans, a navy button-down, and blazer. My eyes unabashedly roam over him. He catches me watching him and smirks.

"Evening Fischers," he drawls, slapping Dad on the back as a hello before he kisses Mom on the cheek, nods at Cari, and takes the seat next to me. "Calliope."

"Kane," I return, my eyes steadfastly locked on his. I swear the temperature in here just rose twenty billion degrees. He slips his hand onto my thigh under the table and squeezes. Smiling at him, I pick up my water. I need to keep my hands busy right now because I want to reach over and run my fingers through his beard, grip his cheeks, and slam my lips against his. It's been far too long since I've kissed him. *How the hell am I going to be able to work so closely with him and not jump his bones?*

Thankfully, chatter starts and it gives me the opportunity to get my mind off the sexy as hell man sitting next to me. Dinner is going well. The food is amazing, as usual, and the conversation is flowing when my phone buzzes. Slipping it out of my dress pocket, I quickly open the message and read it.

KANE: *The things I want to do to your delectable body. Did you wear that low-cut dress for my benefit?*

CALI: *I wasn't even aware you were coming but know I always dress for you*

KANE: *Pink lingerie?*

CALI: *Of course. I wouldn't wear any other color*

KANE: *When will I see you next?*

CALI: ***shrugging emoji***

"No texting at the dinner table, Princess," Dad says, snapping my attention to his.

"Sorry, Daddy."

"Sorry, Daddy," Cari mimics from next to me. "You're such a suck hole."

"You're just jealous that I'm Daddy's favorite."

"Are not," she snaps. "Why did you have to move home?"

"Because I got a job," I snarl back. "What's it to you, anyway? Aren't you and Finley going on a gap year soon?"

"Yes, we leave in six weeks, three days, and seventeen hours."

"Excited much?"

"Like you wouldn't fucking believe."

"Language, Cari," Dad berates her.

"Yeah, Cari, language," I tease back.

"Cali, don't sass your sister. You're not too old for me to spank you," Dad says.

My eyes widen when from next to me and under his breath, Kane murmurs, "She'd love that."

"Sorry, Daddy," I say and under my breath I whisper, "Behave."

Kane smirks at me, picks up his scotch, and turns to Dad. The two of them talk about something to do with a golf game this week. Golf is the most boring sport ever, chasing a little white ball into a hole seems monotonous, boring, and stupid if you ask me.

"Cal, honey," Mom says, bringing my attention away from the boringness of listening to Dad and Kane talk about golf. "What are your plans for your last weekend of freedom before you start your new job?"

"Fern and I are having a quiet one. We'll drink some wine, rearrange things at our place to fit all my crap in." My voice quivers at the end of my sentence when I feel Kane run his hand up my thigh under the table and between my legs. His fingertip brushes over my panties and I flinch at the unexpectedness of this. My knee bangs into the table, the cutlery and glasses rattling, and everyone turns their heads to stare my way. Kane included but he also has a sinister smirk on his face.

"You okay, Princess?" Dad asks, his voice laced with concern.

"Fine, Daddy, just a shiver." '*Cause your best friend is a fucking deviant and he will pay for that.* "I'm just going to use the restroom."

Standing up, I quickly race to the restrooms. I can't believe he just did that, in front of my parents no less. He needs to pay and as I walk away from the table, a plan for payback forms. "Game on, Heatherington, game on."

CHAPTER 35

Kane

That was too much fun, but from the look in Calliope's eyes as she walked away from the table, I think she's planning something and I might be screwed. I say bring it on, I cannot remember the last time I felt this alive and it's all due to the woman who just left the table. A hand gripping my shoulder garners my attention from the sexy woman walking away from us. "Thank you, Kane."

"Why are you thanking me?" I ask Garrick.

"For bringing my princess home. I was worried about her living in that big city all alone. Some smug asshat trying to take advantage of her big, beautiful heart. She should be here at home, where I can watch out for her."

"You do realize she's twenty-three now and all grown up, right?"

"Yep, and any asshat who wants to win her heart needs to go through me first." He taps his chest and has that 'don't mess with my daughter' look on his face.

Nodding at him, I pick up my drink and as I bring the glass to my mouth, my eyes bulge. It occurs to me, I'm the asshat who needs to win him over. Then another thought hits me like a freight train. I need to figure out how to tell my best friend I'm the asshat falling in love with his daughter!

"From that look, buddy, you just realized that one day, you'll be in the same predicament as me when Finley is older. Be thankful you only have one daughter."

"Yep, so screwed." *On both accounts*.

My phone pings with a text. Picking it up, I open the message and when I see the text, my eyes once again bulge. They widen farther when from beside me, Garrick hisses, "Did you just get a nudie pic?"

"No," I quickly refute, exiting out of the image because Garrick does NOT need to see his daughter like that. Calliope, the dirty little minx, just sent me an image of her upper body in nothing but her blush-pink bra. Her gorgeous tits are covered in pink lace and her lips are in a sexy as fuck pout, thankfully you cannot see her face. I do NOT need Garrick finding out about us like this.

"What's going on over there?" Jayne asks. "You're looking a bit flushed, Kane."

"It's nothing, Jayne," I say, waving her off. "I'm fine,

your husband is just being a Nosy Nancy."

Garrick leans into me. "Are you keeping a secret from me, Kane?"

"No." *Yes.* "It was just a wrong number."

"I call bullshit but just know, I'm happy to see you getting back out there." He takes another sip. "It's about time you started dating again."

"Dating?" Jayne sits up straighter and focuses on the two of us. "Are you seeing someone, Kane?"

Just as Jayne asks that, a smirking Calliope returns, taking her seat next to me. "So, what are we talking about?" she sweetly asks, her eyes flicking around the table.

"Kane's dating someone," Jayne excitedly says, clapping her hands. Yes, she claps her hands like an excited teenager. "But he's being all coy." She looks at me and squints. "Is it someone we know?"

Quite well. "If you must know—" But before I finish that sentence, Bitchifer appears out of nowhere like an apparition from hell.

"Kane, darling," she singsongs in that tone that grates on my nerves. "Yes, do tell, whom have you been fucking?" She eyes me like she knows something but surely, she doesn't. I feel Calliope stiffen beside me but before I can say anything, Michael does.

"It's no concern of yours, Danica." He makes sure to emphasize her first name. "And you're not welcome here, so run along." He flicks his hand in a shoo manner.

"Are you going to let our son speak to me like that, Kane?"

"MY," I emphasize that word, "son is free to say

whatever he likes. First Amendment and all that. Plus, Michael is an adult now and I happen to agree with him, you're not wanted here." Then I turn my attention to Jayne and hope that Calliope doesn't hate me for what I'm about to announce. "And for the record, yes, I'm seeing someone. She's the most amazing woman I have ever met and she makes me happy, happier than I have ever been. It's new and wonderful but for now, I, well we, want to keep it between us."

"I knew it!" Finley shouts, slapping the table. "I knew something was up, you've been so freakin' happy these past few weeks. You've clearly been getting some."

"Finley," I berate her, "that's enough."

But my daughter being my daughter, ignores me and looks to Calliope. "Cali, babe, I'm tasking you with 'find out who Daddy's banging' duty." She says this just as Calliope takes a drink and she chokes and splutters on the sip she just took.

She wipes her mouth and composes herself and looks to Finley. "Sure, Finley, I'll add it to the bottom of my 'To-Do' list but I have a feeling, I'll be busy handling more important marketing matters."

"When did you get so boring?" She doesn't give Calliope a chance to reply before she tacks on, "at least keep an eye out for any secret rendezvous or meetings he has."

"Sure, Finley, I'll keep an eye out for who—"

"How tacky," Danica sneers interrupting Calliope, "dating someone when we aren't even divorced."

"And I'm sure you haven't dated anyone since you left, huh?" I snap back at her.

"What I do doesn't matter," she snaps, pissed off that it's been thrown back at her.

"You keep telling yourself that, Danica. Now, if you don't mind, we're trying to have a nice night."

"Kane, you can't keep ignoring me. I'm not going anywhere." She crosses her arms, stamps her foot, and huffs.

"I can and I will, Dan. You need to accept that we are over and you're not wanted here. Just sign the papers and move on … I have." Under the table, I feel Calliope's hand slide onto my thigh, giving it a light squeeze. Her touch calms the rage building inside me and I know that I didn't overstep with my announcement. I know she has my back, no matter what's thrown at us.

"The kids want me here," she whines.

Both Michael and Finley scoff. "Yep, they clearly want you here. Take the hint and leave. Better yet, sign the papers on your way out." Looking to Jayne and Garrick, I smile. "I'm suddenly not in the mood, I think I'm going to head home. Thanks for a great night." I look to Calliope. "Sorry to ruin your welcome home dinner, but know I'm happy to have you on board. I'll see you at the hotel Monday."

Before anyone can protest, I stand up and exit the dining room. Danica always has to fucking ruin everything but I will not let her ruin this for me. For the first time in years, I'm happy and I refuse to let this happiness go.

CHAPTER 36

Cali

When Kane confirmed he was seeing someone, I nearly choked on my tongue. But Kane being Kane, he kept the 'us' part out of his confession and watching him walk away just now, it hurt. It hurt to see him so upset. I wanted nothing more than to follow him and make sure he's okay, but I can't. Pulling my phone out, I shoot him a text.

CALI: *Are you OK?*

Staring at my phone, I will it to ping in my hand and for him to let me know he's okay, but it doesn't make a peep.

Knowing that I need to give him time, I place my phone down and focus back on the table but in the time I was in 'Kaneland' Danica is gone, as are Finley and Michael.

"Well, that was interesting," Mom says. "But I am happy to hear Kane is dating someone." She focuses on me. "Cali, honey, you will have to keep an eye out and let me know if you discover who he's seeing, right?" She looks to Dad. "I wonder who it could be?"

Dad looks less than enthused, the complete opposite of Mom. "Mom, who he's dating is none of my, or your business for that matter. I'm there to work, not contribute to the Silverbell gossip train."

"Ohh, honey, you've been away for far too long. The gossip will always be here and it's best to get it from the source … or his marketing manager. For me, keep an eye out … please? I want to make sure whoever he is with is worthy of him. After that woman, he deserves all the happiness in the world."

"Amen to that," Dad adds. "But whoever this lady is, she must be someone pretty special because when he was talking about her, I've never seen a glint in his eye like there was."

"Maybe it's a he," Cari interjects. The three of us snap our heads to her. "What? I'm just saying."

"Now don't go spreading gossip like that," Mom says. "That's how rumors start," she pauses, "but even if he is, love is love. Now, Cali, hon, would you like a lift home?"

"Thanks, Mom, I'd like that." My phone pings and I quickly pick it up. I smile when I see it's from Kane.

KANE: *I'm fine, Sunshine … just wish I could hold you*

and shout it from the rooftops. I hope I didn't overstep with what I said. I can only imagine the conversation you're having right now

CALI: *Cari thinks you're seeing a man. Dad's happy and Mom, well, she's just Mom and wants the gossip*

CALI: *And for what it's worth, I loved every word you said about secret me ... and I feel exactly the same way.*

CALI: *Did you want to sneak over later?*

KANE: *I'd love that ... will text when I'm on my way*

"What's got you grinning, sis?" Cari asks, leaning over the table to try and see my phone.

"Just Fern," I nonchalantly reply and thankfully she buys it.

"Silverbell ain't ready for you two gals to be living together. Mom, watch the rumor mill go into overdrive now. It'll be all 'Fern and Cali did this' and 'Fern and Cali did that' blah, blah, blah."

I don't need Fern for that. Shaking my head at my sister, I find myself grinning at her, ohh to be young and innocent again. "Sis," I offer, throwing my arm around her when we meet up, "I think you're just jealous that you've never made the rumor mill."

"I'll have you know—"

"Nope," Mom interrupts, "we do not need to rehash that weekend ever again."

My eyes widen. "What did you do? And why do I not know about said shenanigans?"

"I'll tell you later," Cari says, bumping my shoulder. Meanwhile, Mom shakes her head, muttering to herself about 'needing strength and praying to the Lord and never being able to walk into St. Michael's without turning red' ever again.

"St. Michael's?" I mouth to Cari and she just shrugs. Then my eyes widen when I remember what happened. "That was you?" I shout. Cari nods, a huge grin on her face. "Who knew my lil' sister was such a badass?"

"Well, one of us has to be. You're squarer than a square." *If only you knew, little sister, if only you knew what I was hiding.*

Mom and Dad drop me off and I head inside. I find a note from Fern sitting on the kitchen counter saying she's spending the night at Tucker's. This makes me smile more than it should because it means when Kane comes over later, we will have the place to ourselves.

Pouring myself a glass of red wine, I head into the bathroom, it's pamper time. Bringing up Spotify, I click play and "Time After Time" starts playing, as much as I love Cyndi's original version, this version by Quietdrive is pretty awesome.

After shaving my legs and trimming the lady garden, I run a bath. While the tub is filling, I quickly do a nudie dash to the kitchen and top up my glass. When I get back, I pour in some jasmine-scented bath crystals and sink into the tub. Nothing beats a hot bath with a glass of wine after shaving.

Leaning back, I close my eyes and sip on my wine. Excitement builds for when Kane comes over later and my clit begins to throb. Needing to ease the itch, I place my glass behind my head on the ledge and slide my hand down my body as I lift one leg out of the tub, resting it on the edge. My nipples instantly harden as I brush past. Slipping my finger between my folds, I twitch when I brush over my clit. Pushing my finger inside, I moan when I hook it around, rubbing that sensitive bundle of nerves. Sliding my finger out, I circle my clit before slipping it back inside. Squeezing my breast with my other hand, I tug on my nipple and out of nowhere, my orgasm thunders through me. Moaning and splashing about, I thrust my finger in and out as I ride my climax out.

Once I'm back on Plant Earth from Planet Orgasm, I reach behind me, grab my glass, and take a sip. With a contented sigh, I sink back into the water, I finish my wine and relax.

When the water cools, I climb out, slather my body in lotion, and slip on the infamous pink satin dressing gown. Pouring myself another wine, I head back to my room to read while I wait for Kane to arrive. I'm on my second glass of wine when my phone pings.

KANE: *Be there in 5*

CALI: *Door's unlocked, come on up. Fern is out **wink wink***

KANE: *Be there in 3*

A snort-laugh erupts at that message. Getting up, I check to make sure I look okay and I head into the kitchen to wait. Finishing my wine, I top it up and decide to pour a glass for Kane. Turning around, I reach into the upper cabinets where Fern keeps the wine glasses, lifting onto my tippy-toes, I grab the glass.

"Well, that's a beautiful sight," Kane says from behind me, scaring the absolute shit out of me. I didn't hear him arrive and I squeal in fright. The wine glass goes flying, landing on the tiles, and shattering on the floor. I just now realize that when I was reaching up, my gown rose, exposing my naked ass and my cheeks heat in embarrassment … and arousal.

Kane walks over to me and scoops me into his arms, placing me on the countertop.

"What did you do that for?" I ask.

"Can't have you cutting your foot. Where's the dustpan?"

"Cupboard by the pantry."

He kisses the tip of my nose, turns, and grabs the dustpan. A few minutes later, he's cleaned up the broken glass and is standing between my legs staring into my eyes. "Hi," I murmur.

"Hi yourself," he replies. "That was quite the view to walk into."

"I'm sorry, I was hoping to have a glass of wine waiting for you but instead—"

"I got to see your sexy naked ass."

"Yeah, that."

"Feel free to be like that anytime I arrive. You know how much I love you in this pink number."

"Is pink your favorite color, Kane?"

"Calliope in pink is my favorite color."

"Duly noted. Now, would you like a glass of wine?"

"I'd love one, but first, I need to do this." Before I can ask what he wants to do, he grips my cheeks in his palms and presses his lips to mine. Covering his hands with mine, I close my eyes and push my tongue into his mouth. He allows me access and as they duel it out, a guttural moan builds in the back of my throat. Kissing Kane is fast becoming a favorite hobby of mine. He breaks the kiss and stares at me. His gaze full of hunger and heat. "I swear, each kiss gets better than the last."

"Mmmhmpf," I reply with a nod.

He kisses my forehead and then steps back and over to the open wine glass cupboard. He pulls one down—without smashing it—and pours himself a glass. Ever the gentleman, he tops mine up before handing it to me.

"A toast," he offers, raising his glass, "to us."

"To us," I repeat and smile. With my eyes locked on his, I watch him take a sip and swallow. Who knew watching someone drink wine could be so sexy?

He places his wine down behind me and offers me his hand. Placing mine in his, he pulls me off the counter and my gown falls open slightly. "Are you naked under there, Sunshine?" he asks, slipping his finger under the satin and pulling it to the side, baring my breast. "You are naked under there. Were you waiting for me, Sunshine?"

"No," I reply shaking my head. "I was waiting for my other boyfriend to arrive."

"Well, lucky for me, I got here first." He takes my wine from me and places it on the counter next to his. He pulls the tie on my robe and it falls open, exposing me to him. "Fuck, Calliope, I swear each time I see you like this, I'm dreaming."

"If this was a dream, would you feel this?" Grabbing his hand, I press it to my breast. "Or this?" I slide his hand down my abdomen to cup my pussy.

"If this is a dream," he whispers, "best fucking dream

ever."

"Well, baby, it's about to get even better."

Slipping the gown off my shoulders, it flutters to the floor leaving me naked before him. He's still holding his hand between my legs, I was hoping for a little more action, but the night is still young so I take things into my own hands. Dropping to my knees, I make quick work of his pants and free his cock. His glorious rock-hard cock. The tip glistens, begging for me to lick, so I do. Leaning forward, I open my mouth and suck the tip before sliding his shaft deeper into my mouth. He hisses from above as I begin to bob my head back and forth, taking him deeper and deeper each time. He threads his fingers into my hair and begins to guide me. Leisurely, he pumps himself in and out of my mouth before pulling me off him.

"As much as that is amazing, I think you need some attention too, Sunshine."

Shaking my head, I lick my bottom lip, his gaze traces the movement. "I'm good, I've already pre-gamed, therefore, this is all about you."

"You pre-gamed, eh?"

"Yep, now, let me finish your warm-up and then you can take me to bed for the grand finale."

"As you wish." He thrusts his cock back into my mouth and I finish what I started.

We grab the bottle, our wines, his pants, my robe, and head into my room. We snuggle on my bed together and until the wee hours of the morning we drink wine and chat about anything and everything. We don't make it to the grand finale, but I still had an amazing night … and morning. I woke with Kane between my legs and with a slight delay, we finally made it to the finale before Kane had to sneak out and head back to his place.

Later that afternoon, I'm in the kitchen making lunch when there's a knock at the door. Fern still hasn't come home from her sleepover but she has a key, so I don't think it's her. When I answer, I see a delivery girl with a large, shiny black gift bag held between her fingers. "Are you Calliope Fischer?"

"That's me."

"This is for you." She hands me the bag, smiles, and walks away.

"Thank you," I shout after her. She waves over her shoulder and climbs into a nondescript van and drives away.

Walking upstairs, I place the bag on the counter and look inside. All I see is pink tissue paper and a notecard. Picking up the card, I turn it over and read.

My little Sunshine,
Every girl deserves gorgeous underwear at work.
Five sets. Five days.
I hear your boss likes pink.
Yours,
Kane

A grin appears on my face and I quickly tear at the tissue paper, and as per the card, there are five stunning Monty's lingerie sets in different shades of pink. Grabbing my phone, I shoot off a thank-you text to Kane. I've just placed the garments away when my phone pings.

KANE: *I was hoping you'd model them for me.*

CALI: *Five sets. Five fashion shows.*

KANE: *You're going to make me wait???*

KANE: ***sad face emoji***

CALI: *You'll be fine ... but feel free to come over for a replay of last night*

KANE: *Currently I'm golfing with your dad*

I can't help myself, so I quickly rip off my shirt and bra and slip on my satin robe. Standing in front of the mirror, I lower it down and expose my nipple and quickly snap a photo and send it to him.

CALI: ***sexy image***

KANE: *Sunshine, you don't play fair*

CALI: *I never said I did*

I start to feel bad about what I just sent so I quickly send another text.

CALI: *But seriously, thank you ... you really didn't have to*

KANE: *You're welcome. We can call it a signing bonus*

CALI: *I hope the other staff don't get signing bonuses like this???*

KANE: *Nope, just the special ones*

CALI: *You really do know how to make a girl feel special. I cannot wait to work with ... and under ... you*

KANE: *I'm looking forward to working with ... and over you too*

KANE: *Ohh, and pink lingerie is part of your uniform, even when we aren't at work*

CALI: *So bossy ... but luckily for you, I love pink lingerie* *so I think I can abide by that rule ... plus my boyfriend loves me in pink*

After texting with Kane, I log on to the Monty's website and order myself a few more pink sets, you know, for the work uniform and all that.

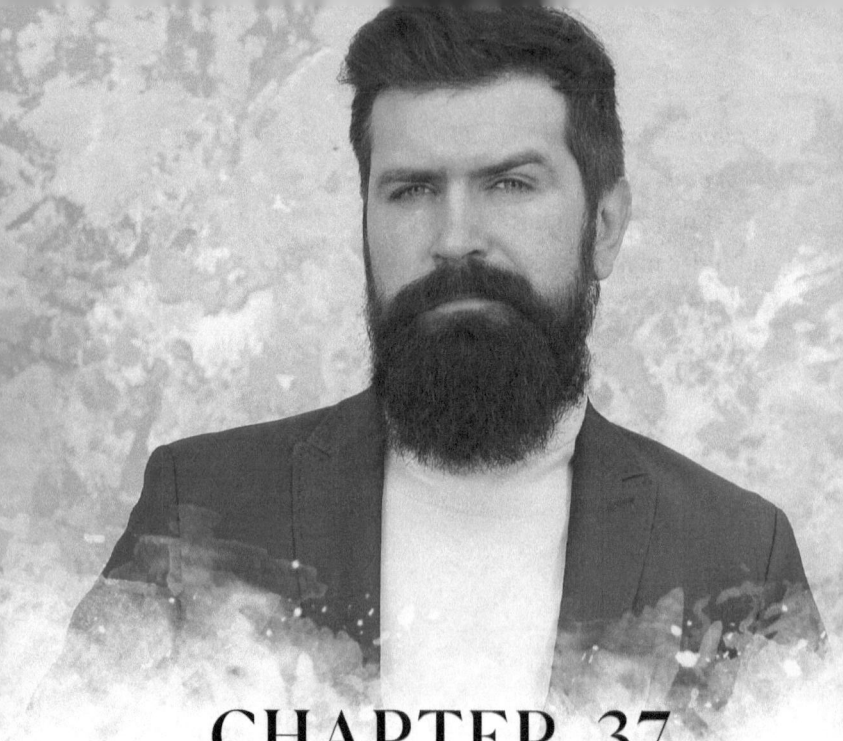

CHAPTER 37

Kane

... six weeks later

"That was close," Calliope whisper-giggles from her spot under my desk. Calliope has been working here for six weeks now and I can unequivocally say, she is the best hire ever. She has been a great asset to The Clifton, and to me. Her ideas are bold and she shows a confidence that I haven't seen in an employee in a very long time.

We maintain a professionalism—well, sort of—but

with it being a Sunday afternoon, we thought we'd be okay. However, my loving children Finley and Michael stopped by to demand I come home for dinner since I've been working so hard lately.

Yes, I have been working hard, but I have also been partaking in sneaky office rendezvous with a certain sexy employee of mine. Under the desk blow jobs have become a trend this past week, and it's a trend I hope continues. Whether it's me in her office or her here—like now—one of us always gets a happy ending.

Agreeing to be home for dinner, the kids leave me to 'get back to it' and with the coast now clear, Calliope resumes what she was doing before we were interrupted. "Sunshine," I growl, because knowing my daughter, she will rush back in with something super important she forgot to tell me, but I soon lose my train of thought when she wraps her lips back around my dick.

Once I've come down her throat—without any further interruptions—she kisses me on the lips quickly and exits my office. Leaning back in my chair, I have a contented smile on my face and I feel fan-fucking-tabulous ... and it's all to do with the sexy as hell minx who just blew— literally—into my office.

Now that Calliope and I are a couple, albeit a secret couple, I'm thinking about asking Alex to start the divorce proceedings again. It's not like I'm planning on marrying the girl anytime soon, but should it come to that, I don't want me still being legally married to Bitchifer to come between us. No more Mr. Nice Guy, this divorce will happen, no matter what.

CHAPTER 38

Cali

*... **three weeks later***

"I'm pre-annoyed." I huff, dropping into my chair across from Fern who conveniently, for me, was in my office waiting after my meeting with the other department heads. The bitch in housekeeping was saying what we all think about Kane and I just had to sit there, playing dumb. Pretending I haven't licked him from head to toe or had him thrusting into me from behind as I'm bent over my desk. Right now, I'm so glad to be living and working with her so I can vent in person. Venting just isn't the same via FaceTime.

"You're what?" she questions, confusion all over her face.

"I'm pre-annoyed because I know as soon as *he* arrives, I have to pretend like we haven't seen each other naked, and I have to act like I don't want him with every fiber of my being while all those other skinny, ho, slutbag bitches fantasize about my man."

Dropping my head to my desk, I groan when images of his mouth pressed against mine in a kiss that left me breathless and wanting to jump his bones—again—flashes before my eyes. But I can't jump his bones right now because it's a workday and we are trying to keep a sexual distance at the hotel, but have you seen the man? He's hot as hell and I'm a red-blooded woman who can't get enough of her secret, silver fox boyfriend.

"And by he, I'm guessing you mean the hottest guy in town, who you're secretly banging, but you're both stubborn and pigheaded and keeping what is glaringly undeniable between the two of you a secret?" I silently give her 'the look'. "Puh-lease," she sasses, "you know I'm right."

"Whatever." I make a 'w' with my fingers.

"May I just point out, you didn't deny the attraction or jumping bones part of that comment."

"Don't make me pre-annoyed at you too."

"You love me … now, wanna talk about it?"

"No … it will just piss me off again."

"And what exactly are you pissed off about?"

Staring over at her, I run through everything that's

pissing me off right now. I don't even know where to begin but as I think about it, I think I'm mostly pissed at the secrets. I'm keeping how I really feel about him hush-hush and we all know, secrets always come out but there are so many variables relating to our secret. It's not just me I have to worry about—there's my dad. His kids. Our work colleagues. My dad. Him finding out scares me the most. I don't want to disappoint him but most of all, I don't want to ruin a twenty-plus-year friendship, but I've never felt this way about anyone before. I know it's selfish but I want the happily ever after, ugh. I'm such a bad person.

My day after my morning freakout continued to spiral and not even dinner with Kane, hidden away in his office, fixed it. If anything, that dinner made everything worse because Dad, well, he caught us in the act.

CHAPTER 39

Cali

"What the fuck is going on here?" Dad bellows from the entrance to Kane's office.

Kane and I both freeze.

My eyes widen.

My heart stops beating in my chest.

Kane's hands grip my ass under my dress tighter.

My chest rapidly rises and falls as my breathing intensifies with fear.

We've just been busted … by my dad, no less.

Looking over my shoulder, I swallow deeply when I

see my dad standing in the doorway, glaring at the two of us. I was secretly hoping it was someone else who just so happens to sound like Dad when he growls. The first thing I notice, his forehead vein is beginning to form, that vein only appears when he's angry—really, really angry—and right now, he's livid.

There's no hiding what we were doing. We were about to have dessert—each other—after our romantic dinner for two. I'm currently straddling Kane on the sofa in his office and our lips were pressed together, kinda hard to deny what was happening.

"Daddy," I plead just as Kane, says, "Garrick," his voice strained.

"Shut the fuck up, asshole," Dad growls at Kane, his eyes locked on his best friend. I've never seen him look at his best friend with such contempt before. His gaze snaps to mine. "Calliope," he snarls my name, "get the fuck off him."

Ohh shit, he just full-named me, I know I'm in trouble now.

"Don't speak to her like that." Kane defends me as I climb off his lap, rearranging my dress to recover my tits before I turn around and walk over to my fuming father.

"Daddy, please," I beg, reaching for him but he steps back and away from my touch. He's staring daggers at Kane over my shoulder right now and he's looking right through me, and that hurts. His face is red with anger and his forehead vein is now pulsating. He's beyond pissed and looks like he's ready to Hulk out.

Stepping in front of Daddy, I try to get him to look at

me but his glare is still focused on Kane. "Daddy," I shout, "look at me … please!" He lowers his gaze to mine and for the first time in my life, he's not looking at me with adoration. I don't recognize the look on his face right now.

"Calliope." There's my full name again. "Please tell me why I just found you dry-humping your boss?"

"Ummm," I draw the word out but I know I can't lie to him, not with the evidence before him, so I tell him the truth. "I'm the woman Kane has been seeing."

"What the fuck?" he growls, shaking his head in anger. His face getting redder and redder with each shake and his forehead vein is throbbing like never before.

"Daddy," I plead, "let—"

"Am I being punked right now? Is Ashton Kutcher about to jump out?"

"No, Daddy, this isn't a TV show. This is real life." Taking a deep breath, I look over to Kane and smile. He returns my smile and stands up. As he walks over to us, I look back at my father. "Daddy, Kane is the Prince Charming who you told me I'd meet one day and sweep me off my feet."

"But … how? What? What the fuck?"

"Daddy," I sweetly say.

"Do not Daddy me, Calliope Victoria," he roars. He just full AND middle named me. He only uses that when I'm in trouble, big, big trouble and right now, I'm in the deepest of deep shit a daughter can find herself in. I don't think I've ever seen him this mad at me before.

This isn't how I wanted him to find out. This is the complete opposite of how we wanted him to find out. Kane and I both knew when he did, there'd be fireworks. I just didn't expect to be caught in the act per se, and the fireworks be more of a bomb exploding.

"Faaaaaark" he growls, shaking his head. "How the fuck did this happen?" Dad yells, and I'm pretty sure the whole of Silverbell heard him just now. "Tell me!"

"That's enough, Garrick," Kane snaps, pulling me into his side and resting his hand on my waist. He gives me a gentle squeeze and kisses the side of my head in that 'I've got your back' reassuring way.

Dad tracks the movement and clenches his jaw. He's mute and the silence is unnerving, considering a few moments ago he was screaming at us.

"Garrick—" Before Kane says anything further, Dad rears his hand back and slams his clenched fist into Kane's nose. Blood sprays everywhere. Dad punches him again and this time, Kane stumbles backward and falls to the floor, dropping with a thud to his ass.

Covering my mouth with my hands, I stand here, watching Dad looming over his best friend. His shoulders are rising rapidly and he's breathing like a raging bull ready to charge. I know I need to go over to Kane, to help him, but I'm frozen with fear.

"She's my daughter, you asshole," he angrily yells. Anger is radiating off him. His fists are clenched by his side, and I can hear him grinding his teeth. He takes a step forward again as if he's going to jump on top of Kane and launch into a full-on attack, but Kane raises his hand in a stop motion. Surprising me, and Kane, Dad stops moving.

"I know she's your daughter, Garrick, but Calliope and

I …"

"You and her what?" he sneers, those four words are laced with venom.

"We … we're, Calliope and I are seeing each other. As she said, she's the one I mentioned a few months ago."

"I'm sorry, I swear I just heard you say that you've been seeing my daughter for a few fucking months now."

Kane is silent and I'm still frozen. Dad takes another step toward him and finally my body moves. Pushing past Daddy, I put myself between the two men. I eye Dad before turning around to help Kane up. Reaching out, I offer him my hand, he places his in mine and I pull him up. Kane nods his thanks and from behind me, Dad growls like a wolf about to attack.

Spinning back around, I use my body as a buffer between Kane and Dad. A surge of adrenaline courses through me because I find the strength to stand up to Dad. "That's correct, Dad." I reach behind me and take Kane's hand. I lace our fingers together and step beside him. Dad watches us intently; he clenches his jaw and continues to breathe deeply through his nose. "Daddy, Kane and I have been seeing each other for a few months now."

"You fucking bastard, she's my little girl," he bellows, shoving Kane and accidentally bumping me in the process. Kane growls when he sees me stumble. Dad takes another menacing step forward, but I step between the two of them and raise my hands. Pressing my palm into each of their chests, pushing, I stop them both from attacking one another. Both of their hearts are racing erratically under my palms. Dad's chest is heaving under my touch. *Shit, I hope he doesn't have a heart attack from this.*

"Garrick," Kane voices, but Dad ignores him. He just shakes his head and stares daggers at us, his gaze flicking back and forth between the two of us. Another growl from deep in his throat breaks the silence. I'm worried he's going to hit Kane again but instead, he scoffs and throws his hands up in the air. "I … I can't do this."

Before Kane or I can say anything, Dad turns around and storms out of Kane's office, slamming the door behind him. The door I wish we had closed earlier.

Blinking rapidly, I stare at the doorway Dad just stormed through. My eyes well with tears and then I collapse to my knees and cover my face. "He … he hates us," I cry into my hands.

"Sunshine," Kane coos as he drops down next to me. He pulls me into his lap and holds me tightly. He whispers sweet nothings but it does nothing to abate the hollowness I feel.

"Did I just ruin your friendship?" I tearfully ask him.

"You didn't ruin anything, Sunshine. He just needs time."

"But—"

"Nope." He shakes his head and presses his finger to my lips. "No buts. I know him, he needs time to process."

"What if he never processes?"

"He will," Kane tells me but from the look on his face, I don't know if he believes it himself. Cementing my fear that us being together has ruined their friendship.

It's been four days and Dad hasn't spoken one word

to me or Kane. He won't answer my calls. My texts are left unread and when I stopped by the house, just now after work, he made some lame excuse and left without kissing or hugging me, leaving Mom confused.

Obviously, he hasn't told her yet, but Mom being Mom takes one look at me and she immediately knows something's up. "Let me get some wine and then you and I can chat."

Nodding, I follow her into the kitchen. "How did you know?" I sadly ask, leaning against the countertop while she pours our wine. Mom hands me a glass and I chug half of it back before Mom's even taken a sip. She refills my glass and escorts me outside. It's a beautiful evening and the sunset is gorgeous. It's oddly calming seeing the world so beautiful and peaceful when my world is anything but beautiful and peaceful right now.

Mom tucks her legs underneath her and takes a sip. "So, who is he?"

"Who's who?" I nonchalantly ask, staring into my wine glass.

"The boy who's swept you off your feet and has your father all grizzly-like."

A laugh escapes me at Mom's description of Dad, but then the guilt slams into me. "Ohh, Mom, I was so happy and now, I'm all confused."

"Before we get into things, who is the young man who has stolen my baby girl's heart?"

I choke on the sip of wine I'd just taken when Mom refers to Kane as a young man. After composing myself, I look to Mom and mumble, "It's Kane."

"Kane who, honey? Is he new in town?"

Shaking my head, I swallow deeply. "It's Kane Heatherington, Mom."

"Ohh," she replies, before bringing her glass to her lips and chugging the whole thing back. She quietly stands up and heads back inside, returning a few moments later with the open bottle, and another. She refills her glass and then mine. She sits back down next to me, reaches over to take my hand, and squeezes it in that mom kind of way. "Okay, tell me everything, Cali."

Taking another big sip, I breathe in deeply and I tell her everything and I mean everything, starting from my date with Seth and bumping into Kane. Us becoming friends. Me becoming a stripper and how Kane found me when he was prematurely celebrating his divorce.

When I'm finished, Mom places her wine down on the table before us. She takes mine and pops it down next to hers and then she pulls me into a hug. The mom hug of all mom hugs and it's just what I need right now.

"Ohh, honey, I have so many questions but the most important one is, are you happy with Kane?"

Nodding, I grin at her. "Happier than I've ever been before, Mom. He's become my everything."

"You deserve a love like that and Kane is a lucky man."

"But what about Dad?"

"You know he's a stubborn mule when it comes to you girls. Give him time, he'll come around. It's not every day you find out your daughter is in love with your best friend."

"Mom, I'm not in love with him." She eyes me but I'm not in love, am I? It's too soon for the 'L' word. It's just the honeymoon, all-consuming phase of a relationship. Love will come but it's not here yet … I don't think. "Surely, he knew about my crush?"

"Cal, honey, he's a man. It took him a long time to get the hint that I liked him, he's not the quickest when it comes to love."

This causes me to laugh. "But what do I do now?"

"Give him time. Now that I know, I can work on him, but I think you and Kane need to be honest with him. Tell him everything."

"Even about the stripping?"

"Everything, honey, no more secrets."

Nodding, I play that phrase 'no more secrets' over and over in my head and realize she's right. "Fine, I'll tell him everything but, Mom, we were only keeping it a secret because we didn't want this to happen."

"You know what they say about secrets."

"I sure do, I'm currently living the consequences of keeping secrets." Looking over at her, I reach out and take her hand. "Thanks, Mom."

"You don't need to thank me, I'm your mom. This is what I'm here for, but I do have one question …"

"Shoot."

"What's it like kissing Kane? The ladies and I at the country club have always thought he was delectable."

"Mom," I chastise. "I'm not telling you that but I will say, he leaves me breathless."

"Just like your father does to me."

"Moooom," I screech, "a daughter doesn't need to know that."

"Doesn't need to know what?" Cari asks, dropping between us.

"How Dad kisses," I tell my sister.

"Eeeeew," she growls and fake gags. "I think I'd rather go back to my homework."

Mom and I both laugh as Cari leans forward and grabs my glass of wine, taking a sip. Mom grabs another glass and the three of us finish the bottle of wine and then I head home. Dad didn't return while I was there but the next day, he summons me to Kane's office 'to talk'.

CHAPTER 40
Cali

Walking toward Kane's office, my heart begins to race. This is it, it's time to face the music but when I reach Kane's office, it seems Dad and Kane started without me because when I walk in, Kane and him are already discussing us. "... I'm sorry you found out how you did, Garrick, but Calliope and I are seeing each other and she—"

"She's my baby girl," he interrupts, "how could you?" He stands up and when he spins around, I come face-to-face with my dad.

"Hi, Daddy."

"Calliope," he says by way of greeting and I note that it's still my full name. Not Cali or Princess, it's still Calliope.

"Kane was just telling me the story of you two."

Nodding, I walk into Kane's office and over to him. He kisses my forehead and I close my eyes. Breathing him in and hoping I have the strength for this conversation.

"How could you let this happen?" Dad asks again.

I'm not sure who he directs the question to, I open my mouth to reply but Kane beats me. "How could I not?" Kane voices. "Calliope is the most amazing, strong, fun, spontaneous person I have ever met." He looks to me and with that glance, I feel every word he just spoke and then he adds, "and I love her."

"What?" Daddy and I both screech at the same time. Dad's tone laced with anger, mine with shock.

Kane spins me to face him, grips my cheeks, and says it again, "I love you, Calliope Fischer."

"Unfucking believable," Dad vents, while I stammer in utter disbelief. "You … you love me?"

"Yep." Kane nods. "I love you, Sunshine."

I rapidly blink and process his words. He stares into my eyes and all the love and feelings I have for him bubble to the surface. Ever since Mom mentioned love last night, I've been thinking nonstop about if I do love him and I realize in this moment that I do. I do love him. A smile graces my face because he feels what I feel, this is no longer some crush. It's real love. Reaching up, I cover his hands on my face and murmur, "I … I love you too, Kane."

Leaning forward, I press my lips to his and kiss him,

cementing our voiced out loud love for one another. Sliding my hands around his shoulders, I deepen the kiss, slipping my tongue into his mouth. Completely forgetting my dad is here but I soon remember when Dad shouts, "Time out. Time-fucking-out."

Kane and I pull apart, he winks at me and when I turn my head to look over at Dad, I see him mimicking the timeout motion with his hands. This causes my smile to widen and I have to hold back a laugh. I don't know why I find that funny but now isn't the time to be laughing, especially with Dad still glaring intently at both Kane and me. "Let's just back the fuck up. Back this fucking truck up."

Pursing my lips, I hesitantly turn around to face Dad. "Yes, Daddy?" I innocently say, I may as well try and milk my luck with him. I've never seen him this angry before, not even when he caught Raven and I kissing, but Raven isn't his best friend and I was only a kid. This is a little more serious than that. "Let me get this straight, you two have been sneaking around and are dating ... and apparently now are in love?"

We both nod.

"My daughter and my best friend."

We both nod again.

"My best friend and my daughter are together."

We nod again, neither one of us game to speak. He nods his head. Up and down, processing everything. With each nod, his anger seems to be dissipating and I'm ever so thankful for that. I look over to Kane. "I think we, well, I need to tell him everything."

"There's more?" Dad runs his hands through his hair

and laces his fingers over his head. Shaking his head side to side, his eyes widen. "Please don't tell me you're pregnant!"

"No, no babies, but I think you better take a seat." I nod to the armchair next to him. Dad looks to the chair and then back to me. "Please?" I ask again, and thankfully, Daddy drops into it.

"I'll get you a drink," Kane offers.

"Make it a double."

Kane steps away from me and instantly I feel the loss of his body. He walks over to the wet bar and pours a drink for Dad. He hands it to him and Dad knocks it back before shoving the glass to him again. "Another," he demands. Kane takes the empty tumbler and refills it. Handing it back to Dad before he takes a seat.

I stand here awkwardly, suddenly not sure what to do. Do I sit? Do I stand? Do I leave the two of them alone and let Kane tell him everything? What the fuck do I do? Kane senses my unease and taps the sofa next to him. Okay, I'm sitting.

Walking over, I sit down next to him. He takes my hand in his and brings it to his lips, that one little kiss calms me, that is until Dad opens his mouth and growls, "Okay, start talking, Calliope."

We're still on the Calliope bandwagon BUT at least he's talking to me again, and at least Daddy's vein hasn't appeared today. I take a deep breath as nerves and angst filter through my veins as I begin to tell him everything. "When I was a little girl ..." and for the next few minutes I fill Dad in on my childhood crush and all the secrets I've been keeping from the moment I left Silverbell for New

York.

"Let me get this straight, you've had a crush on Kane since you were little. You lied about how great New York was. Became friends with my best friend behind everyone's back. You also became a stripper and then you ..." he points to Kane, "... got a lap dance from my daughter, and then you both fell in love?"

"That's the gist of it yes." I nod and study Dad. I can't read him now but the fact his forehead vein is still MIA, I think it's all going to be okay.

"Why did you do it?"

"Dad," I scoff and roll my eyes, "you cannot help who you fall in love with. If I remember correctly, you told me that when I fall in love, it will be the most all-consuming feeling in the world and you will stop at nothing to have that feeling."

"No, not that, the stripping? Why didn't you say anything? Mom and I would have helped you." Then he looks to Kane. "And you," he grumbles, "how could you let her strip?"

Kane holds his hands up defensively. "Hey, I didn't find that part out 'til a few months ago. If I had known when we first ran into one another, I would have stepped in."

"And by stepping in, you mean falling in love with my princess?"

"That came after. When I saw her in that room, I was shocked, but I saw her in a different light that night and—"

"Yeah, a half-naked light," Dad jokes.

"Daaaad," I draw out the word but the fact he just cracked a joke gives me hope that all will be okay. "Are ...

are we okay?"

"It's a lot to take in, Princess." *Yes*, I internally cheer, we're back to Princess. "It's not every day you find out your daughter was a stripper or that she and your best friend are in love." He looks to Kane. "You do really love her, don't you? You're not just fucking about? It's not some mid-life crisis bullshit?"

"Very much so, Garrick." He lifts my hand and kisses my knuckles, reaffirming the love he has for me. "I love her to the moon and back."

Dad nods but doesn't say anything further. "Your mom's going to kick my ass for throwing a punch, I assured her my brawling days were over."

"I think she'll give you a pass this time," Kane says and I nod in agreement.

"Ummm, she already knows, Dad."

"What?" he hisses.

"I told her last night and she seemed to be okay with it when I told her you hit Kane, but for the record, please don't hit him again."

"I'll only hit him again if he hurts you." He looks to Kane. "This is where I give you the 'you hurt her, I kill you talk' and I don't give a flying fuck that you're my best friend. If anything, I will hold you to a higher standard because I know what a true jackass you can be, after all, you are my best friend." We all laugh at that joke. "But in all honesty, I couldn't ask for a better man for my Princess." Then he chuckles. "Now I know why your mother reminded me last night that Grandpa never liked me in the beginning—"

"Because you're a jackass," Kane teases.

"Says the jackass," Dad teases back. "But getting back to my point, as a parent, you only want the best for your child, and it's hard to see them grow up and fall in love. And I know I cannot dictate who she loves, I can only guide her. Looks like I just so happened to guide her into the arms of my best friend."

"That you did." I nod, agreeing with Dad.

"It's not as hard to say this as I thought it would be, but I'm happy that you're both happy. Will it take time to get used to the PDA, yes, but if you can keep that to a minimum, I think everything will be okay."

"Thanks, Dad, Kane and I appreciate that. We didn't mean for this to happen or for you to find out how you did, but your best friend is kind of awesome."

"And your daughter is amazing," Kane adds, kissing my knuckles again.

"That she is," Dad says with a huge grin on his face. He lifts his glass and finishes off his drink. He slams the empty tumbler down on the table and stands up. "Okay, so, I'm going to go. I'll let you two get back to work but if I can offer one piece of advice to you, Kane?"

"Sure, what is it?"

"For the love of God, please close the fucking door in the future. The image of you two dry-humping will forever be etched into my mind. No one, especially your mother needs to see that."

"Please don't ever mention dry-humping and Calliope in the same sentence again," Kane tells him.

"And, Dad, we promise to be more locky, locky with the doors."

"Good, good." He nods in agreement.

Dad turns to leave but I quickly jump up and slide my arms around his waist, hugging him from the back like I sometimes do. I may be twenty-three but I'm still a daddy's girl at heart. "I'm sorry, Daddy," I whisper into his back. He stiffens for a moment and it hurts but after a few beats, he relaxes. He pulls my hands away and spins to face me. "We didn't mean to hurt you," I whisper, my eyes welling with tears again.

"I'm not hurt, Princess, just shocked." He swipes under my eye and wipes away a stray tear and pulls me in for a hug. He holds me tight and when he squeezes me in that 'dad' way, I know we'll be okay. "This was the last thing I expected to discover when I came here the other day."

"We really are sorry, Garrick," Kane says from behind me. "We didn't purposely deceive you, or anyone for that matter. We just wanted to see what it was between us before imploding everyone's world. I still can't believe it myself to be honest, but it is what it is. As I said before, Garrick, your daughter is fucking amazing, it was hard not to fall for her."

"Of course she's amazing, she's my daughter." He pauses. "And I'm sorry too."

Pulling back, I stare up at him. "Why are you sorry?"

"For punching your … boyfriend." He pauses. "Wow, that was easier to say than I thought it would be." He looks to Kane. "I really am sorry for punching you, but you hurt my princess and I'll do more than just punch you in the nose."

"Duly noted, but I'm not planning on hurting her, Garrick. She's one of a kind and I'm never letting her go."

"Love has turned you into a pussy," he teases. Then looks intently at us both. "I expect both of you for dinner on Friday night."

"Of course, Daddy, we'll be there."

"Good, because you can tell everyone together that you two are an item. No more secrets."

"Garrick, if you don't mind, I'd like to tell the kids before everyone gets together. Maybe we can do a cookout at my place instead of going out? Just in case there are fireworks."

"Will you do your slow-cooked brisket and get Finley to make her famous double chocolate fudge brownies?"

"Brisket yes, but I cannot ask my daughter to make you double chocolate fudge brownies with the news I have to share with them."

"Fine … but the brisket better be the best fucking one you've ever made."

With that, Dad departs, leaving Kane and me alone. "Well, that went better than expected," Kane says. "It was only a few days of silence."

"Aaaaand he only punched you twice," I offer, "but how have you been explaining the black eye?" I run my finger gently over the bruising.

"I've been telling the truth. Told them my girlfriend's dad punched me."

"Such a badass," I tease.

"But I'm your badass, now come here and kiss me better."

"With pleasure."

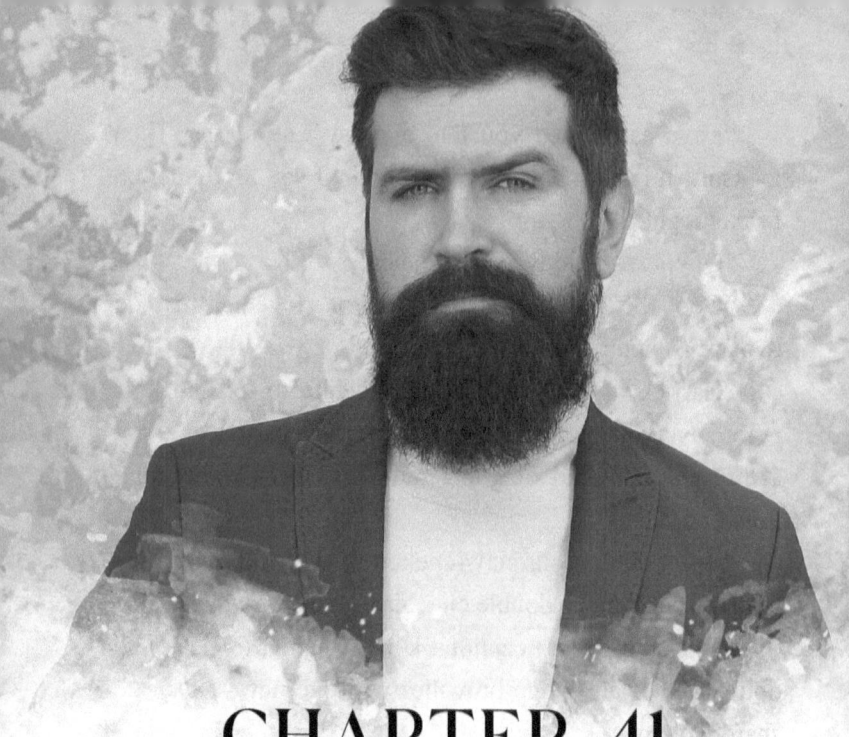

CHAPTER 41

Kane

Waking up in Calliope's arms is wonderful. It would have been fucking amazing with her lips around my dick but I can hear Fern puttering around, so it's probably for the best that I woke up naturally.

After leaving The Clifton last night, Cali and I came back here, grabbed a bottle of wine, and then had a nice relaxing bath together before I took her to bed. We made sweet, sweet love 'til the wee hours of the morning before drifting blissfully off to sleep in each other's arms. *Man, I sound like a chick.*

"Good morning," My Sunshine, mumbles sleepily from next to me.

"Good morning, Sunshine. Sleep well?"

"I always sleep well when you're with me. How about you?"

"I too sleep well when you're in the bed with me, but I was hoping to be woken up with your lips wrapped around my dick."

"How could I have done that when you were awake before me?"

"Semantics," I reply with a shrug. "You could always just suck it now and we can pretend I just woke up?"

"I think that can be arranged." Pulling the sheet back, she situates herself between my legs and grips my shaft. "You're already half hard."

"That's 'cause your naked body was pressed against mine."

"You do love me naked. I'm not sure what you like best, me naked? Or me in pink lingerie?"

"I love you both ways equally but less talking, more sucking."

"I'll bite it off," she playfully replies, raking her teeth over the tip, causing me to hiss. "Mmhmm," she murmurs over my cock. "I think you liked that, Mr. Heatherington."

"I like anything to do with my cock and you, so have at it, Sunshine … but maybe a little less teeth. I'm kind of fond of my dick."

"I'm kinda fond of it too." To prove her point, she sticks her tongue out, runs it up the side of my shaft, circling her tongue through my slit. Opening her mouth, she sucks the tip and then slides my dick into her mouth.

"Fuck, Calliope, your mouth is heaven." She smiles around my shaft and then moans, the vibrations ricochet through my cock and then I realize what she's doing. "Are you pleasuring yourself, Sunshine?"

"Mmmhmpf," she confirms, sucking harder on my dick.

She ramps up her efforts and I'm about to come when the door to her room flies open and quickly slams shut. Looking up, I see Fern standing against the closed door with her hand covering her eyes. "Ummm, fuck, shit, ummm, Cal, your mom and dad are here."

"Think you could have knocked?" Calliope says, my cock popping out of her mouth as she grabs the sheet to cover us once again. "You can uncover your eyes now."

"Sorry, I panicked but can I say, Cal, your ass is looking phenomenal."

Calliope snorts. "Umm thanks. Can you let them know we'll be out in a sec?"

"Umm, you just said we."

"Yeah, I did. Dad kinda caught Kane and I the other night."

"No fucking way," Fern hisses and jumps onto the bed and crosses her legs, getting comfy for a chat. "Guess that explains the shiner there, now, Cal. Tell. Me. Everything."

"Calliope will tell you everything later," I tell her. "You think that maybe you can leave so we can get dressed and greet our guests?"

"Ohh yeah, sure." She hops off the bed and walks to the door. With her hand on the knob, she looks over her shoulder. "For what it's worth, I'm glad you two aren't going to be hiding it anymore. I can tell you two are head over heels for one another. A love like that shouldn't be hidden but, Kane, you fuck my girl over and I don't give a flying fuck that you're my boss, I will fucking de-nut you."

Before I can reply, she steps into the hall leaving Calliope and me alone. Calliope turns to me. "We can finish that ..." She points to my somehow still hard cock, "... later. For now, we need to meet the 'rents."

"I've met your parents," I emphasize the word parents, "plenty of times before."

"Yes, but this is kind of the first official meet the 'rents as my boyfriend and not dad's BFF."

"Riiiight."

"And you don't want to do that with a boner, so how about you think about Dad naked and deflate that beautiful cock of yours, and later, I'll finish what I started."

"That sounds wonderful but, Calliope, please never mention my dick and your father naked in the same sentence ever again."

"Deal." She places a quick kiss on my lips. Jumping out of bed, she quickly dresses and heads out to greet her parents.

Falling back to the mattress, I stare up at the ceiling and laugh. The past week has been crazy but I wouldn't change a thing, well, maybe I'd change the getting punched part. My nose still hurts like a bitch but finally admitting how I really feel about Calliope was a weight lifted and at the same time, it made me whole again.

This may have started in secret but now that it's out, I'm going to shout it from the clifftop because being in love with someone like Calliope Fischer is the best feeling in the world.

CHAPTER 42

Cali

"So, do we like call you Mom now?" Finley asks me after Kane and I inform my sister and his kids that we're dating. We are all sitting in Kane's backyard, the brisket is brisketting away, the guys all have beer, and us girls are all drinking wine. This is the first get-together with Kane and I officially as a couple and I have to say, it's been smooth sailing. Everyone has taken the news of us well. I love being able to be openly affectionate with Kane and I have to say, I'm a fan of PDA when it's coming from Kane. A butt squeeze here, a peck on the cheek there. Here a kiss, there a kiss, everywhere a kiss kiss.

"No, Cali will be just fine. I'm still me … I'm just with your dad."

Looking to Konrad and Michael, they're both quiet. "Boys?" Kane asks them, obviously sensing what I'm sensing. "Are you both okay with this?"

Michael slaps Konrad on the back. "That'll be fifty bucks, brother, told ya he was dating a younger woman."

"That doesn't answer my question," Kane growls at them, clearly missing the smile on both their faces.

"Dad," Michael says, slapping him on the shoulder. "I'm fifty bucks richer and you're happy. Can't get any better than that."

Nodding, he looks to Konrad. "Fine by me," Konrad nonchalantly replies with a shrug. "I just want you to be happy, Dad. She seems to make you happy, so I'm happy, plus Cal is a cool chick."

"Thanks, Konrad. You're pretty cool too."

"What about me?" Michael cries.

"Meh," I tease with a shrug. "But seriously, I'm happy to know that you guys are accepting of us. I was worried your dad and I being an us would somehow ruin things. Make everything awkward."

"Takes more than a feisty chick to scare me off," Konrad says. "Just know," he adds, pointing his beer bottle at me, "I'm not calling you Mom when you two get hitched."

"Hold up," my dad shouts, "time out," once again making the timeout hand motion. "They just started dating, let's hold off on the wedding and babies talk."

"Hold up." Kane repeats Dad's sentiment and hand

motions. "Who said anything about babies?"

All heads turn toward me and they all have that 'is she knocked up' look in their eyes. "I'm not pregnant," I murmur and to reiterate that fact, I lift my wine and drink what's left. "Who needs a refill?" I ask, but I don't wait for anyone to answer. I stand up and head inside to refill my glass and process the conversation that just transpired.

With the refrigerator open, I stare into it. I hadn't thought about marriage or having kids with Kane in a while, but now it's all I can think about. Will he even want to have more kids? His are all grown up, does he want to do that all over again? Do I want kids? When I was little my dream wasn't to marry a prince and have babies, I was going to be a kick-ass marketing executive with a doting husband ... I guess kids were in the picture but do I still want that? Can I have that being with Kane? The wine bottle is right there but I don't grab it, I just stare at it and think about marriage, babies, and Kane.

Hands slide around my waist. "You must be looking for something well-hidden because you've been staring in there for a few minutes now. Everything okay, Sunshine?"

"I'm, yep ... ummm." I close the fridge door, pull out of his embrace, and walk away. "I need a moment." Before he can protest, I exit the kitchen, open the front door, walk across the porch, and sit on the top step.

Staring down at the path, I pull my knees up and rest my chin on them. Suddenly, there's a presence next to me and then an arm is draped over my shoulders. "What's up, Sunshine?"

"Nothing, I—"

"Bullshit, babe, you were gone faster than a toupee in a hurricane. Please talk to me." He pauses. "Was it the marriage? Or baby talk? Or both?"

Turning my head, I stare over at the man that I love more than anything in this world but words elude me right now. This isn't the time or place for this conversation, but it's out in the open now.

"Talk to me, Sunshine. What's going on in that beautiful mind of yours? What's got you hiding out here?"

"You were right," I whisper, "the marriage and baby talk scared me a little. We haven't discussed that. What if we want different things, I …"

"But what if we want the same things?"

"What do you want?"

"You." One word. Three letters and he utters it with the force of a 747 taking off. "What do you want?"

"You," I repeat, "any way I can have you but, Kane, what about marriage and babies?"

"What about them?"

"Do you want to get married again? Have more kids?"

"To be honest, I never thought about it before but I'm not opposed to either. As long as I have you, that's all that matters."

"You want more kids?"

"If you do. I'd love nothing more than to see your stomach swelling …" he slides his hand over my flat, nonpregnant stomach, "… with a child that we created together, but I'm also happy to have your stomach flat and encased in sexy pink satin and lace. I just want you, Calliope Fischer."

"Kane," I tearfully reply. "No one has ever loved me like you do. You make me feel like I'm your whole world."

"You are my whole world, Calliope, and I wholeheartedly agree, no one loves me like you do. You're the cookie to my dough."

I can't help but laugh. "There isn't an ounce of dough on you, Mr. Silver Fox."

"Fine, you're the macaroni to my cheese."

"Much better."

"Glad you finally approve but, Calliope, whatever happens … happens. I love you, just focus on that and if the rest is meant to be, it will be."

"Okay, and I love you too … corny comparisons and all."

"You haven't seen anything yet. I'm the milk to your shake. You're the flip to my flop. The bumble to my bee. The—"

Covering his mouth with my hand, I shake my head and grin. "I get it."

"Just one more," he mumbles against my palm. Nodding, I remove my hand from his mouth. He lifts his and reaches over to cup my cheek. "You are my sunshine, Calliope. My only sunshine. You make me happy. So fucking happy."

"I think I like your version of that song best."

"Me too, Sunshine. Now, let's get back out there before they think we ran off to Vegas to get hitched because you're pregnant with triplets."

Hand in hand we rejoin the barbecue, just as the brisket is ready. Kane cuts up the meat while Mom and I arrange the salads and rolls. Everyone has a plate and we are all sitting around the table, eating, chatting, and laughing. There's no more talk of marriage and babies. It's just two families together having a night under the stars.

"You know, Kane, as far as 'I'm sorry for banging your daughter' briskets go, this one is fucking good," Dad says, shoveling another mouthful into his mouth.

"Garrick," Mom berates Dad, smacking him in the stomach. "You did not just say that."

"What?" Dad scoffs, some of his prized brisket flying out of this mouth. "It's a good brisket."

"I'm referring to the part about our daughter. Yes, we're happy for them, but I never want to hear you talking about banging and them again."

"But—"

"No buts, Garrick. Now apologize."

"Sorry for saying your 'I'm sorry for banging your daughter' brisket is good."

"How about we all stop with the apologies and just enjoy the rest of the evening?" Kane says.

"Agreed," Mom and I say in unison.

Thankfully, after that, the rest of the evening goes smoothly and there's no more banging talk, well, that is until it's just Kane and me. We've just climbed into bed when he says, "Sooo, Sunshine, shall we bang?"

CHAPTER 43

Kane

... six months later

"**A**re you fucking kidding me?" I bellow down the phone.

"No, Kane, I'm not fucking kidding you. Like we predicted, Bitchifer refused to sign the papers, again, but don't fret, this time, to quote you, 'we aren't backing down'. This time we will take it before a judge and unless she pulls some miracle out of her ass, in as little as thirty days, you sir, could be divorced."

"I'll believe it when I hold that signed piece of paper in my hot little hands. Alex, you have permission to throw everything into this. I want to be rid of Danica Heard."

Hanging up from Alex, I walk upstairs and into my bedroom. I've already showered and I'm waiting on Calliope. Tonight, we are all heading to the country club for my forty-sixth birthday. I would have been happy to just stay at home, order Chinese, and chillax on the back patio, especially when I walk into the en suite bathroom and see my woman in the sexiest pink—of course—lingerie set. "Fuck me, Sunshine, you are a vision," I voice as I step behind her and rest my hands on her hips.

My gaze tracks down her body's reflection in the mirror. I want nothing more than to pull at the petite bows sitting on her hips with my teeth, remove her panties, and have my way with her before we get to dinner, but I know Calliope, she won't allow that to happen before we go out.

My gaze finally lands on her beautiful face and we silently stare at one another in the mirror. Lifting my hands, I cup her boobs and squeeze before gently tugging on her nipples through the lace of her bra. "Is this new?" I whisper, biting her earlobe.

"You know it is," she breathlessly pants, grinding her ass into my crotch. "You sent it to me with a card that read 'Happy Birthday to Me.'"

"Ohh, yes, yes I did … and I have to say, seeing you in this, is the best birthday present. I cannot wait to unwrap you later."

Spinning around, she drapes her arms over my shoulders. "Would you like a little peek now?"

"Do we have time?" I ask, my cock thickening in my pants at the thought of peeling Calliope out of this sexy set.

"It's your birthday, do you care if you're late?"

"Fuck no," I declare as I slip my finger under her bra strap.

"Uh-uh," she tuts, stepping back. "I'm running this unwrapping, now, go and sit on the bed or the armchair, birthday boy's choice, while I finish up."

"Fine," I relent, "but hurry up."

Walking into the bedroom, I unbutton my pants and remove my shirt. Dropping on to the edge of the bed, I flop back and stare at the ceiling, eagerly awaiting my present.

The beat to "Closer" by Nine Inch Nails begins to play and immediately I lift up to my elbows and I have to say, I like, no fucking love, what I see. Calliope has covered herself with THAT robe and she's leaning against the doorframe to the en suite, arching her back and pressing her tits out. Her hips sway side to side in sync with the music. Pushing off the frame, she spins around and shakes her ass at me. Leaning forward, the robe lifts, exposing her G-string-clad ass. She snaps back upright and spins to face me. Her hips, once again, rocking side to side. She takes a step toward me and I sit up straighter. I don't know where to look.

Her sex fueled face.

Her long, lean, sexy legs encased in the shoes I bought her for graduation.

Her panty and robe covered mound.

Or her hidden cleavage.

Calliope is a complete sex bomb.

As if she senses my turmoil, she undoes her robe and

slides it off her shoulders. It flutters to the carpet, leaving her in her heels and lingerie.

"I thought I was unwrapping you?"

She shrugs at me and runs her hands seductively over her body, brushing her breasts before sliding them back down her sides. She grips the little bows at her hips and pretends to tug. A groan slips free. As sexy as this is, I'm ready to combust. She takes a step closer and I reach out, pulling her into me. She squeals and I bury my face in the valley of her tits. "You smell like heaven," I growl into her—my—breasts, rubbing my face in them. Biting her nipple through the material, she moans and presses herself into me farther. I can't help myself, I lift her up and lower her to the mattress, covering her body with mine. I kiss her roughly on the lips before kissing my way down her body. Over her breasts—which for the record was hard to do— down her stomach before licking along her panty line.

With my teeth, I pull at one of the bows on her side before doing the same to the other one. Pulling away the material, I look between her thighs, she's already turned on. Her lips are glistening in the light and I need to taste her.

Lowering my head, I lick her from taint to clit, circling her little bundle of nerves with the tip of my tongue before sliding back down to her entrance. Spearing my tongue into her, she cries out at the intrusion. "Kane," she moans as I begin to thrust my tongue in and out of her. Just when she's on the brink, I pull back, my beard coated with her juices.

"That was the best appetizer, Sunshine, but I think it's time for my main course." Before she has a chance to move, I free my straining cock, pull her to the edge of the bed and with a flick of my hips, I push inside her.

"Kane," she pants as I piston my hips back and forth. My cock sliding in and out.

"More," she cries.

"Harder," she demands.

"Fuck me, Kane. Fuck me now," she shouts, lifting her leg, like I did the first night we did this. I rest it on my shoulder and continue to thrust in and out of her.

"You close, Sunshine?" I ask, not sure I can hold off much longer.

"So close," she whines.

Pressing my finger onto her clit, I circle it with the pad of my finger and it sets her off. Her muscles clench down on my shaft and she comes. Her body stiffens and she lets go. She screams as pleasure courses through her veins. Seeing her come undone sets me off and I follow, emptying myself inside her.

Lowering her leg, I stare down at her. Her hair is fanned out beneath her. Her cheeks are flushed pink. Her chest's rapidly rising as she catches her breath. "Happy birthday, baby," she pants. "I hope you liked unwrapping your present."

"I fucking loved it and I hope I get to unwrap it again later."

"That might be in the cards but first, you need to feed me so I have the energy for you to unwrap me again later."

"I like the sound of that." Pulling out of her, I offer her my hand and we walk back into the en suite. "Shower or sponge bath?"

"I can't be assed taking my shoes or bra off so sponge

it is."

Turning the sink faucet on, I grab a cloth from under the vanity and wet it. Dropping to my knees in front of her, I clean her up. When I'm done, I press a kiss to the top of her mound.

"Kane," she snaps, slapping my head. "Enough, we're going to be late otherwise."

"It's my birthday, I'll kiss your cunt if I want to."

"Keep using the 'c' word and it'll be closed to you forever."

"Fine, it's my birthday, I'll kiss your pussy if I want to. Better?"

"Much, now feed me so you can have my cunt for dessert later." My eyes widen at her use of the 'c' word but if I know Calliope, she just did it to keep me on my toes. Truth be told, she can use any word in the world, as long as I have her, I'm fine with any language.

We are all standing by the bar, having a night cap before heading home. I thought I'd gotten out of the traditional song but when Garrick orders Macallan 30-year for the men and Glenfiddich Winter Storm ice wine for the ladies, I know it's about to happen.

"Happy birthday to you …" they all begin to sing as does everyone else in the bar. Looking around, I smile when I see all those I hold near and dear to me are here to celebrate my birthday. They have just finished cheering after singing and I'm on top of the world, but that feeling quickly dissipates when Bitchifer comes barreling toward us.

"Happy birthday, husband," she singsongs, pushing

Calliope from my side to kiss me on the cheek. She grabs a glass of ice wine from the bar top and raises it in a toast before chugging it back.

"What the hell are you doing here?" I growl through clenched teeth.

"I'm here to wish you a happy birthday, silly. My invite to dinner must have gotten lost in the mail."

"Ever think that maybe you weren't invited?" Calliope hisses, stepping back beside me, sliding her arm around my waist.

"Run along, little girl, the adults are talking." Danica flicks her hand in an 'off you go' motion.

"You need to leave," My Sunshine growls and seeing her so alpha is a real turn-on.

"Sunshine," I say, pulling her into my side. "It's fine. Danica is an adult; she knows when she's not wanted."

"Ohh, how precious, you're fucking her. You have no respect." She pauses, looks Calliope up and down, disdain written all over her face.

"Says the one with no respect," Calliope sneers. I can feel the anger building in her body. She has repeatedly told me how she hates what Danica has done to me and the kids, but seeing her so protective of us warms my heart and is a total turn-on, my cock is at half-mast seeing her all growly.

"Are you going to let your little plaything speak to me like that?"

"She can speak to you however she wants, we're all adults here."

"Danica," Calliope says her name calmly, "you're causing a scene, there's a time and place for this conversation and at Kane's birthday dinner, which you weren't invited to I might add, isn't the place."

"Scene?" Danica shouts, "I'll give you a scene." She reaches to the counter and grabs a glass of wine and throws it in Calliope's face. Everyone around us gasps.

"What the hell, Danica?" Michael snaps. Grabbing a napkin from the bar, he hands it to Calliope. "Are you okay, Cal?" he asks. Calliope nods and wipes at her face. Michael turns to his mother. "Apologize to Cal now."

"Excuse me? Are you sticking up for this trollop?" She pauses, and then adds, "And stop using my first name, I'm your fucking mother."

"Danica," he emphasizes her first name, "this trollop …" he looks to Calliope, "… I don't mean that." Then he turns back to Danica. "As you called her, she's been more of a mom in the last six months than you have my whole life, so just fucking stop."

"Don't speak to me like that, Michael." She looks to me for backup. "Are you really going to let him speak to me like that?"

"He's an adult, he has a right to an opinion and it just so happens to be an opinion that I agree with."

"What about you, Finley?" Danica sneers. "Are you okay with this young, skanky, gold digger being your new mommy?"

"Yep, I'm A-O-fucking-kay with it, Danica." My sassy daughter adds emphasis to her mother's first name, and it has the desired effect. Danica's mouth drops open in shock that two of her three kids are defending Calliope and not her. If Konrad was here, I know it would be three for three.

Not getting what she wants from the kids, she turns her attention back to Calliope, who hasn't uttered a word since Danica threw the drink on her.

"What have you got to say for yourself, you gold digging little bitch?"

Calliope stiffens beside me. She's on the verge of tears and when I hear her choke back a sob, it hurts. I hate this is happening to My Sunshine but before I can reply, Michael steps up and defends Calliope once again. "Danica." He once again sneers his mother's first name. "Cali is the best thing to ever happen to Dad ... and to us. Now do us all a favor and fuck off. We don't need or want you here anymore. The divorce is almost final. Just sign the fucking papers and move the fuck on. We all have, it's fucking time you do too."

"But ... but ..." Danica stammers and that's when she realizes everyone here is Team Calliope and Kane. "Ugh, fine, I'll sign the fucking papers. I don't have time for this Podunk bullshit town."

"That's the best birthday present you can ever give me. Now, fuck off, Danica, we're about to have cake."

Turning my back to her, I take Calliope's hand and we walk to the other side of the bar. Garrick, Jayne, and the kids follow and when we're on the other side of the bar, I take Calliope's cheeks in my palms and with my thumbs, I swipe away her tears. "Don't cry, baby, she's not worth it."

"I'm not crying over her, I'm crying because she ruined your birthday," Calliope tearfully cries.

"No, Sunshine, she didn't. That woman can't ruin anything because she's nothing to me. All I need to be happy is you and my kids." Garrick clears his throat in that 'what about me' way. "And my best friend and his wife."

"You mean that?"

"Yep, every word. You're it for me, Sunshine." Before I know what's happening, I drop down to bended knee and take her hand in mine. "Calliope Victoria Fischer, you are my sunshine. You are my everything. Will you marry me?"

Everyone gasps and the entire bar falls silent. Calliope stands there, staring down at me open-mouthed and wide-eyed. She's mute, not uttering a word. Everyone's gaze is on the two of us. Time feels like it's ticking by so slowly. Then a smile appears on her face and she utters one word, "Yes."

"Really?" I question, not quite believing she said yes.

"Yes," she repeats, nodding and grinning at me. "Yes, I'll marry you. You're my everything too, Kane." She takes a deep breath and shouts for those in the back to hear. "Yes, I'll marry you."

Jumping up, I grip her cheeks in my palms and kiss her, cementing our engagement. "I don't have a ring," I mumble against her lips.

"I don't need a ring. I just need you."

"This is the best birthday present ever. Thank you for loving me."

"No," she cries, "thank you for loving me like you do."

CHAPTER 44

Cali

... almost a year later

Today is my wedding day.

Today I marry the man I've had a crush on since I was a little girl.

Today I marry my dad's best friend.

Today I'm the bride and all eyes will be on me—cringe.

But most of all, today I marry my best friend. My lover. My everything.

All my worries about Kane and I being an us were for nothing. Sure, most people were shocked and only two punches were ever thrown—thankfully—but it goes to show just how strong Dad and Kane's friendship is because it was strong enough to survive his best friend falling for his princess.

"My God, Princess," Dad says from behind me, "you look beautiful. When did my baby girl grow up?"

"Thanks, Dad," I reply, turning to face him. "You look pretty spiffy too."

"I hate wearing monkey suits, but seeing you like this makes the uncomfortableness worth it. Just know, anytime you want to make a run for it, you give me the signal and I'll whisk you away. No questions asked."

"Appreciate that, Dad, but I want this with every fiber of my being. My heart beats for him and only him."

"That's beautiful, Princess, but did it have to be with my best friend?"

Shrugging at him, I walk over to the sofa in the room and sit down, my dress poofs around me, cocooning me in Swarovski-crystal-covered lace. My butt has just hit the cushion when there's a knock on the suite door. Dad answers it as he's closer, plus I just sat down.

"Delivery for a Calliope soon-to-be Heatherington."

"Thanks," Dad tersely says to the delivery boy. He shoves the box at Daddy and runs away.

"You just caused that kid to shit his pants."

"I didn't like the way he was looking at you."

"Dad, you don't like the way any male looks at me. You elbow my fiancé anytime he looks my way."

"I'm your dad, it's my prerogative. When you have kids, you'll see."

"Dad, you know you won't be getting any from me. Kane and I have repeatedly said, no kids for us."

"You sure about that, Princess? The bond with a child is the most amazing thing in the world. I'd hate to see you miss out on what I have with you and your sister. You two are my best creations and I want that for you."

"I'm sure, besides, I have Konrad, Michael, and Finley." And that's true, those three people mean everything to me and they treat me with respect and love … even if Konrad is older than me. "I know they aren't mine biologically, and after today I'm technically their mom, but I care for them in a different way now. I can't explain how it changed or when it did, but my love for Kane flows through to them."

"I think I understand but I have to admit, there's a part of me that's sad I won't get to be a grandaddy to your kids."

"I can always convince Konrad, Michael, and Finley to call you Grumpy?"

"I'm not Grumpy," he sneers with a scowl.

"Case in point, old man. Now, gimme my present." I stretch out my arm and wriggle my fingers in the 'gimme, gimme, gimme' kind of way.

"Finally, bridezilla appears."

"Hardy har har, Daddy." It's been a running joke lately, everyone waiting for me to flip my lid because I'm so meticulous with everything. But that's why lists were made and I made deadlines early. It's like fate is on #TeamKanopie or would we be #TeamCalane? Nickname aside, everything has been smooth sailing and in a few short minutes, I will officially become Calliope Heatherington.

Daddy hands me the box, I'm about to lift the lid when

there's another knock. Once again, Dad answers and once again it's the same kid. "I have another delivery for the bride?" he shyly says.

Without saying anything, Dad outstretches his hand and the kid places a smaller box on Dad's palm. The kid is looking directly at me and he smiles. "You make a stunning bride," he quickly throws toward me before he hightails it out of here.

Earning himself a growl from Dad, I shout out a "Thank you," as Dad slams the door closed.

"Little punk-ass, flirting with a woman on her wedding day." Laughing at Dad, I hold out my hand for present number two. He hands the new gift to me and since it's smaller and currently in my hands, I open it first.

Inside is an envelope with my name handwritten and beneath that is a beautiful silver key ring. My eyes well with tears when I see 'Mrs. Heatherington' engraved on it. Wiping at my eyes, I open the envelope and pull out the notecard, and as I begin to read, my eyes once again well with tears.

Cali,

You have made our dad happier than we've ever seen him before. Sure, one of your new stepsons is older than you, but age is just a number.

We've been the awesome foursome for a while now but after today, we'll be the awesome fivesome ... welcome to

the family Momma Cal.
Love
Konrad, Michael, and Finley
PS. We promise never to say Momma
Cal again

A laugh spills free and I run my finger over the engraving on the key ring.

"You okay, Princess?" Dad asks, handing me a tissue.

Nodding, I dab at my eyes, careful not to smudge my makeup. "Yeah, my new step kids are pretty awesome."

"Well, they had a good role model in their dad … and his best friend."

"That they did, but I think it's mostly from my future husband."

"Let's agree to disagree." We both laugh. "What's in the other one?" He points to the bigger box.

"I'm not sure. How about I open it?"

"That's generally how presents work."

Lifting the lid my eyes widen when I see the logo on the box inside the box—Christian Louboutin—and I immediately know what this gift is from Kane. Opening the second box, I reveal my new shoes. My breath hitches and my eyes once again well with tears as I lift one of the gorgeous shoes. Before me is a pair of "Very Lace" Louboutin open-toe pumps. The off-white lace and mesh upper matches my dress perfectly and are the perfect accompaniment to my dress, with the red sole offering a splash of color just for fun.

Seems my fiancé has been sneaking a look at my browsing history. I found these dream wedding shoes a few months ago but I would never spend that much on myself. However, it seems, my almost husband does. Instead, I spent more than ever on the pink lingerie and garter set that I'm wearing underneath my dress. I cannot wait for Kane to see the latest pink set I bought. Over our time together, I think Kane has bought me every available pink set from Monty's and by now, he's probably a major shareholder in the company.

Placing the stunning pumps back down, I pick up the card, flip it over, and read.

My Sunshine. My soon-to-be-wife,
Every girl deserves a gorgeous pair
of shoes on her wedding day.
Hope they're the right ones.
I can't wait to marry you.
Yours forever,
Kane Xo

"Kane," I tearfully mumble to myself.

Placing the card down, I kick off my slippers, remove my new shoes from the box, and slide them onto my feet. It's like I'm Cinderella at the ball and my Prince Charming has just slipped 'the' shoe onto my foot. They fit me perfectly. Standing up, I walk over to the mirror and lift my dress to gaze down at my feet.

"How the hell are you going to walk in those things without breaking your neck?" Dad asks me. "Is he trying to kill you before you're even married?"

"Dad, these are the comfiest shoes ever and as if he'd kill me, he loves me. Besides, if he killed me, you'd kill him, and then Mom would kill you, and it'd just be one big mess, and we all know Cari won't clean up a bloody mess. We're lucky if she takes her plates to the sink."

"That was quite the mouthful and I think I got it all. Consensus, no one is killing anyone 'cause Cari won't clean up."

"That's about right."

"We really have some weird conversations at times."

"That we do, Daddy, that we do."

"Okay, well, I'm going to quickly find your mother but I'll be back in time to walk you down the aisle."

"I'd appreciate that … I'd hate to have to kill you for being late."

Dad shakes his head, mumbling to himself about his daughter being a smart-ass. He walks out of the room, leaving me alone to stare at my feet in the mirror. I cannot believe he did this. Wanting to thank him now, I grab my phone, snap a pic, and send it to him.

CALI: *Thank you so much, you really shouldn't have*

CALI: *I'll have to find a way to say thank you later **wink wink***

No sooner have I sent my thank-you text and my phone pings.

KANE: *You're very welcome*

KANE: *You can thank me by wearing nothing but them*

while we consummate our marriage

 CALI: *I don't know if I can wait 'til tonight*

 KANE: *I'm sure we can find a corner at the reception*

 CALI: *Mr. Heatherington, are you proposing what I think you're proposing?*

 KANE: *I've already proposed to you, Mrs. Heatherington ... it's our wedding day, in case you forgot*

 CALI: *How could I forget when I just received the ultimate wedding shoes ... I can't wait to parade them for you*

 KANE: *If it involves you and a sexy pair of heels, I'm there*

 CALI: *I thought you liked me in pink?*

 KANE: *Ok, new plan, you can thank me by wearing pink lingerie AND your new sexy heels while we consummate our marriage*

 CALI: *Deal*

 CALI: *I cannot wait to marry you*

 KANE: *I can't wait to marry you either*

 CALI: *PSSSST. I'll be the one in white*

 KANE: *PSSSST. I'll be the one with eyes only for you*

Reading over Kane's last message, a goofy smile breaks free. I can't wait to marry this man. He's my Prince Charming, no one, and I mean no one, loves me like he does, and now, I get to marry my prince and spend the rest of my life loving him back.

The door flies open and Fern comes bouncing into the room. I notice her lips are puffy like she's been making out with someone and her cheeks are flushed. She's been suspiciously absent lately. I think she has a new man in her life … a man who sends her sunflowers on the fifteenth of each month. Her gaze lands on mine and her smile widens. I forget all about her and her mystery man when she sings, "It's time, Cal, let's get you hitched."

CHAPTER 45

Kane

Standing here at the altar, waiting for my bride, I'm nervous as all hell. Normally, my best friend would be by my side as my best man but right now, he's on father of the bride duty. Instead of Garrick by my side, I have my two sons standing with me today. I could really do with a best friend pep talk from him right now, and as if sensing my inner turmoil, Konrad reaches out and squeezes my shoulder. "Just breathe, dude. You don't want to pass out before the ceremony."

Staring at my eldest, I take a breath as he suggests and

oddly, it calms me.

"Better?" he asks.

Nodding, I smile. "Much." My gaze flits to Michael. "Thank you both for standing up here with me today, I really appreciate it."

"We wouldn't be anywhere else," Michael says, then his face turns to stone. "Last chance to run away, Dad. I've got a car and like five bucks to my name, but I can get you out of here, just say the word."

Shaking my head, I laugh at the serious look on my son's face. "Only place I'm running is down that aisle to meet Calliope."

"You're so whipped," Konrad teases.

"When you meet the one, you'll be whipped too," I nonchalantly say with a shrug, and I mean it. I don't remember being nervous like this on my wedding day to Bitchifer, guess that should have been a sign that it wasn't right, but I was young and dumb. Now, I'm old and know better.

"Dad, Momma Cali will be here before you know it. Just be patient," Michael casually says before stepping back into line.

"Momma Cali, really?"

"I thought we said we'd never call her that again?" Konrad complains to his brother, playfully smacking him in the chest. Before we can discuss them calling her 'Momma Cali' any further, the wedding music starts.

Turning my attention to the end of the aisle, I smile when I see Fern and Cari coming toward us. They look beautiful but my eyes are locked on the entrance behind them.

Waiting for My Sunshine to appear and then, she's there. She's beaming and I've never seen her look so stunning. I'm not sure what I like best, Calliope in a wedding dress or in nothing but pink lingerie.

Suddenly she's before me. "You look stunning, Sunshine."

"Thanks, it's the shoes." She sticks her foot out and turns it side to side. The photo didn't do them justice and now I can't wait to see what they look like wrapped around my waist, the heels digging into my ass as I pound into my new wife.

The minister clears his throat, and never before have I been happy to be interrupted because I cannot be sporting a hard-on in front of the minister, my best friend—who is also my bride's father—or our family and friends.

Nodding, I take Calliope's hand and we face the minister. "Dearly beloved …" and before I know it, he's announcing us as husband and wife and I get to kiss my bride. Gripping her cheeks in my palms, I press my lips to hers. For a few brief seconds, we just hold our lips against each other's but then she presses her tongue into my mouth and it's game over for me. Pushing mine into hers, I slide my hand around to her waist and dip her backward so I can kiss her deeply.

It's not appropriate for the public but this is our first kiss as husband and wife and I want it to be memorable. Breaking the kiss, I pull her upright and we gaze into each other's eyes. "I love you, husband."

"I fucking love you, wife."

Pulling her into my side, I press a kiss to her temple and

I feel her body relax as she wraps her arm around my waist. Sliding my hand into hers, we walk down the aisle as our guests blow bubbles all around us.

This is the happiest day of my life and it's all thanks to the woman beside me. I wasn't even this happy when I held the official divorce papers from Bitchifer in my hand. Calliope is my everything and I cannot wait to grow old with her by my side, but first, we're going to celebrate with our family at the reception before I whisk her away to Hawaii for a two-week, pink-lingerie-filled honeymoon at Luxe, Lanikai Beach in Hawaii.

We have just arrived at the hotel and are checking in. I'm pissed off and sexually frustrated right now. Calliope and I have been married for almost twenty-four hours and I have yet to fuck her. My dream of stripping her out of her sexy as fuck dress hasn't come to fruition and I'm being a snarky fuck.

Calliope is looking around the lobby when a commotion breaks out. "… you're not welcome here anymore," a man growls.

Calliope turns to face the commotion and her eyes widen in glee. She steps forward to get closer to the action, not caring about being seen. "But—" the woman cries.

"No buts. You are trespassing and you need to leave. The next time you step foot on a Luxe property, I will contact the authorities and have you charged."

"Oh. My. God, Kane," Calliope whispers, when I join her. "This is like I'm watching a live action *Days of Our Lives* … are they shooting a special in Hawaii or is this fight really real?"

"When do I have time to watch that crap?"

"Shhhh." She covers my mouth with her hand. "This is getting good."

"… desperation for something you can't and never will have. I don't love you anymore, Scarlett. I've moved on and you need to as well."

"With that whore?" she screams at him, garnering more than just Calliope's, and dare I say, my attention. "She has a kid, why would you want that?"

"What I want doesn't concern you anymore. You need to leave." He pauses. "Now." That seems to stop her in her tracks but this psycho chick doesn't back down. She gets right up into his face, Calliope grips my arm, waiting to see what happens next. "You'll come crawling back when she leaves you."

"You keep telling yourself that."

The guy turns his back to her but she's not giving up. "You're a fucking fool, Hunter. You and that whore deserve each other. I hope you both die."

"Wow, that escalated quickly," Calliope whispers as we stand here and watch the crazy lady drive off. "I wonder—"

"Wife, how about we create our own private show for two? Let's get up to our room because I have plans for you."

She turns to face me, and fuck me sideways, I'm the luckiest man in the world. She takes my hand and drags me toward the elevators. "Let's go, husband."

After a quick and sexually-filled elevator ride, we enter the honeymoon suite and now that we're finally here, I cannot wait to ravish my wife. She looks to me and I can see nothing but hunger reflecting back at me in her gaze. "Now, dear husband of mine, I have a surprise for you. Hand me that small suitcase so I can prepare. You go make yourself comfortable, I'll be out in a few minutes."

Handing her the suitcase, she smiles her thanks, then lifts to her tippy-toes and presses her lips to mine. Her arm wraps around my neck, pulling me into her, her body pressing against mine. My cock, which has been semi-hard for the last twelve hours, hardens instantly. My minx of a wife slides her hand between us and cups my dick, squeezing. "The things I'm going to do to you, dear husband of mine …" she mumbles against my lips before stepping away from me. "Pop the bubbly, I'll be right back."

Taking the handle of the suitcase, she walks into the master bedroom and leaves me standing here with a rock-hard dick, blue balls, and excitement for what's about to happen next.

CHAPTER 46

Cali

Oh. My. Fucking. God, I'm ready to combust. Sexually, I mean. Kane and I are now in Hawaii on our honeymoon and we still haven't consummated our marriage. Our ceremony went off without a hitch but after that, everything that could go wrong did go wrong.

The travel agent popped into the reception—gotta love small towns—to let us know that she fucked up and our flight was leaving that night, not the following night like we planned. We had to cut out of the reception early to make our flight. Then there was a storm and we were delayed … twice, and finally, we were in the air. We contemplated joining the Mile High Club, but I chickened out at the last minute. I didn't want our first time as a married couple to be a quickie like that, plus, have you seen how tiny airplane restrooms are? I want our first time as Mr. and Mrs. Heatherington to be perfect so reluctantly, we held off.

And now, I'm hiding in the bathroom changing into an outfit that I hope will make up for the wedding night sex we missed out on. I'm positive he currently has a massive case of blue balls because I have a serious case of blue clit right now—damn you travel agent for fucking this up for us. I contemplated bringing yesterday's set and my wedding dress, but Fern being the amazing best friend she is, handed me a sexy as hell pale-pink negligee, saving the day. So instead, I just packed my garter, my new shoes, and my gift from Fern.

Stripping out of my travel clothes and underwear, I slip the silky material of the negligee over my head. It slides down my body and fits like a glove. Pulling the garter up my leg, I slide it into place and then I put my new shoes on. Tousling my hair, I slather my lips in pink lipstick, rearrange the girls so they look perky, and stare at my reflection. Blowing myself a kiss, I turn toward the door—it's time to put on a sexy show for my husband.

Bringing up Spotify, I connect my phone to the speaker system in the suite and press play on what I like to think of as our song, "Closer" by Nine Inch Nails. Pulling the double doors open, I enter the suite with flair and my eyes home in on my sexy as hell husband. He has his back to me but with the dim lighting in the room, he can see me in the reflection in the glass of the floor-to-ceiling windows.

He turns to face me. "Fuck me, you're a vision, Sunshine."

"And you, sir, are overdressed."

"Well, you better come and fix that for me … wife."

"With pleasure … husband."

Swaying my hips seductively side to side, I make my way over to him. His eyes lock on the swish of my hips and in this moment, I'm thankful to have been a stripper. Miss Rhi really knows how to bring sexy to the simplest of tasks. Stopping before him, I take the glass of champagne he's holding and take a sip. Taking another, I pull him by the collar to me and press my lips to his, transferring the liquid from my mouth to his.

"Callagne is my new favorite drink," he murmurs against my lips.

"Personally, I'd like to try dickagne before the night is over."

"That can be arranged, but first, I think I need you to help me with my clothes."

"I can definitely help with that." With my eyes locked on his, I undo his buttons one by one. Once they are all undone, I run my hands up his chest and across his shoulder blades, sliding the material down his arms and off. It flutters to the carpet and I take a moment to appreciate the man before me.

"Like what you see?"

"Very much so … but I'll like it much better once these," I slip my finger into his waistband and tug, "are gone."

"Well, have at it, Sunshine."

Dropping to my knees, I unbuckle his belt, pop the button, and lower his fly, then I pull on his pant legs and tug them down. He kicks them off, leaving him in nothing but his boxer briefs, his extremely tented boxer briefs. Licking my lips, I take his briefs off in one fell swoop. His cock springs free, the tip leaking and right in my face, begging for me to suck, so I do. Wrapping my lips around the tip, I hollow my cheeks and suck.

"Fuuuuuuuuuck," Kane growls from above. "Your mouth feels like heaven, Sunshine, how the fuck did I get so lucky?"

"I think I'm the lucky one," I pant. "I now get to do this for the rest of my life." Sucking him back into my mouth, I relax my throat and take him all the way in.

"Fuuuuuuuuuck," he hisses again, threading his fingers into my hair and guiding my head back and forth. Lifting my hand, I cup his balls and gently massage. They tighten in my grasp and I know he's close so I suck hard, but he pulls back, his cock popping out of my mouth. "Sunshine, the first time we come as a married couple, it won't be down your throat … but we will definitely be doing this again. Now get up and press your back to the window."

Standing up, I do as I'm asked. Pressing my back to the cool glass, I lift my arms over my head, elongating my body. Kane's eyes run over me and I can feel the intensity of his stare all over me. He traces his fingertip down my neck. "The things I'm going to do to you."

"I think you're all talk."

"Is that a challenge, Sunshine?"

"If it means I get to ride your cock, then yes, challenge

accepted."

"What am I going to do about the dirty mouth of yours?"

"I have an idea or two of what you can fill it with but first, fuck my pussy and make me come all over your cock." I don't know where my dirty talk comes from, seems Kane is rubbing off on me, but I have to say, my words turn me on. Him too, going by how stiff his cock is between us.

"Yes, ma'am, I will be happy to fill you as you've requested." He slides his hands up my thighs and his eyes widen when he feels my bare ass. "No panties?"

"Not this time."

He growls and my already thrumming clit reaches a crescendo, I'm ready to combust. I have never wanted Kane as much as I do right in this moment. He feels it too because he lifts me up, taking the majority of my weight, and nudges his shaft at my entrance. It effortlessly slides in due to my high level of arousal. We both moan and I slide down to the hilt. He presses me back into the window and we thrust our hips back and forth. I'm slightly worried that we're going to smash through the window but the sensations pouring through my body overpower that worry, and I focus on Kane and the pleasure he's giving me.

"Yes," I mewl when he lowers his head to my cleavage, sucking a nipple through the silk. "I'm … I'm close," I pant, and when he bites my nipple, that's the detonation I need. A tsunami of pleasure crashes through me. My body quakes as the most intense, amazing and every other adjective for a fucking fantabulous orgasm engulfs me. I scream, hugging Kane to me tighter as my orgasm continues to flow.

My release sets him off and he grunts through his

orgasm. Growling, "I fucking love you," as he pumps his hips, milking everything from his release. His body stills and he rests his forehead against mine, both of us breathlessly panting.

"That," he pants, "was fucking amazing and totally worth the wait."

"Mmmhmpf," is all I can manage as a reply. I'm spent, emotionally and physically. The climax was intense, it took my mind, body, and soul. I've never felt like this before and it's all because of the man currently holding me up. "Take me to bed," I whisper.

"I don't think I have it in me to go again tonight."

"Good, 'cause you nearly just fucked me to death. I need to recharge before I can even think about doing that again."

"Fuck, I love you, Calliope Heatherington."

"And I fucking love you too, Kane Heatherington. Now take me to bed."

Without a word, he walks us into the master suite. He pulls the bedding back with me still attached to him, and he climbs in. Together, with our bodies wrapped around one another, we drift off to sleep after the best sex of our lives.

They say love can be all-consuming and I would agree. Kane is my everything and I cannot wait to grow old with the man who loves me like no other. I finally got my happily ever after and I'm never letting it go.

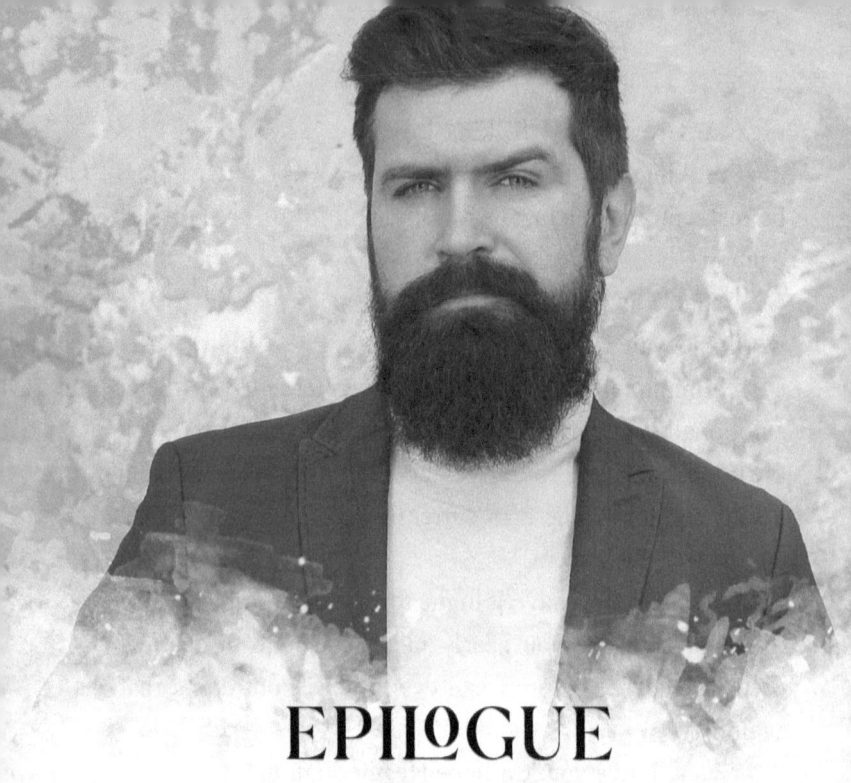

EPILOGUE

Kane

... six years later

"**O**h. My. Fucking. God, I hate you Kane-fucking-Heatherington. Your dick is never coming near my vagina ever again!" Calliope screams, clutching my hand tightly in hers as another contraction hits. In a few more pushes, we are going to meet the new addition to the Heatherington family.

Yes, Calliope and I are about to become parents. We had agreed we didn't want to have kids together; we were happy just the two of us. However, fate, well, she decided that seven was a much better number for our family. Yep, this is our second surprise baby. I'm turning fifty-two this year and will now have five children, two of which will be under one. Who knew Calliope would be so fertile while breastfeeding our daughter, Vi? It seems the first time we had sex after Vi was born, we conceived surprise baby number two. And today, we welcome him, or her, into the world.

Vi is currently hanging with Grandad Garrick and Grandma Jayne. If I thought Garrick was protective over his princess, you should see him with his granddaughter. I can't wait to see what he's like with this one.

"Okay, Calliope," the doctor says, "I can see the head, one more push and your bundle of joy will be here."

"I can't do it," she cries. "Kane, I …"

"Sunshine, you are amazing and yes, you can do it."

"Kane—"

"Nope," I interrupt her, "you can do this and you know why I know you can?"

"Why?" she cries.

"Because I love you and our love has given us two miracles, and I promise that as soon as the doctor is free, I'll get the snip."

She laughs and all the angst in her body dissipates. "You're a goofball and I love yo—" She doesn't get to finish because another contraction hits.

"Push," the doctor shouts just as Calliope grips tightly to my hand and pushes with everything she has. Then the most amazing sound, a newborn crying, echoes through the air. "Congrats, it's a boy."

"We have a Ryder," my beautiful, amazing wife cries. "Kane, we have a boy." The doctor places our son on Calliope's chest and she looks down at our baby boy. "Hi, Ryder. I'm your mom and this sexy silver fox here is your daddy. You may have been a surprise, but as soon as I saw that positive symbol waving its sparkly pregnant jazz hands at me, I knew you were the final piece to the Heatherington puzzle." She presses a kiss to his forehead. "I love you, buddy."

Even though I've done this four times before, this time is different because I know it's the last. As I stare down at Calliope holding our son, I realize that Ryder here completes us. Just like she said, he's the last piece to our puzzle and I could not be happier. Don't get me wrong, I love my other children dearly, but Ryder here, it feels like he was the addition we didn't know we needed.

We've just arrived back at her room and I sit here, watching my amazing wife hold our son. "You did good, Momma." I lean down and kiss her forehead.

"He's perfect, Kane." She takes my hand and squeezes. Looking up at me, she smiles. That little lip lift fills my heart with so much joy and love. Then she whispers, "I love you."

"Back at ya, baby." Leaning down, I press my lips to hers just as the door to the room opens.

"Cut it out, you two … unless you want to give me a third grandbaby," Garrick teases as he and Jayne walk in. Of course, Vi is snuggled tightly to his chest.

"Hardy har har, old man," I tease my best friend … and father-in-law. Still blows my mind that technically he's my FIL, but I wouldn't change a thing. Calliope was the missing piece of my heart, and our two kids filled my heart to overflowing. "Our baby-making days have come to an end. I'm booked for the snip-snip next month."

"You're a brave man. No way is anyone coming near my balls with a knife."

Jayne smacks him in the stomach as I mumble, "Pussy," earning myself a similar whack from Calliope. Grunting from my wife's attack, the door flies open and Finley, Cari, and the boys enter the room.

"Where's my baby brother?" Finley shouts, startling Ryder, but Calliope quickly settles him with a quiet shhh and a kiss on his wee little nose.

"How did you know it was a boy?" I ask as she literally pulls her baby brother from Calliope's arms.

"I said from the beginning it was a boy. You guys now have the million-dollar family, but please tell me this is the last one?"

"Yes," Calliope and I both utter at the same time.

Winking at her, I climb onto the bed next to my amazing wife, and pull her into my side. She snuggles into me and I look around the room. Our nearest and dearest are here and the atmosphere is full of love and laughter. The Heatherington family is now complete, and I cannot wait to live out the rest of my days with my wife and my five children by my side. I'm one lucky son of a bitch.

The End!

Wanna know what secrets Fern is hiding from Cali? Find out May 2023 in **Never Let Me Go**.

If would like to know more about the fight Cali and Kane witness on their honeymoon between Scarlett and Hunter, you can in **Secrets and Sunrises** which is available now.

Acknowledgements

First and foremost, I need to thank *Alex* and *Sophie* for creating Silverbell and inviting me to be a part of this project, I have fallen in love with this fictional town and I can't wait to read everyone's story. Also a shout out to my fellow Silverbell authors, thanks for joining the journey with me.

Rebecca Barber, you have become one of my most favorite people. I'd be lost without you on my team, feel free to send me chocolate dicks anytime.

My beta babes, *Wench* aka *Tara, Stephanie, Vi, Kayla* and *Bec* thank you for helping me make this story everything that it is. You're input and feedback is priceless and I'm so thankful to have you on my team.

Karen Hrdlicka from *Barren Acres Editing*; thank you for everything that you do for me. You've been with me since the beginning and I'm so grateful to have you on Team DL and I cannot wait for the day that I get to squeeze you in person. PS. Kane is yours, after thirty books, you finally got to claim your man.

Lisa; thank you once again for checking all my I's are dotted, my T's are crossed and there's no extra e's or s's.

Alex; Thank you. Thank you. Thank you for the beautiful, stunning, amazing cover. I'm so in love with it. You took the image and created something that captured Cali and Kane to a T.

And to Lou, thank you for making the inside just as pretty as the outside and putting up with my nit picking on the formatting but I thank you because I absolutely love it.

To my husband, *Troy*, and my munchkins, *Piper and Kade*. You all put up with deadline wife/mum and you still talk to me. I couldn't do this without you guys. You three are my biggest cheerleaders and I love you all long-time.

And finally, *you, my reader*. Thank you again for taking a chance on lil old me. My characters and I love it.

Cheers,
Dana XoXoX

Playlist

Love Me Like You Do – Ellie Goulding
You are my Sunshine – Christina Perri
Wannabe – Spice Girls
In the air Tonight – Phil Collins
Self Esteem – The Offspring
King and Lionheart – Of Monsters and Men
Closer – Nine Inch Nails
Complicated – Avril Lavigne
Right Here Waiting – Richard Marx
Just the Two of Us – Grover Washington
Awake My Soul – Mumford & Sons
One of them Girls – Lee Brice
Lipstick – Dan + Shay
I Will Wait – Mumford & Sons
Hold My Hand – Lady Gaga
Midnight Blue – Lou Gramm
Two of Us – Birds of Tokyo
Bruises – Train feat. Ashley Monroe
The A Team – Ed Sheeran
To Be With You – Mr. Big
Start of Something Good – Daughtry
Something I Need – OneRepublic
Half of my Heart – John Mayer
Never Tear Us Apart – Bishop Briggs
Between the Raindrops – Lifehouse feat. Natasha Bedingfield
Here's To Us – Halestorm
What If – Five for Fighting
Somebody Like You – Keith Urban
Superman (It's not Easy) – Five for Fighting
Battleships – Daughtry
I'll Be You Man – James Blunt
Time After Time – Quietdrive
100 Years – Five for Flight
You and I Collide – The Time Keepers
Drops of Jupiter (Tell Me) – Train
How Did You Love – Shinedown

This playlist can be found on Spotify.

IMOGEN WELLS

Embers of You

KENNEDY

Time is a healer, or so they say.

But time has done nothing to heal my wounds.

Forced back home after six years, I must now face everything I ran from.

Grief, feelings for those I once loved and a threat I thought I'd left behind.

But there is one person I've never been able to hide from.

One person who can crumble all my walls.

Asher King.

ASHER

Life is good. A good job, good friends and sex on tap.

What could possibly go wrong?

Kennedy Scott, that's what.

After six long years, she's returned to Silverbell and with her comes feelings I've tried to forget and secrets I thought were buried.

Now, I have to stop history repeating itself or risk losing it all.

Whether you're sunshine or grumpy, light or dark, the seemingly quiet and quaint town of Silverbell Shore welcomes you and all your deepest, darkest, forbidden secrets.

available for preorder

Silverbell Shore Books

Careless Whispers - *Alexandra Silva & Sophie Blue*
Love Me Like You Do - *DL Gallie*
Embers of You - *Imogen Wells*
Finding Hope - *Sophie Blue*

Also by DL Gallie

STANDALONES

Antecedent

Doc Steel

Oops

Off the Books

Fractured:A driven world novel

Deck…the Balls

Secrets and Sunrises

Love Me Like You Do

Never Let Me Go

I Pucking Hate That I Love You

A Pucking Good Christmas **details coming soon**

Seven Nights

Seven Kisses

* * *

FALLING NOVELS

These men make it hard not to fall for them

Falling for Dr. Kelly

Falling for Dr. Knight

Falling for Agent Cox

Falling for Agent Cruz

Falling:The Complete Collection

* * *

THE UNEXPECTED SERIES

When it comes to love, expect the unexpected

The Unexpected Gift

The Unexpected Letter

The Unexpected Package

The Unexpected Connection

The Unexpected series: The Complete Collection

* * *

THE CASTAWAY GROVE COLLECTION

Love has arrived in the Grove

Oasis

Unequivocal Love

Five Words

Broken Rules

…and a few more to come.

The Castaway Grove Collection, Vol 1

* * *

THE LIQUOR CABINET SERIES

Liquor has never been so disturbingly saucy

Daiquiri Dream (prequel*)

Malt Me (Book 1)

Tequila Healing (Book 2)

Wine Not (Book 3)

The Final Shot (Book 4)

The Liquor Cabinet: Series boxset

*Only available in the boxset

About the Author

DL Gallie writes spicy romance with elements of comedy and suspense. She currently lives in Central Queensland, Australia, her husband and two kids but has lived in many different places around the world and within Australis. She and her husband have been together since she was sixteen, and although they drive each other crazy at times, she couldn't imagine her life without him.

Shortly after her son was born, DL began reading again. With encouragement from her husband, she picked up the pen and started writing, and now the voices in her head won't shut up.

DL enjoys listening to music, drinking white wine in the summer, red wine in the winter, and beer all year round. She's also never been known to turn down a cocktail, especially a margarita.

FIND D.L. GALLIE ON
FACEBOOK ~ INSTAGRAM ~ BOOKBUB
GOODREADS
dlgallieauthor.wixsite.com/dlgallieauthor
dlgallieauthor@outlook.com
Sign up to my newsletter

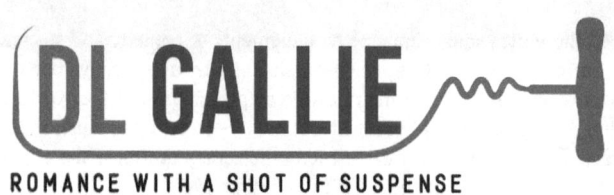

ROMANCE WITH A SHOT OF SUSPENSE
AND A DASH OF COMEDY